MW00436345

LINEAR TACTICAL SERIES

SHAMROCK

USA TODAY BESTSELLING AUTHOR
JANIE CROUCH

SHAMROCK: LINEAR TACTICAL

This book is dedicated to my parents...
For the love you've provided so many of your "children".
I may have been the first, but I certainly was not the last.

•

"There was a time I asked my father for a dollar
And he gave it a ten dollar raise.
When I needed my mother and I called her,
She stayed with me for days"

CHAPTER 1

VIOLET COLLINGWOOD HAD THOUGHT the tiny, windowless room where her kidnappers had held her for the past three days was the worst place she could possibly be.

She'd been so very wrong.

In that room, there'd been little light and just a hole in the ground for a toilet. The only way she'd known how much time had passed was by the arrival of meals twice a day: a couple of protein bars and some water.

Sitting in the dark by herself for hours, not knowing if she was going to live or die, had given her a lot of time to reflect on how she'd gotten there. What she could've done. Should've done.

Two men had grabbed her as she'd walked from her evening class to the parking area across campus. She'd almost been to her car in the garage when they'd pulled up.

She should've been more aware. Her brother, Gabe, was always telling her she needed to be more aware of what was going on around her. She'd always thought he was just paranoid, that his time as a Navy SEAL had made him hyperaware of danger.

But being hyperaware was better than being kidnapped and held in a dark, airless room somewhere.

Were they holding her for ransom, hoping her brother would pay money for her return since he was CEO of Collingwood Technology? Maybe they didn't know that Gabe put almost every dollar they had back into the company. He didn't have a lot of liquid assets.

He would do anything he could to get her back, but if they were asking for millions of dollars . . . Gabe didn't have that sort of money. At least, not if they expected him to be able to get to it quickly.

She'd kept her ear to the door—*literally*—since being shoved in the room, sometimes able to catch the sound of conversation. When it was quiet, she'd nearly dislocated her shoulder trying to break through the door, and she'd bloodied her fingertips trying to feel for any cracks in the wall that would suggest some sort of structural weakness.

She was putting those chemical engineering classes she'd been taking for the past three years to a use she had never expected. The effort kept her from giving in to terror and despondency.

There was nothing more in the world she wanted than to get out of that dark room.

Or so she'd thought.

But that was before they'd stripped her naked and put her in a cage. Now she'd give anything to be back in that dark room. At least there, no one had paid attention to her.

There had been some big argument outside the door: men yelling at each other. She'd strained to pick out any words. A *Mr. Stellman* was mentioned repeatedly, but she had no idea who that was. *Death*, *kill*, and *money* were also mentioned, as well as every variation she'd ever heard of the *f* word.

Nothing at all about that screaming match had made her feel any better, even when she'd heard a door slam.

The door to her room had opened a few moments later. The light streaming in had momentarily blinded her, causing her to fall hard to the ground as she tried to scurry backward.

A man, tall and beefy, with blond hair that fell over one eye, was on her in just a few steps despite her attempt to get away. He reached down and grabbed her hair in his fist, dragging her back to a standing position.

"Maybe we're not allowed to taste you for ourselves, but that doesn't mean you can't make us some money." His voice was breathy, excited.

"Wh-what?" she whispered.

"Take off your clothes. It's time for you to earn your keep around here like everyone else."

Violet didn't know what he was talking about, but she sure as hell wasn't going to take off her clothes.

The door was wide open for the first time in days, so she made a run for it. She threw all her weight at the guy, who lost his grip on her. But she was barely halfway to the door before he tackled her to the ground.

"I don't think so." His breath was hot in her ear as he laughed. Violet squirmed to try to get away again. His hips thrust up against her. He was definitely turned on.

She stopped moving and just lay flat on the floor. She didn't want to rub against him any more than she had to.

"Aw, come on, don't stop all your wiggling on my account." His hand reached between them and grabbed her buttocks, squeezing and kneading roughly. Violet whimpered before swallowing the sound. She didn't want to show him any weakness.

But tears leaked out of her eyes as he ground himself against her and yanked her head up by her hair so he could slide his other hand around to grope her breasts as brutally as he had her ass. She'd have bruises on her flesh, courtesy of his roughness and her pale skin.

Vomit pooled in her gut as he continued to dry hump her, his much bigger body pinning her lower half down, his grip on her hair keeping her head and torso pulled upright at an unnatural angle.

Violet had never known such helplessness in her entire life. She'd been terrified when the two guys had grabbed her in the parking lot, but even that had been a shocked, detached kind of fear.

This was so much more impossible to bear. The grunting of the man on top of her as he thrust and rubbed against her over and over. The pain in her breasts as he pinched them.

She gagged when he thrust his tongue in her ear, his loud breathing all she could hear.

If I put a raspberry pastry cream with a touch of lemon zest in the puits d'amour *rather than jam, it would add the depth of flavor I've been missing.*

She grabbed on to the thought with every bit of mental energy she had, allowing it to force everything else away.

Lemon zest. How much? I don't want it to overpower the rest of the French pastry.

The zest from one lemon, plus the juice, would really give it the zing it's been missing.

"What the hell are you doing?"

An icy voice from the doorway jolted her back into the

present. For a second, Violet's dazed mind thought that the man was talking to her.

"Stellman said *hands off*, Randy," the guy from the door continued. "Do you know what he's going to do to you if he finds out you fucked her?"

Randy let go of her hair and threw her head down. It crashed against the floor with a thud that caused everything to blur for a moment. She concentrated on breathing, on dragging enough air into her lungs to keep from hyperventilating. At least her neck wasn't being held at that impossible angle anymore.

"I'm not fucking her, Dillon, for God's sake. I'm just getting to know her a little better." Randy used both hands to squeeze her buttocks in a punishing grip for a few more seconds before getting off her.

Violet just lay with her cheek on the floor, watching Dillon in the doorway, afraid to move or do anything that would draw attention back to her. Distantly, she could feel a tear leak out the corner of her eye and run across the bridge of her nose before dropping. Dillon just stood in the door, arms crossed, watching her with calculating eyes.

"Whatever," he finally said, turning from the door. "If we're taking her to The Barn, get her ready. We're late, and the other girls are already in the truck."

Randy grabbed her by the arm and hauled her to her feet. "Shall we try this again? Take off your clothes."

She couldn't do it. She tried, even brought her fingers to the buttons of her blouse, but she couldn't get them to work.

Randy's fist crashed into her stomach.

The shock hit her first as she struggled to drag in any oxygen. Then the pain exploded through her body. Violet doubled over, coughing, sure she was about to die.

Randy's hand was in her hair once more, snatching her

upright. "I won't hit you in the face because Stellman doesn't want you hurt for whatever reason. But believe me, there are lots of ways I can bruise you without leaving any obvious marks. Now take your damn clothes off," he seethed.

This time, her fingers worked. Shaking, but they worked. Randy watched it all, sneering the whole time. She balled up her clothes and put them on the floor. There wasn't anywhere else to put them.

Randy just kept looking at her, licking his lips. Then he grinned. "Natural redhead."

Violet was pretty sure she was going to vomit. She forced herself not to cower or give him the satisfaction of covering herself with her hands.

She just wanted to go home to her tiny apartment in Idaho Falls. She'd even go live with Gabe. Her brother was completely overbearing and didn't understand her at all, but at least she wouldn't be here.

Randy grabbed a small box he'd dropped on the floor and tossed it to her. Cleaning wipes. "Here. You can clean yourself up, or I can do it for you."

She immediately took out the cold wipes and began to drag them across her body. She definitely didn't want Randy doing it.

Being clean again after three days of no shower or running water felt wonderful. But she would've stayed filthy for the rest of her life if it meant stopping whatever plans Randy had for her tonight.

When she was done, he came and stood right in front of her. For one horrified moment, she thought he was going to kiss her.

She couldn't bear that. She didn't know why that particular thought seemed so repugnant to her when five minutes ago she'd thought Randy was going to rape her. But she could not stand it if he kissed her.

But instead he slipped some sort of heavy necklace around her neck, so short it was almost a choker. It had some sort of locket in the center.

"Transmitting device. I will be able to hear every single thing you say tonight. And if that's something I don't like, even so much as your name, you can bet I'll pay Dillon off, and I'll make you wish you were dead a hundred different ways before I finally kill you."

He smiled—almost friendly—and opened a piece of mint gum before applying pressure to her jaw so she was forced to open and he could pop it in.

"Got to have fresh breath for your customers."

As she began to chew, spearmint flavor flooding her mouth, her body began to shake. She clutched her arms around herself, trying to hold back the tremors. It was August, not cold enough for her teeth to be chattering. She clenched down on the gum.

"Let's go!" Dillon roared from outside the door.

Randy grabbed her arm and yanked her forward, out the door. She looked around to try to get her bearings, to see if she could figure out where she was. A house somewhere, obviously, from all the rooms and the furniture, but she had no idea where.

Randy dragged her through another door into a garage. A small moving truck was parked inside, the back door rolled open.

Inside, half a dozen women in various states of undress sat in a line, staring blankly at her and Randy.

On the other side of the truck was a large cage—actually a crate used for training dogs. Randy pulled open the door and threw Violet inside. It was big enough for her to sit up in, but she couldn't stretch out her legs. She fought down the panic coursing through her system.

"You keep the hell quiet, or this will be your permanent place of residence." Randy shut the cage and padlocked it.

He stepped back and pulled the rolling door of the truck down, blowing her a kiss right before his face disappeared from view.

And then there was nothing but the sound of her own quiet sobs as she wished she were back in the dark room she'd so desperately wanted to get out of.

CHAPTER 2

AIDEN TEAGUE HAD INFILTRATED some of the worst hellholes on the planet. During his time as an Army Green Beret, his main job had been to scout ahead of his team for information and to make contacts.

Over the course of those years, he'd had to befriend some pretty questionable people in order to make sure his team's mission was completed successfully. It was a good use of his talents. He had a natural affinity for languages, an ingrained understanding of cultural nuances, and the sort of presence people just seemed to respond to. Or at least, bad guys responded to.

He'd never expected to be using these skills again after he'd gotten out of the army a little over four years ago.

He'd thought his infiltration days were behind him. Somehow, sitting in a private club everyone called The Barn, Aiden didn't think he would be using any of the five other languages he spoke besides English. Although a crash course in hipster criminal slang would probably help him a great deal right now.

He'd been undercover for just over three weeks,

pretending to be a dirtier version of himself—someone who owned a weapons and survival training facility but did some smuggling on the side. He was here, like everyone else, because he was interested in buying information about weaknesses in the US air defense system. A man named Gordon Cline, a government employee who obviously didn't mind selling out his country for money, had been discovered putting together the sale of this highly classified information.

Cline wasn't the problem. He was low-level and could be taken out of play at any time. There was a much bigger fish Aiden had been sent to reel in, somebody named Stellman. Nobody knew who he was or what he looked like, and those who found out tended to end up dead.

Aiden didn't normally do undercover work. He now worked at Linear Tactical, the survival, self-defense, and weapons training facility he and some of his army brothers had opened four years ago. But when his former commanding officer had come asking for help a month ago, Aiden had agreed.

They'd all thought it would go much more quickly. But Cline, bless his traitorous fucking heart, had been drawing out the sale of the information for as long as possible. He was courting as many criminals as he could in order to auction the information off to whoever was willing to pay the most.

And Cline loved strip clubs. That's how Aiden had found himself at the fifteenth one in as many days.

He was damn tired of seeing naked women. Not something he ever thought he'd find himself thinking. But evidently, he was the only one, because this private party was packed. Some were people Aiden had seen before in the past couple of weeks, some strangers.

Still no sign or mention of Stellman.

This building, neither a club nor a barn, was privately owned and situated in the far outskirts of Reddington City. Aiden had lived in Wyoming for more than four years and had never known this place existed. The building was basically a series of smaller rooms all surrounding a main meeting area. There were two dancers currently up on the stage in the main room. Unlike regulated strip clubs, where dancers always had at least a little bit of clothing on, no matter how sheer, the women dancing here were completely naked.

Except, of course, for strategically placed pieces of elastic around their waists or thighs to hold the money the men gave them. And by the looks of it, they were making a lot. The two on the stage certainly were.

Aiden had no problem with any woman who chose to make a living that way. As for what went on in the back rooms . . . There was a lot more lawbreaking going on in this place than just the selling of government secrets. But he wasn't here to break up a prostitution ring, so he'd just ignore that for now. He'd definitely be mentioning The Barn to Sheriff Nelson once this was done. Let the Teton County Sheriff's Department handle it.

Aiden sat back in his seat and watched everything going on around him. He just wanted to go home. The tumbler in his hand was filled with water, not the tequila or gin everyone else assumed. He had no interest in lowering his guard. This night was shaping up to be just like all the others since he had gone undercover: too much playtime, too little business. He was getting damned tired of it.

Cline was sitting over at a corner booth, a nearly naked woman on either side of him cooing and playing with him. No doubt pay-to-play was the only way Cline saw action.

But instead of enjoying them fawning over him like he usually did, he was staring down at some damned napkin.

Aiden had strolled by earlier to talk to Cline, trying to get a better look at what was keeping the little computer nerd from his normal partying ways. The napkin had symbols written on it, almost gibberish—or some sort of code.

But gibberish to Aiden was obviously something damn important to Cline, the way he was staring at it.

Aiden had talked to the other man for a minute, trying to get any info he could, but he'd had to walk away and leave it alone when Cline got agitated. That was the tricky part about undercover work, balancing the push and pull with the overall goal. Aiden didn't want to blow his cover over something that might be meaningless.

Hell, everything here tonight seemed pretty meaning-less. Like always. Like they were being directed to this particular place as part of a script for a play none of them knew they were characters in.

He was tired. Getting a good night's sleep in his own bed—for the first time in days—would probably be a more effective use of his time than sitting around here. But first, he had to try to grab Cline's napkin. He cursed again this group's paranoia. Everyone had to leave their cellphones and all weapons at the door. No pictures of any wrongdoing.

Or in Aiden's case, no ability to call for backup if things went to shit.

He needed that napkin. His gut told him it was the key to everything. Aiden always listened to his gut, even when it meant he was going to be stuck in this shithole for more hours as he attempted to gather the needed intel and get that damned napkin. There were five hundred other places he'd rather be. He took a sip of his water and tried to mentally fortify himself for the hours to come.

Then he saw *her*.

Nothing about her should've drawn his attention. She had on a short, white silk robe, so she certainly wasn't as naked as many of the other women in the room. She wasn't moving in any seductive way that would draw overt attention to herself. The opposite, in fact. He couldn't even see her face clearly because she kept looking over at the main door like she might decide to stroll out of it at any second.

Proving she had good judgment.

All he could see was that deep auburn hair falling down around her shoulders. He wanted to see her face. Her eyes.

Hell, if she was going to be one of the dancers on stage, at least it would make this night more bearable.

A guy was holding her arm tightly while talking to a number of other girls. Aiden had met him, but he was pretty low on the totem pole, so Aiden hadn't spent much time with him. What was the guy's name? Ross? Rick? Something with an R.

The second man he'd come in with was standing near the door in the shadows, watching everything happening around him. Aiden hadn't met him at all, just glimpsed him a few times. The man never talked much to anyone. Maybe he was just Randy's muscle.

Randy. That was the guy's name.

The women Randy had brought in with him—all in various states of undress—had scattered after a word from him, looking for buyers of their wares: lap dances or more. Only the redhead had stayed with him. Probably because he had yet to release her arm.

Aiden still hadn't seen her face. He was surprised at how fiercely he desired to do so. He forced himself to look away from the woman to check on Cline. The geek still sat in his booth, sulking, staring at that damned napkin.

That piece of paper was the objective. Not some woman, no matter how sexy that hair and lush body might be, her curves barely covered by the short robe. Aiden forced himself to angle his chair so he had a better view of Cline and less of the redhead.

But a disturbance from her direction drew his attention back a few minutes later. Randy had pushed her up on a little mini stage surrounded by four or five men in chairs, drinks in their hands. Her robe was now off her shoulders, the garment only staying on her body because of the tightly knotted belt at her waist. Delicious, plump breasts were partly visible under the cascade of hair.

Her gaze was still glued to the ground, hair covering her face.

Randy obviously wanted the woman to dance or entertain the men—to make money—but even when, face mottled in anger, he grabbed her chin forcefully and said something Aiden couldn't hear, the woman still didn't move.

Randy reached for the belt of her robe and gave it a tug. It came loose, and the robe floated to the ground at her feet, leaving her completely naked.

Aiden couldn't turn away. Her waist was small before curving out to softly feminine hips. Her legs were perfectly full, no sort of ridiculous thigh gap younger women were so often obsessed with.

Aiden had traveled all over the world in the army and seen all types of female shapes and sizes. As a result, he liked a woman soft, with curves that enticed him to stay and play for a while.

This one was damn near perfect, in his opinion. One hundred percent beautiful, lush woman.

But instead of teasing the men with her nakedness or showing it off, she immediately dropped down and yanked her robe in front of her, covering herself.

Randy looked like he was going to lose his shit completely as he snatched it away again. The men around him chuckled, and one called out encouragement to the woman, just angering Randy more. He fisted her hair in his hand and yanked her head back.

Aiden was on his feet immediately when he finally saw her face.

This woman was in trouble.

She didn't look like the other girls. She may be naked like them, but everything else about her screamed she didn't belong here. She had neither the jaded, worldly look that some of the dancers had, nor the blank, empty stare that blanketed the features of the others.

The look in this woman's eyes was clear: terror.

Randy said something in her ear that leached away whatever color she'd had in her face. Then she nodded, and the hand that had been grabbing for the robe he held out of her reach dropped back down to her side.

Frustration coursed through Aiden. There was nothing he wanted to do more than march over to the woman, grab her, and get her out of here. He wasn't sure what was going on, maybe someone had talked her into this, or maybe something much worse, but she shouldn't be here. Not with that look in her eyes.

But he couldn't. He couldn't go over there and play white knight when the persona he'd been so painstakingly building was of a criminal and a traitor to his own country. Aiden Teague, weapons smuggler, was not someone who gave a shit if some young girl was scared.

And she was young. Couldn't be more than twenty-two or twenty-three to his thirty-three.

But if he made the move every instinct in him was screaming to do—which included putting Randy in the hospital for manhandling her—all his undercover work would be for nothing.

People might die if that happened.

So just like he had when missions had gone wrong in the army, Aiden improvised. Because there was no way in hell he was going to ignore what was happening to this woman. He walked directly over to Randy.

"How much for the whole night?" He forced a calm, almost bored tone he definitely didn't feel.

Her eyes, a ridiculously bright green now that he was close enough to see them, widened before her gaze dropped to the floor. Tremors were starting to rack her shapely body, and he hated the words he was forced to say.

All he knew was that she was safer with him than she would be with anybody else in this entire building.

One of the men who had been watching her on the stage protested about Aiden getting her for the whole night, but Aiden ignored him.

Randy yanked her closer, almost causing her to stumble.

"Aiden." Randy smiled like they were old friends. "You're into the redheads, huh? Yeah, she's for sale, but not for the whole night. She's only here for two hours. And sorry, buddy, but she doesn't fuck. No sex."

The man who had protested scoffed and left, the others following. There were too many women here available for sex to get in a bidding war over one who wasn't.

Randy was still yanking on her hair, holding her head at an awkward, painful angle. Aiden was pretty certain he was going to have to break that hand at some point.

But right now, he just forced himself to pull on his undercover role. "No sex? That sounds pretty boring. Or like one of you might be some sort of cop."

The guy laughed a little nervously. "Whoa, man, no need to go all Sherlock on me. Nobody is a cop, you know that. And just because there's no sex doesn't mean it has to be boring." Randy pushed her forward. "Look at her. I'm sure you can think of other body parts to use to make it interesting."

His grip on her hair was forcing the woman's face up, but she wasn't looking at Aiden. Her eyes were darting all over the place. And her trembling was a full-on shaking now. She was close to a breakdown. He wasn't sure what would happen if she lost it right here, but it wouldn't be pretty.

He needed to get her away from Randy and figure out what was going on.

"That's true. Lots of options." He forced himself to give Randy a wink. "But I want her for the whole time she's here. I don't share, so no one else touches her. So how much?"

They settled on a price. Not much more than Aiden would have paid to take a woman out for a nice night on the town. Randy was obviously glad to get anything at all. Aiden didn't care; he just wanted to get the woman away from him before she collapsed.

"Remember, no sex," Randy said, running a finger along her neck. She shuddered again. "And no marks or bruises either."

Aiden looked down at the bruises that were already marring the skin on her breasts. Finger-shaped bruises. He smothered the rage threatening to overwhelm him. Losing his temper now wouldn't help her situation. He gestured to her breasts with his hand.

"Looks like someone already got around to bruising your merchandise." More forced boredom.

Randy winced, then grinned a little as he leered at her breasts. He'd obviously been the one to put those marks on her creamy flesh.

Aiden would definitely be breaking this man's hand. Probably more.

Randy waggled one eyebrow. "She must bruise easily. Just no *more* marks, okay?"

Aiden let out a sigh. "I don't want to have to pay for the dings somebody else put on the rental. So don't be pissed and try to blame these on me in a few hours."

Hopefully, Aiden would have her out of here in a few hours. As soon as he could get her alone to talk, he could ask her if she was here under duress.

Aiden gave him the money and raised his eyebrow when the guy still didn't take his fist out of her hair. "You planning on joining us? If so, I want my money back."

Randy yanked the woman close and whispered something in her ear, then finally let her go, pushing her toward him. "Like I said, she'll be leaving in two hours. Enjoy."

Trying to keep himself between her naked body and the rest of the men in the room, Aiden led her back to the rooms Randy directed them to. What exactly he was going to do with her, he had no idea.

CHAPTER 3

REMEMBER, I'm listening to everything you say. Everything.

Randy's whispered words in her ear finally put Violet over the edge. She'd held it together in the cage in that dark truck for the eternity it had taken to get here. She'd tried to talk to the other women in the vehicle with her, but they'd ignored her.

She'd held it together, even through her chills, as Randy had walked her inside the building along with the other women. Having on that robe he'd tossed at her as he pulled her out of the cage and truck had neither reassured her nor gotten her any warmer.

"Make money," he'd said to the other women once he got them across the room. "Or no prize."

Violet had no idea what the *prize* was, but evidently the thought of not getting it was truly upsetting to the women. One had begun to cry and rub her arms before another had stopped and tried to comfort her in another language. Then they'd scattered.

Randy's use of short direct words made Violet wonder if

perhaps none of the women spoke English. That would also explain why they wouldn't talk to her in the truck.

Violet had no idea where they were, and although she was thankful The Barn wasn't literally a *barn*, she was under no misconception that this place was safe. It seemed to be some sort of private strip club or something.

Dillon had just stood inside the door and stared at her, arms crossed over his chest. His dark gaze was almost as menacing as Randy's wandering hands. She could almost feel the quiet evil radiating off of him.

Then Randy had pulled her over to the little stage and told her to dance. Violet would've laughed if she weren't afraid it might turn into some hysterical cackle she wouldn't be able to control. She was an *engineer*, for God's sake. She didn't know how to dance at all, much less do some sort of sexy strip tease.

Yanking down her robe just caused her to freeze further. She'd kept her gaze on the floor rather than the leering men all around her.

When Randy had ripped it off her completely, she'd dropped and pulled it up over her torso before she could even weigh the wisdom of that move.

"If you don't make some money, I'm going to be the one getting my money's worth from you later tonight, in ways I promise will be much worse than a couple of lap dances," Randy whispered in her ear as he yanked the robe away, leaving her completely naked once again.

The chills worked their way through her body again. She tried to force them back, to think through the numbing fear starting to overwhelm her. There was a buzzing in her ears and she clamped her teeth down on the gum that had long since lost its taste.

She couldn't dance for these men. Just staying upright

took every bit of her concentration. If she passed out, only God knew what would happen to her body. But her breaths were coming in short, panicked gasps, blackness engulfing more and more of her vision.

"How much for the whole night?"

Randy's painful yank on her hair and the deep voice pulled her back from the abyss she'd been about to fall into. Yet she still took in the conversation between Randy and the tall, dark-haired man who'd come over to *buy* her like it was from a distance. The chills coursing through her body turned into shudders.

She once again managed not to laugh hysterically as Randy insisted on no sex. What, was this guy going to dry hump her like Randy had? Somehow she didn't think so.

This guy was so much more deadly than Randy. Not because of his size or muscles. It was the aura around him. Maybe not sinister, but definitely dangerous.

Violet tried to keep it together, tried to stem the hysteria bubbling up inside of her, but it was too late now. No thoughts of lemon zest were going to save her psyche this time. Randy and the man exchanged money, and Randy whispered his threat before pushing her toward the dangerous man, keeping her robe.

The man was leading her somewhere, but Violet didn't know where. She couldn't seem to control her body, and the room was slowly starting to spin around her.

She heard a noise that sounded out of place, some sort of high-pitched cry. A keen, almost animal-like. And it was getting louder.

Maybe this place really was a barn, and some poor animal was getting slaughtered.

It wasn't until the dangerous man spun around and

pressed her naked body up against the wall that she realized that it was *her* making the sound.

His hand slid into her hair, but it wasn't brutal like Randy's had been. He pulled her face against his chest, cutting off the noise.

She should be appalled, should pull away. But all her brain could seem to process was the soft warmth of his black T-shirt against her face. It was the gentlest thing she'd felt in days.

"Hang in there, Firefly. Just until we get to the private room."

His voice was deep and low in her ear. His arms were around her body, not trapping her, but supporting her. Right now, they were the only things keeping her upright.

"Take a few deep breaths with me. In. Out. No one can see you."

As the spinning stopped and strength returned to her legs, she realized he was telling the truth. The way he had positioned their bodies, no one could see her at all with him pushed up against her. Not that anybody was watching anyway. There were a lot more interesting things to see here than one woman about to pass out.

She had no idea why this man was being kind to her—he had just spent money to use her in any way he wanted except intercourse, and the clock was already ticking—but she couldn't make herself move away.

His arms stayed wrapped around her loosely, not forcing her to remain near him if she wanted to move away. He was shielding her, and God, she needed that, just for a second.

"There you go," he murmured again. "Find your center. You can do this."

She finally eased back from him the rest of the way until

she was no longer touching the softness of his T-shirt. She looked into his eyes, soft brown with green and gold flecks, as he looked back, obviously weighing the odds of her having another breakdown.

She was trying to weigh the same thing.

Conversations continued all around them. Nobody had even noticed what was going on. Except Randy. When Violet finally worked herself completely away from the man's chest, the first thing she saw was Randy glaring at her. He tapped his ear, and she got the message. He was listening.

The man with his arms around her may not be cruel, but he also wasn't going to be any sort of savior. Randy wasn't going to allow it even if the guy was so inclined. But why would a man who bought a woman for sexual favors be so inclined anyway? She stepped completely back from him, and his arms fell to his sides.

"I'm better now," she whispered. "Thank you."

"Look, are you all right? Are you in some sort of trouble? You don't seem too happy to be here."

Out of the corner of her eyes she saw Randy rapidly approaching. Obviously, he'd been telling the truth about the transmitter.

"No, I'm fine. Really." She had to think of a reason she'd be acting like this. "Just low blood sugar or something."

Randy stopped his approach, and Violet let out a sigh of relief. She'd take the stranger over her kidnapper.

The stranger nodded his head, but his eyes narrowed. He'd noticed Randy's approach also.

"Private room now," the man whispered. "Time to get my money's worth. Your boss said no sex, but that mouth looks very tempting."

She flinched at the words. Maybe some part of her had

hoped he was a sort of white knight after all. But he wasn't looking at her, he was glancing over at Randy, who was now grinning like an idiot. Obviously, the thought of her being misused gave him a thrill.

The room he pulled her into was tiny. It held a loveseat and a wooden chair around a small stage with a stripper pole in the center. As soon as they were in and the door closed behind them, he grabbed a remote control and pressed some buttons. Sultry music with a thick, heavy beat flooded the room.

"I bought you," he said, voice like ice. "Now dance."

CHAPTER 4

THOSE GREEN EYES looked at him with just the slightest suggestion of betrayal before she masked it.

Good, he wanted betrayal. That meant she trusted him a little. Or had, until he'd ordered her to dance.

She began walking away from him, toward the stage, but he grabbed her arm and pulled her back with him until they were both sitting on the small couch.

"That's right, baby, work that pole."

Now confusion filled those green eyes. If he wasn't mistaken, Randy had some sort of transmitting device on her person somewhere. The other man had definitely been about to step in when Aiden had asked her if she was under duress, then backed off after she'd told Aiden that ridiculous lie about low blood sugar.

"Yeah, spin around like that. I love to see a hot woman like you on the pole."

Since her body was completely naked except for that necklace, the piece of jewelry was Aiden's best bet for the transmitter. She was still looking at him like she couldn't quite understand what was going on.

He pointed at the locket, then brought his finger to his lips in a quiet sign before raising both eyebrows. The best sign language he could figure out.

Those expressive eyes grew wide before she nodded frantically.

"Yeah, arms up. Let me look at you." He hoped his words were close enough to what someone would be saying if he was watching her put on a show for real. The crassness was already cringeworthy.

"Tell me your name, hotness."

She shook her head frantically. He nodded, then pointed at her so she would provide some sort of answer.

"No names." She did a great job of putting just enough breathiness in her voice to make it sound like she was really moving against the pole, even as she sat sideways on the couch and pulled her legs up and wrapped her arms around them.

There was nothing more he wanted to do than offer her his shirt, but if Randy burst in, that would be nearly impossible to explain.

"What am I going to call you then?"

"I like what you called me before," she said.

"Hotness? Baby?"

"Firefly."

He smiled. "All right, Firefly. I'll have no problem remembering that with all that red hair. I'm not quite as shy as you, so you can call me Aiden Teague."

"You're Irish?"

"Irish enough my friends call me Shamrock. That, and I'm pretty damn lucky."

She rested her head on the back of the couch, closing her eyes for a second. She looked exhausted. Like she was on her last reserves. Like she needed someone to take over whatever battle it was she was fighting because she couldn't do it anymore.

And Aiden couldn't do a damned thing to help her if he was going to keep his cover.

"Are you lucky?" she asked without opening her eyes.

"I'm here getting to watch those gorgeous curves of yours. I would say I'm the luckiest bastard in this place."

Her eyes opened at that, as if to see if he really thought she was sexy. Under any other circumstances, she would have to wipe the drool from his chin if he was watching her naked body. He nodded and shrugged in apology at the same time. She was definitely sexy.

This situation definitely was not.

He wished he weren't in this undercover situation alone. Wished the bastards he was trying to catch weren't so paranoid that they'd taken all phones at the door. That was the rule, no communication or recording devices allowed at any of the potential meets. It was one of the ways Stellman's identity had remained a secret for so long. No chance to record or snap a picture of the man.

God, he wished he had some way to communicate with this woman. He knew she was in trouble, but what sort? Was she being trafficked? Or was Randy her pimp, and she was having second thoughts?

She definitely didn't look hard enough to be a prostitute. But then again, none probably did when they first started.

"Why don't you come on over here and let me get a closer look at you. See if you taste as good as you look."

Her tiny flinch, even though she knew he was acting, broke his heart. "N-no sex, remember?"

"Yeah, but there's plenty of other stuff we can do." His words made him want to vomit. Her eyes were closed again, her head leaning against the couch back. He reached out and touched her small foot, the closest part of her body to him. Her eyes flew open, but she relaxed when he just stroked her foot softly. "Let's put that mouth of yours to work."

The tremors began wracking her body again. Tears poured out of eyes that looked at him with utter devastation. She pointed to her chest, then held her wrists out as if they were shackled.

He nodded. Definitely not a prostitute. She was in trouble and needed help.

He couldn't leave her. Screw Operation Sparrow. Screw stopping Cline from selling his secrets. Major Pinnock would have to find another way to catch this Stellman guy. After all, Major Pinnock had been his commanding officer in the army that had taught him the most important lesson in his life: you never left a fallen comrade behind.

Aiden had once carried one of his injured Special Forces brothers over his shoulder for two miles to get him out of enemy territory. This shouldn't be nearly as difficult. And it was definitely enemy territory.

"Don't be scared, Firefly. I'm going to help you." He reached up and took her hand and squeezed it gently in his, leaning forward and nodding so she would know he understood what she was telling him.

"Really?" she mouthed, hope lighting her eyes.

He took his finger and crossed it over his heart.

He added another line for Randy's sake. "I'm going to show you just what I like. You are as soft as you look, aren't you?"

He motioned for her to turn so he could look at the locket necklace. It was bolted with a special lock, just like he'd feared. Aiden wouldn't be able to get it off her without Randy becoming aware of what he was doing. That meant leaving with her before Randy came back in the room would be nearly impossible. He'd definitely notice the change in noise if they left this room.

Aiden stroked a hand over the impossibly soft skin of her shoulder as she turned back around. The only way to get her out would be to follow Randy out of the main room when he left with her, then break her out. Hopefully, Aiden could get some of his Linear team to help.

He wished he could communicate the plan to her, let her know what to expect. Of course, he also wished he had access to his phone or his Glock. Both of those would solve his problem also.

Instead, Aiden did what he could: held her hand as their time went on, every once in a while saying something obnoxious to preserve the roles they were playing. At the end of the two hours, knowing they were running out of time, he unfastened his belt and pants.

She remained balled up next to him as she had the whole time, but at least she didn't tense at his actions. Until Randy burst through the door a few minutes later.

"It's time to go."

Aiden forced himself to keep his head lying back on the couch, legs sprawled out in front of him, the very picture of a man who'd had his sexual needs fulfilled. "Just like you said, Randy. Lots of other talented uses besides sex."

Randy tossed the robe at Firefly, who quickly scrambled into it. "Time to go," he said again.

She looked at Randy, then back to Aiden. He wanted more than anything to be able to reassure her. But there was no way he'd be able to get her out with Randy right here and his muscle guy waiting at the door.

"Thanks for a good time, sweetheart." He smirked and winked. "I hope to see you again soon." So much sooner than Randy expected.

He grit his teeth as the other man yanked her up with a punishing grip on her arm and marched her out the door. Five seconds later Aiden had his pants buckled and was following behind him.

The main room was chaotic. The party was winding down. Everyone had gotten louder as the drinks and women had been consumed more freely. Randy and his guy were gathering up the women they'd brought, Randy's hand now gripping Firefly's hair again.

He was going to break every damn finger in that hand.

Aiden forced a smile as someone came up to talk to him about a possible business venture. He angled his body so he could keep an eye on Randy.

That was when he saw Cline out of the corner of his eye. The man had gotten up from the booth where he'd been sitting earlier and was talking to some other people: two men Aiden didn't recognize and a few women standing next to them.

Cline was still playing with that damned napkin.

When someone made a joke, and everyone laughed, one of the women eased closer to Cline, and he put the napkin in his blazer's pocket. The woman locked her lips on his and a few seconds later was easing that same blazer off Cline's shoulders and tossing it onto the booth seat.

The group laughed again as the woman trailed her fingers down Cline's arm until she had his hand, drawing him toward one of the back rooms.

Aiden waited to see if anyone in the group would go through the blazer once Cline left, but they paid no attention to it whatsoever. They just continued to talk and laugh, walking away from the booth.

This was too good an opportunity to pass up. If Aiden was going to burn this cover helping Firefly, the least he could do was get that info on the napkin first.

He was casual with his movements as he made his way over to the table, then picked the napkin out of the pocket with nimble fingers. He glanced down at it to make sure it was the same one he'd seen before.

Still the same gibberish symbols. He had no idea what they meant but prayed Major Pinnock would. He folded the napkin into his own pocket, then headed toward the door, picking up his pace when he realized Randy and Firefly were already gone.

"What I'm telling you is that my phone has been messed with," someone yelled near the lockers at the front of the club. "If you're going make us give up our stuff, the least you can do is make sure it's safe. This locker was open!"

Shit. Aiden needed to get to his own locker and the keys to his car inside so he could follow Randy. He rushed forward to see a short man yelling at the big hulking guy in charge of locker supervision.

Any other time Aiden would've appreciated the sight of an unarmed, much smaller man running his mouth at a bouncer, size extra-huge, sporting a SIG Sauer P226 at his shoulder. Not now. Aiden moved around the screaming man only to stop short when the bouncer held out his arm.

"Nobody goes into the lockers until we get this sorted out." His deep voice matched his massive size.

Fuck. "Dude, I've got an emergency that needs to be handled right now."

Bouncer shook his head and actually drew his weapon.

"Your emergency is going to have to wait until after I deal with this asshole. Nobody touches the lockers until we get this cleared up."

"I just want my keys. I'll come back for the rest."

The bouncer shook his head and went on to tell both Aiden and the screaming little guy that security was going over the footage of the cameras covering the lockers to see if there had been any foul play. Until then, everyone just needed to go back into the main room and enjoy the entertainment or wait outside.

When Aiden realized the big guy wasn't going to budge, he ran out the door. His only hope was stopping Randy in the parking lot and praying to God he was still loading the women—*Firefly*—into a vehicle.

But when he got to the parking lot, he couldn't find Randy or the women anywhere, despite searching both sides of the building.

They were gone.

And Aiden had no idea where.

CHAPTER 5

AIDEN PUNCHED the large weighted bag suspended from the ceiling of the Linear Tactical sparring center again. And again. Then stepped back and performed a complicated series of kicks that attacked the bag from all sides.

He didn't pull either his punches or his kicks, although it would eventually leave him bruised even through the protective gear he wore. He did another series of punch-kick combinations, even as he recognized that punishing himself wasn't going to help Firefly.

But he would be goddamned if she was going to be the only one to have bruises.

It had been two and a half days—*fifty-eight hours*—since he'd last seen her, last seen those green eyes trusting him to get her out from whatever was happening with Randy. Was she still waiting for him to show up? Did she think everything he'd tried to communicate was a lie?

Was she even still alive? Aiden punched the bag harder.

The second he'd finally gotten his belongings from the locker and made it to his car, he'd called Sheriff Nelson. The sheriff had sent someone to watch The Barn the two nights since, but not only had Firefly not been back, no one had. Evidently, until there was another private party, The Barn would remain empty.

Cline certainly wouldn't be hosting any more parties. He'd been arrested yesterday. After he was tried for treason, he wouldn't be seeing any women—naked or otherwise—for a long time. The true criminal had been using Cline as a distraction for law enforcement, then gotten himself killed two days ago after torturing Charlotte "Charlie'" Devereux, the girlfriend of one of Aiden's best friends.

It all had to do with that code Cline had written on that damned napkin at The Barn.

Like Aiden's gut had told him, those symbols were at the center of it all—in a much worse way than anyone could have possibly anticipated. The symbols had been part of the code needed to access and manipulate eight unmanned combat drones.

Aiden going back to get it had potentially saved thousands lives.

All it had cost was Firefly. Every mission had a price. He'd just never meant for her to be the one to pay it.

He'd replayed that night a thousand times in his head, balancing his choices and the decisions he'd made. If he had moved thirty seconds quicker, he would've gotten out of the building before the little man had started screaming. He would've saved Firefly.

It had been a long two days. Aiden wasn't used to second-guessing his decisions.

He shifted his weight and moved into a sliding side kick that would've ripped the bag from the ceiling if it weren't so well anchored. Even being part of the team that had rescued Charlie and killed the man trying to sell access to the drones hadn't relieved this gnawing in his gut. The advanced self-defense class he'd taught this morning hadn't either, nor had trying, unsuccessfully, to gather more info about Randy. Nobody seemed to know anything about him except that he and the other guy, Dillon, sometimes showed up with women or drugs or guns.

Fucking jack-of-all-trade criminals.

Somebody had to know how to get in touch with him. Until Aiden found that person, his criminal undercover persona would stay alive. Until he could find Firefly. Or at least until he could find Randy, who Aiden would happily beat the shit out of until he told them where to find her.

He couldn't stand to think about the state she would be in. He had no idea why the no-sex rule had been in place or how much longer it would hold.

He just had to find her.

"Is there a certain number of times you're going to hit that bag before it gives you the answers you want?"

Aiden hadn't heard his friend and army buddy Finn Bollinger come in. "What are you doing here? I thought you were at the hospital with Charlie. Is she awake yet?"

They'd had to keep her in a medically induced coma a couple of days to help with the swelling in her brain from the beating she'd taken while refusing to give information to her torturer.

"She's in and out. Her mom and Jordan Reiss are with her right now." Finn scrubbed a hand over a jaw that definitely needed a shave. "I'm here because Major Pinnock called and asked me to meet him here. You too. He's in the conference room."

That's where this had all started, with Major Pinnock asking for help to stop Cline and find this guy Stellman. Aiden didn't care about that anymore. "I'm not going after Stellman, Finn. I respect the hell out of the major, but I'm only going back under to try to help this woman. That's it." He'd already told Finn all about Firefly.

Finn held the bag as Aiden took a few more shots at it. "I think you'll want to hear Pinnock out. He's bringing someone with him who might have information about your girl."

That was the first even remotely good news he'd heard. Aiden stopped punching the bag. "Who?"

"Gabriel Collingwood. Remember him from the military?"

Aiden reached up and grabbed the Velcro strap of his fighting mitt with his teeth and pulled it loose. "Sure, from those crossover missions we did with his SEAL team. He got out of the navy, right?"

"Yeah, like seven years ago when his parents had died. He took over Collingwood Technology."

Aiden ripped off the other glove. "What's Collingwood got to do with any of this?"

"His company is the government contractor that had the access code to the drones. That second set of symbols Charlie saw was from Collingwood's company. Stellman was blackmailing him for the information."

Aiden grabbed a bottle of water. "Fine, but why is he here now? He should've notified Pinnock he was under duress way before today."

"I'll let Gabe tell that story. But I think you might find it interesting."

Aiden doubted it. "And why's that?"

"Because of how Stellman was blackmailing him to get the information. He kidnapped Gabe's sister."

～

Violet Collingwood.

An hour later, Aiden was staring at a picture on his computer tablet of the woman he knew as Firefly. His Firefly was Violet Collingwood, Gabe's younger sister.

In the picture on his screen she was laughing, standing next to her brother, whose cheek she'd obviously just smeared icing on. Gabe's look into the camera was exasperated. Hers was impish. So very different than the woman Aiden had seen at The Barn, when she'd barely been holding it together.

What was happening to her right now? What had happened to her last night? Had Randy taken her to another private gathering where she'd been at the mercy of whoever had "bought" her? Aiden's fingers tightened around the tablet until he was forced to set it down so he didn't damage the computer.

Gabe Collingwood had the same bloodshot eyes and unshaven cheeks as Aiden, the same burning fury that had already gotten the man out of his seat twice and pacing. It was a helplessness that went against everything he'd ever been trained to do.

The Linear conference room was full of men of a similar nature: Gabe, Major Pinnock, some guy Gabe had brought with him, as well as Aiden and Finn.

Aiden had already reported to them all about what had happened at The Barn. He hadn't elaborated on Violet's appearance, but he hadn't withheld details just to save Gabe's feelings either. The man would make the best decisions if he had as much information as possible.

Aiden didn't flinch when he told Major Pinnock that not only had he been willing to blow his cover, but he had been in active pursuit of blowing it when he'd lost sight of

Randy and the women. He'd do the same thing again to save Violet.

He gave Gabe a pointed look. "Why didn't you notify Pinnock immediately if you were being blackmailed? Most contractors of your company's nature have contingency plans in place for that sort of thing. Doesn't yours?" Maybe if the other man had enlisted help when he'd first found out about Firefly—*Violet's*—kidnapping, she wouldn't still be in jeopardy.

Gabe didn't flinch. "We have contingencies in place for *me* being under duress and needing a way to signal the military, but I made the decision not to inform Pinnock right away."

Aiden's hands clenched into fists under the table. "Oh really? And how did that work out for you? How did it work out for Violet? Oh wait, she's still being kept against her will and suffering God knows what even as we speak."

Gabe slammed a hand down on the table. "You think that because you've met my sister for a total of two hours that you know what's best in this situation? What's at risk? You were ready to jump ship on your cover at the first sight of trouble."

Aiden's chair flew backward as he stood and leaned his weight on his fists on the table. "I was willing to do *whatever I had to* in order to get her out of there. Obviously, that's more than you're willing to do."

Aiden couldn't get his hands on Randy at the moment, but he'd be more than happy to beat the shit out of Collingwood instead. Who the hell would just leave his sister in a situation like that if he had the means to help her?

Finn grabbed his shoulder and Aiden spun around. "What?" he barked.

He knew he had no reason to yell at Finn, but Jesus,

why were they all standing around in here talking rather than *doing* something?

But what could be done?

"Gabe saved Charlie's life," Finn said.

"What?" he asked again, wrenching his tone into something more reasonable.

Gabe sat down in his chair, Aiden and Finn following suit.

Gabe ran a hand across his face, rubbing his eyes. "Once Stellman proved he had Violet and told me he was going to kill her if I didn't provide the access codes for the drones, I did what I had to do to save as many lives as possible."

"And what exactly was that?" Aiden asked.

"I gave Stellman the code he wanted but then immediately wrote a shell program and changed where the code would lead."

"That bastard would very definitely have killed Charlie if the code she'd memorized had been fake," Finn said.

Gabe let out a breath. "The fact that she held out as long as she did, giving me time to build the shell program, was amazing."

Finn smiled. "You know how it is. Not all girls are made up of sugar and spice. Some are made of hurricanes, intelligence, cuss words, and courage. That's Charlie."

Nobody in the room doubted the courage and strength of Charlie Devereux after what she'd endured.

"Violet would've been killed too," Gabe said hoarsely. "If I hadn't provided what they wanted, they would've killed Violet. Buying more time was the best option I had."

"And as far as Stellman knows," Major Pinnock continued, "Gabe provided the right code. Unfortunately, Stellman's partner happened to get killed trying to access the drones."

"So you think Violet is still alive?" Aiden whispered.

Gabe nodded. "Yes. I think she's too valuable a tool for Stellman to give up. Using her to control me worked once. He'll try it again."

"Then why would he pimp her out at party for a couple hundred dollars?" Aiden rubbed his forehead, which was starting to pound again. "It doesn't make sense. Someone might recognize her, or like with me, she might be able to get a message out."

Gabe looked over at the man two seats down from him. With dark skin and darker eyes, he had taken in everything said so far without saying much. The warrior in Aiden recognized the warrior in this man. Gabe gestured to him. "This is Kendrick Foster, recently promoted to Collingwood Technology's head of security. He's been separately gathering as much intel as possible about Violet's location."

Kendrick gave them a brief nod. "My team reports that the man you saw Violet with is named Randy Villarreal. He hasn't worked for Stellman for long. We think he took her to that club because he doesn't know who she is and just wanted to make extra money with a pretty face. The fact that Randy told you that intercourse was not an option supports that theory."

Every jaw in the room tightened at the words and the reminder that just because there was every reason to believe Violet was alive didn't mean she wasn't suffering.

"Violet's not like your Charlie, Finn," Gabe said, voice cracking at his sister's name. "She's young, just turned twenty-two last month. And she's not tough at all. She's quiet, just about to finish her chemical engineering degree. Brilliant, but gentle."

Not the type that was going to recover easily from something like this.

"What's the plan?" Aiden asked. "Sitting around waiting for Stellman to blackmail you again doesn't seem very proactive."

"That's why we're here," Gabe said. "We need your help."

"Whatever you need." Aiden meant every word.

Gabe looked over at Kendrick and gestured for him to continue. "We've been scouring and analyzing any data we can on Stellman, Randy Villarreal, and a red-haired female who might be in his company."

"Where are you getting your data?" Finn asked.

Kendrick's eyes were hooded. "Let's just say I haven't spent my entire life in corporate circles. I have contacts."

Aiden didn't care where the information was coming from, as long as it was accurate and helpful. "What are your unmentionable sources saying?"

"Randy was spotted last night at a nightclub outside of Reddington City."

"With Violet?" Aiden doubted it but asked anyway.

"No. He didn't have any women with him. He was purchasing narcotics."

"By the time we got someone to the club, Randy was already gone." Frustration colored Gabe's tone.

"What exactly were you planning to do to this Randy guy if you'd gotten to him?" Major Pinnock asked, eyebrow raised.

Gabe didn't flinch. "Just ask him a few questions about the whereabouts of my sister."

Aiden caught Gabe's eye. "If you do catch up with Randy and need help asking your questions, I'd be more than happy to help with that." He already owed the man five broken fingers.

Gabe nodded, an understanding firm between them. If

they could catch Randy, he *would* tell them where Violet was being held.

"What we did find out," Kendrick continued, "is that there's a private party tonight at an undisclosed location. Similar to the one where you saw Violet—lots of girls available for an evening's pleasure. Whether these women have any choice about it doesn't matter to a lot of these people."

"You think Randy will be there with Violet?"

Kendrick shrugged. "I think he blew a wad of cash on drugs and now wants to make some of that money back. This will look like an easily controllable situation to him."

Hope began to build for the first time since Aiden had realized he'd lost Violet at The Barn. "Okay, so we move in. Call Sheriff Nelson and get law enforcement on the scene." Aiden looked over at Finn, who nodded in support.

"It's not that simple," Gabe said. "First, the location is unknown and evidently there will be all sorts of cloak-and-dagger shit getting people there. Private vehicles with blacked-out windows, no weapons or cell phones allowed. The invite list will be highly selective. We're hoping your cover ID is established enough to get you invited."

Kendrick rubbed a hand over his closely cropped black hair. "I can't say for certain, but I think this event tonight is going to be a human auction. Scumbags there are going to be trying to buy women."

Shit. That was bad. "Look, I'm willing to do whatever you want me to do, but even if I do find her, I'll run into the same problem I had at The Barn. Getting her out with no weapon and no way of calling for backup is damn near impossible."

"We have this." Gabe took out a small box and slid it over to him. Aiden opened it and immediately recognized a tracking device.

Aiden shook his head. "If they're as paranoid as you said, they're probably going to scan everyone for active transmitters. Plus, if you come in guns blazing, Violet and a lot of the other women may get hurt."

"No, storming in won't work," Kendrick said. "And we have every reason to believe they'll be blocking all transmissions from this location anyway, so even if you could get into the building with a tracker on and running, it wouldn't do much good. This tracker is for you to put on Violet once you find her. Put it anywhere on her person or clothing, then turn it on once she leaves."

Understanding dawned. "Then you'll move in on wherever they're holding her."

Gabe nodded. "We're not bringing in law enforcement. I can't take the chance on something going wrong. I want to send in you Linear Tactical guys. If you're still up for missions like this."

"We are," both Aiden and Finn said at the same time. They had no doubt the rest of the guys would feel the same.

"You're the next best thing to my SEAL team—one of the tightest Special Forces groups I've ever worked with."

"We'll be ready," Aiden assured him.

"I want Kendrick as part of the team too." Gabe's words weren't a request. "He'll be my personal eyes and ears. I would be going in also if it weren't for my knee. I won't take a chance on slowing you down."

Aiden turned to the younger man. "Can you keep up?"

One dark eyebrow rose. "Don't doubt it."

Major Pinnock cleared his throat. "Look, I want to get Violet home as much as anyone, but you need to be aware of the other factor here, Aiden. Security is probably as tight as it is at this private party because Stellman is going to be there. We want you to get the tracker on Violet, but being able to ID Stellman . . . we may not get another opportunity like this."

"Not to mention, as long as Stellman goes free, Violet will always have to be looking over her shoulder," Kendrick said.

Aiden looked around at each man in the room. "Then it sounds like tonight is going to be a big night."

CHAPTER 6

MY SIGNATURE ÉCLAIR needs a mixture of both dark and milk chocolate. Milk chocolate by itself would be too sweet. Also, a dash of cayenne pepper might add a unique and unexpected flavor.

Violet felt the pinch on her thigh at a distance. Through eyes that wouldn't quite focus, she watched the man in the gold mask perpetuate the tiny cruelty.

The detached part of her brain knew she was disassociating again. Her mind was hiding from what was really happening here in order to protect her. Reality was too much to process.

This was a human auction and these people were monsters. Masked monsters.

"We need more wine, Timothy. Send the girl to get some more."

The bored request came from the lone woman in the group of monsters, no less evil because of her gender. She was one of the six people Violet had been assigned to serve. The group had "rented" her for the night from Randy to meet their food, beverage, and entertainment needs as they decided if they would bid on any of the people being sold. Violet supposed she should be glad she wasn't one of the people being auctioned off later. And she was thankful. But every time one of these people touched her, she wanted to vomit.

Two of the six people—Gold Mask and Blue Mask— were more violent. But the pinches and stinging slaps to her thighs and buttocks were easier to take than the softer, more intimate caresses of the others. Hands were constantly on her breasts, or between her legs, as she brought them whatever drinks or snacks they wanted.

It had been a relief when her mind had just completely shut down.

In here with her recipes, all the things she wanted to make when she got home, she couldn't feel anything else. She didn't squirm at the monsters' touch anymore—which had just made them laugh anyway. She didn't try to get away when they pulled her down on their laps. Here inside her mind she could survive.

And in here with her was Aiden. Somehow he was in her mind's safe place, even though he had no right to be.

After the night at The Barn with him—Three nights ago? More?—she'd stayed awake all night waiting for his rescue. Was that what he'd been trying to tell her when he'd said he would see her again soon, that he was going to help her? When he'd crossed his fingers over his heart and looked at her with such sincerity in those hazel eyes?

Part of her was still waiting for him to show up, even though it was obvious he wasn't going to. What had happened? Had he even tried? Had he decided she wasn't worth the trouble?

Was he some sicko, like these people, who got off on mentally tormenting others?

By the time her third meal had arrived in the dark room at the house with no sign of Aiden, Violet had just slid into the corner, wrapped her arms around herself, and cried. Having her hopes raised so sharply and then dashed had been so much harder than having no hope at all.

But still she couldn't seem to hate Aiden. Maybe he hadn't gotten her out like he'd crossed-his-heart promised, but he'd at least been gentle with her at The Barn. He could've been so much more cruel, as she knew now.

And at least the money Aiden had paid Randy at The Barn had made Randy happy. He'd left her alone, more interested in the drugs he'd scored than tormenting her. Or maybe Dillon's warnings that Stellman didn't want her damaged had taken root. Randy hadn't set foot into her windowless room since she'd returned from The Barn. Until tonight.

He'd stripped her once again and thrown her in a luke-warm shower this time to wash her hair, leering at her the whole time. There'd been no sign of Dillon as Randy had loaded her back into the cage in the truck, then brought in the other six women. Once again they'd all looked completely blank before Randy had shut the door, leaving them in the dark.

When they'd arrived at the mansion and been escorted to a basement floor, each of the women, including Violet, had been assigned a group of people to serve. Most groups were sitting around on couches and comfortable chairs, waiting for their chance to bid. She'd been running around all night getting them whatever they needed. She endured their petting when she wasn't serving.

One of the men pulled her onto his lap and mangled his hand around her breast, forcing Violet back into the situation. She shuddered as he licked and nipped his way down her throat. "Did you not hear the request for more wine?"

She struggled to get away, which just caused him to grope her a little longer before letting her off his lap, chuckling with his friends. She scurried off to get their alcohol.

A pâte sablée crust for a miniature pie would work well. The shortbread-cookie-type texture would pair well with the multiple types of chocolate. But would it be too sweet?

She refused to let reality back inside her mind. She had no idea how many hours she had left with these people, or if, at some point, each of them would take her into a back room to do whatever they wanted. Would she be killed if she fought? Was she a coward for allowing this to happen to her without screaming and telling them all to go fuck themselves?

Violet had never said those words to anyone in her life. Maybe now would be a good time. Would Randy rush over and stop her if she told the sadistic group of monsters to go back to hell where they belonged? Would he throw her back in the cage?

Just survive.

She heard her brother's voice in her head. That was what Gabe used to say to her after their parents had died, and she'd been so overwhelmed by grief and guilt. After all, they'd been out shopping for a present for her when they'd taken a curve too fast in their car and flipped over the median.

In those hard times, Gabe had pulled her into a hug and told her to *just survive* that day. They would worry about tomorrow, tomorrow.

If staying inside her mind and baking were how she *just survived* this, Violet would take it.

It was better than the alternative.

She retrieved the glasses of wine from the bar and allowed herself to remain wrapped in her own head as she walked back, not really seeing or hearing anything around her. She was handing them out to the monsters when Gold Mask spoke to someone standing behind her.

"Want us to send her back for another glass, Aiden? You can sit with us for a while."

Violet's head jerked around so fast she nearly toppled her entire tray. She would have if Aiden hadn't reached from behind her and steadied it with calm, sure hands.

"Don't want you to spill that," he said.

The monsters laughed. "Oh, I don't know. I'd like to see her clean it up on her hands and knees," Gold Mask said.

That got another round of laughter from everyone. Aiden's eyes narrowed just slightly, but Violet was the only one close enough to notice.

What was he doing here? Oh God, was he here to buy a person like everyone else?

Evidently, she wasn't the only one with that question.

"I didn't think this was your scene, Teague. Thought you were only into weapons sales," one of the men said.

"I am. I'm just here as a favor to my friend Angel to set up a meeting for a different sale."

Aiden squeezed her elbow as he said the word *angel*.

Angel, as in her brother Gabriel? That had been his call sign as a Navy SEAL. Was Aiden trying to tell her he was working with Gabe?

And would she survive if she allowed her hopes to rise only to have them dashed again?

Aiden grabbed the two remaining wine glasses and gave them to the people waiting, then sat down in an empty chair and pulled Violet into his lap. "Firefly and I made each other's acquaintance last week. I promised her we would see each other very soon and have been quite upset that I haven't been able to keep that promise. When I saw her over here with you, I wanted to come over and say hello."

Was he trying to tell her something again, or was it just her mind's attempt to protect her?

"Well, obviously you have a connection with her that we didn't have," Blue Mask said, one of the men who'd been pinching and tormenting her for hours. "I'm a little perturbed that you're taking away our entertainment. Scaring the little red rabbit has been the highlight of my night."

She felt Aiden's fingers tighten on her waist. Not enough to hurt her, but definitely enough for her to know he was angry at the monster's words.

But Aiden's voice was calm. Friendly. "I'll be happy to pay whatever you guys spent on her. I've been thinking about this sweet thing all week. There's no way I'm letting her get away this time." Aiden snuggled her closer. She made no attempt to get away. She still wasn't sure he was trying to signal her with his words, but she would take him over any of the rest of them. Aiden might be a criminal, but at least he wasn't here to buy humans.

Aiden had had ample opportunity to abuse her and he hadn't. So if her choice was to stay close to him or to the people who had been taunting her all night, she would take Aiden every time.

"The auction will be starting in the back soon anyway," the woman muttered, looking at Violet with cold eyes behind her mask. "Shame she's not up for auction. It would be a pleasure to break her."

She felt Aiden's grip tighten on her again, but his face remained neutral. "Not for me. There are so many more pleasurable things to do with someone like her than break her. You know what I would do? I'd keep her in purple lingerie all the time." His eyes met hers. "A deep *violet* color."

Violet's breath caught in her throat. *He knows who I am.* The clues he'd been dropping were real. The relief was almost staggering.

"She'd looked terrible in purple with that red hair," someone said, but neither she nor Aiden was paying them any attention.

Aiden was working for Gabe or with Gabe. Or hell, maybe he was even working against Gabe but just hated Randy more. She didn't care as long as he was getting information about her to her brother. There were so many questions she wanted to ask but couldn't because of both the people and the damned necklace Randy had put on her again.

"Aiden, didn't expect you here."

Speak of the devil.

"Hey, Randy." Aiden didn't get up. "I saw Red here from across the room—who can miss that hair?—and thought I'd come say hello for old times' sake."

"Yeah, well these people have paid for her services tonight, not you. Plus, the auction is about to begin so she'll be leaving. Don't want her to be sold by accident." He grinned.

"I'm heading out in a little while too. I buy weapons, not people." He grinned at the masked group around him. "But hey, no judgment toward you freaks. You do you."

There were a few chuckles, but most of them had already turned their full attention to the stage where the auction would take place.

Randy grabbed Violet's arm and pulled her away from Aiden. "Time to go."

Most of the people not wearing a mask were exiting. Randy propelled her forward into the hallway. She didn't dare look to see if Aiden was behind them.

"Randy, hold up." Aiden stepped in front of the smaller man to stop their progress. "I wanted to see about booking another few hours with Red here."

"She's not currently booking any sessions right now, but I'll get back to you. Or I have quite a few other options if you're interested."

Aiden slipped off his jacket and wrapped it around her naked shoulders. "You should take better care of your girls, Randy. Won't do you any good if they get sick from being out in the cold."

The jacket was big and warm and smelled like Aiden. A clean scent. Everything else she'd smelled since being taken had been dirty one way or another. But his jacket was warm and clean and wonderful.

It covered her nakedness, but more importantly, it almost certainly contained whatever tracking device Gabe was going to use to find her.

"Jesus H. Christ." Randy laughed. "What are you, in high school, giving her your letter jacket? Let me know if you want to talk about some other girls. This one won't be available."

What did that mean? Was he going to kill her? Planning to ask for a ransom from Gabe?

"That's a crying shame. Firefly here is talented and beautiful." Aiden glanced at Randy. "Want to make a quick fifty bucks?"

"Sorry, Teague, the no-sex rule is still in play. There's not enough time for that or . . . other stuff anyway."

Aiden ran his thumb across her bottom lip. Violet couldn't help her slight shiver.

A *good* shiver. She'd forgotten she could even do that.

"I just want a kiss, Randy. If I'm never going to see Firefly here again, I just want one kiss. We never got around to it last time."

"Whatever floats your boat, man. Fifty bucks."

Aiden pulled out his wallet and gave him the money, then grabbed the collar of his jacket and pulled her to him. He obviously didn't care that Randy was standing there blatantly watching or that there were other people in the hallway.

His lips were soft on hers, wiping away all traces of the masked monsters who had kissed her throughout the night, bruising her mouth in their roughness.

He coaxed, nibbling at her lips before easing them apart with his. She expected his tongue to thrust into her mouth, but it never did. The kiss was almost chaste. Like what she would expect at the end of a first date where both of them hoped to see each other again.

His hands slid up from the collar of the jacket to frame her face, just as gentle and softly intimate.

"Okay, Romeo, time's up," Randy said, boredom all but dripping from his tone. This obviously hadn't been the kiss he'd expect someone to pay fifty bucks for.

Aiden's fingers pressed against her face and scalp once more, his thumbs trailing across her cheeks before he stepped back from her.

"Worth it?" Randy asked.

Aiden didn't look away from her. "Every penny. I hope to see you very soon, Firefly. Don't think that I'm going to forget about you."

Randy rolled his eyes. "Later, Aiden. Want your jacket?"

"Nah. Let her keep it."

"Whatever." He grabbed her arm and yanked her down the hallway. Violet glanced over her shoulder and found Aiden watching them before Randy snatched her around a corner.

The rest of the women were waiting in an obedient group by the door that led out to the garage where the truck was parked. They looked at Randy in anticipation, all of them barely able to hold still.

"Good," Randy said. "You all get the prize when you get back to the house."

That was the news they'd all obviously wanted to hear. They followed behind him like ducklings as he led them to the truck.

"Take the jacket off," he said as he opened the cage door and she crawled in.

"No, please, just let me keep it. I'm cold." She couldn't give it up.

"Sorry, nothing comes back to the house except what left with us. Standing rule."

She slid back in the cage. She wasn't giving up the jacket. "Go fuck yourself, Randy."

Well, now she'd said those words to someone.

She knew she was in serious trouble when he didn't say anything back, just set his keys down. She slid as far back as she could go, pulling her legs up, knowing that wasn't going to help in the long run but doing it anyway. When he reached in to grab her, she kicked at him, feeling a sickening joy when her foot connected with his face and he howled in pain.

The joy didn't last long. This time when he reached inside the cage, he had something in his hand. A moment later when her body seized in agonized shock, she knew what it was.

A Taser.

She couldn't make her legs work this time when he reached inside, but she let out a sob when he used the Taser on her again.

Then he grabbed her by the calves and dragged her out. She tried to pull up her arms to protect herself when he got her far enough out of the cage to backhand her, but she wasn't nearly fast enough. The building spun as his fist crashed into her stomach and she retched to the side.

One of the other women must have moved because he turned his focus to them for a moment. "If you move, you lose your prize."

Evidently that threat was enough to stop any of them from trying to help Violet.

He ripped her head up from where she was lying against the floor of the truck, trying to get her breath, and yanked her backward. "I'm the boss, bitch. Nobody else. You'll do good to remember that."

She used her last bit of strength to fight as he pulled the jacket off of her, but it was useless. She watched as he dropped it to the ground after ripping it from her body.

Then he used the Taser on her time after time until she could no longer scream or cry. When he finally stopped and pushed her back in the cage, he didn't even have to lock the door to keep her in.

As Randy pulled the door to the truck shut, the last thing Violet saw was Aiden's jacket lying in a heap on the dirt.

CHAPTER 7

AIDEN HAD to wait an agonizing three more hours before the first private vehicle left to escort people away from the auction. Time passed with excruciating slowness. And since everyone wore masks inside this truly fucked-up masquerade, identifying Stellman in the crowd was impossible. Asking someone to point him out would be a death wish.

This party was very different than the low-class get-together at The Barn. The criminals here, most of whom, ironically, wouldn't consider themselves criminals at all, had power that came from money and prestige rather than weapons and violence.

Aiden collected as many details as he could about as many people as possible. They wore masks, but that didn't mean there weren't identifying clues about them from their actions, words, and conversation.

A blond woman calling herself Sabrina who collected rare red wines. A man nicknamed "Munich" who wore a Harvard class ring. An Asian bragging about his summit of Mt. Kilimanjaro last year on Christmas Day.

Aiden filed away all the information in his brain, using

tricks he'd perfected in the army. Each person got their own room inside the house he built in his mind. When he opened those mental rooms later, he'd be able to retrieve the information.

None of his memories would be usable in a court of law, but they would be a start. They'd give law enforcement something to go on. Because Aiden was damned sure not going to let these people get away with what was going on here today.

But that was tomorrow's problem. Today they would save Violet.

That kiss. Good Lord, that kiss had damn near made him forget about everything going on around them. Made him forget that some of the worst atrocities known to man had been happening in the next room. Made him forget that Randy had been standing there, leering. Made him forget he was kissing her in order to place the small tracking device just behind her ear.

He'd just wanted to keep kissing her.

Violet had understood what he was telling her about her brother, about knowing who she was, about the rescue. She would be as ready as she could be.

Once he could finally leave, and the sedan with blacked-out windows was thirty minutes away from the party, Aiden's phone was returned to him.

He immediately turned on Violet's tracker with it. By the time he met up with his team, they should have her location.

Another thirty minutes later the car stopped to deliver him at the same place that it had picked him up in downtown Reddington City. They'd driven more than an hour, which meant the auction could've been anywhere from a half a mile to fifty miles away.

Aiden got into his own car and drove around for ten minutes just to make sure no one was following him. Then he drove directly to the warehouse Gabriel Collingwood had secured as their home base for this operation.

The familiar faces of his Linear Tactical partners—men he had and would trust with his life—were hard at work when he walked in the door.

"They crossed into Fremont County," Zac Mackay said. He'd been their team leader in the Green Berets and would resume that role tonight. "Tracker stopped about ten miles east of Dunoir. Heavily forested area, no residential houses, so it's off the grid."

"Good," Aiden said as he loosened his tie and prepared to change into his mission fatigues. "No civilians around to worry about."

"How did Violet look? Was she okay? Did you have any problems getting the tracker on her?" Gabe was pacing back and forth, his fists clenching.

Aiden changed clothes as he talked. His team had seen him in less than his boxer shorts, and Gabe and Kendrick didn't strike him as being overly shy.

"Physically, not bad. No broken bones, limp, or anything to suggest internal injuries. Minimal bruising. She was being used as a sort of waitress at the event." Details about the people inside the private party, what they were doing there, and even Violet's exact situation, would have to wait. They weren't pertinent to the mission of liberating Violet. "I gave Violet my jacket but decided to put the tracker on her skin just behind her ear instead."

"Why did you give her your jacket?" Gabe asked. "And why did you plant the tracker on her neck? It had to be difficult for you to place it there undetected."

Aiden pulled a long-sleeved shirt over his T-shirt, then

strapped on his Kevlar vest. "Suffice it to say, giving her the jacket worked in the situation. As did the tracker. Overall it was better than putting it on her arm or somewhere it might be detected."

"But how did you get it there, Teague?" Gabriel demanded. "So help me God, if you've been taking advantage of my sister in this situation . . ."

Aiden stepped up so he was face-to-face with Gabe. Fighting was not going to help now, but damn, it was tempting. "Your sister is strong. She is surviving under circumstances that would mentally cripple most people. She was able to pick up on my cryptic clues."

He hadn't been able to say Gabe's name outright, and saying the word "violet" had been a bigger risk, but he'd had to make sure she understood help was coming.

"That's because she's got an IQ higher than Einstein," Gabe muttered. "Definitely higher than mine. I'm not surprised she figured it out, even under duress."

"She did." Aiden nodded. "And hopefully, she'll be ready tonight and won't be scared when this all goes down. But the details about what's happened to her this week are her choice to tell or not tell. I did what I needed to do in the situation, and it worked. Now let's get her out."

Gabe obviously wanted to argue more. He probably wanted to rant against the world and beat the shit out of someone.

He wanted his sister back, wanted to be able to protect her. Aiden understood.

"Okay," Gabe finally whispered.

"Are we almost ready to roll?" he asked Gavin, who had always been the team's most technically savvy member. Finn and Dorian, the final two members, were double-checking weapons and gear near the door. They were all aware that this mission was outside the parameters of the law.

Not a single one of them cared.

But their intent was not to kill. Although all of them had their personal choice of handguns somewhere on their person, most of the weapons they carried were for the temporary takedown of their enemy—tranquilizers and stun guns.

The plan was to get Violet safe, then call in law enforcement to clean up the mess. They would say they just happened to stumble upon the place during a Linear training exercise.

Amazing how that tended to happen.

"We're good to go, but . . ." Gavin's brows were furrowed as he studied the screen.

"What's wrong?" Zac asked.

"Maybe nothing. Hopefully, nothing."

"Okay, what's the *potential* problem?" Aiden asked.

"I was just looking through the tracker's transmission history. There were some abnormalities with Violet's tracker."

"It's not working correctly?" Gabe came over to study the computer with Gavin. Whatever he saw, he obviously didn't like any more than Gavin had.

"Shit," Gabe muttered. "I double-checked this tracker myself. Didn't want to leave any room for faulty tech or some sort of malfunction. This is one of the most robust transmitters my R&D department has ever made. It should not have been giving off spikes like that."

"I was as gentle as possible with it while placing it on Violet," Aiden assured the other man. "It was definitely functional when Violet left me."

"What would've happened if someone found it on her?" Zac asked.

Gabe scrubbed a hand over his eyes. "Well, it's still transmitting. So if someone found it, then they didn't deliberately destroy it."

"If they found it and left it transmitting on purpose, that would mean they know we're coming," Aiden said. "They'll be ready for us."

A situation their team had firsthand experience with.

"It's possible," Gavin said. "As we all know, that's always possible."

All of the Linear Tactical team looked over at Dorian. He had been the one to pay the price when they'd been ambushed in Afghanistan because the enemy had known they were coming. He'd spent weeks in an Afghani prison and had barely survived.

And even though he had survived, he'd never been the same. He still struggled with PTSD so badly, it was difficult for him to be around people for long periods of time.

The big, quiet man knew what everyone was thinking. He just shrugged. "We go anyway. As long as there is a chance Violet is there, we go. I'll be okay."

"Is there something I need to know about here?" Kendrick asked. "If there might be some sort of meltdown, I'd like to know ahead of time."

"There won't be," Zac said. "Dorian can handle himself just as well, if not better, than every person in this room. Regardless of whether the bad guys know we're coming or not."

Dorian just shrugged again. "As long as I don't have to sit around and make small talk with them, we should be fine. Now, if I'm required to do any sort of entertaining, then yeah, you might have to put me down."

It seemed to be enough to reassure Kendrick. The younger man gave Dorian a quick nod.

Gavin was still studying the computer screen. "Honestly, I don't think they found it, because that still wouldn't explain the inconsistent transmission early on. I don't think they know we're coming."

Aiden didn't like the look on his friend's face. "That's good news right, Redwood? Why are you saying it the way people normally say 'dead baby seals'?"

"The only time I've ever seen a transmitter behave this way was when we had one on someone who tried to climb an electrical fence. Got the hell shocked out of him. The tracker still worked, but it gave off inconsistent readings because of the damage done by the voltage."

Finn shook his head. "Are we saying that there's some sort of fence where they're holding Violet? Or that she made some sort of escape run?"

No, that couldn't be right. There would've been nowhere for her to run at that party, not naked like she was. And if she'd understood what he was saying about them coming for her, why would she have tried to make an escape on her own?

But if not, then how had a bunch of voltage damaged the tracker? The only other way would've been something like . . .

Oh shit. Oh God *no*. Bile pooled in Aiden's stomach. He turned to Gavin, who obviously had already figured out what had happened.

"How many times would she have to be hit to do that sort of damage?" Aiden croaked.

Gabe's fist came crashing down onto the metal table as he put the pieces together himself.

"Jesus," Zac whispered. "Taser?"

Gavin nodded. "Multiple times for it to have damaged the transmitter to this extent. Honestly, we're lucky it's working at all. She must've taken at least one shock straight to her neck near the transmitter. If it had been on, the voltage probably would've blown its circuitry to hell, and we'd have no reading at all."

Hard to be thankful that she'd been tortured by an electroshock weapon multiple times *before* the tracker had been turned on.

"Let's focus, people," Zac said, voice calm, solid. "Location hasn't changed. Objective hasn't changed. And at least now we know that Violet might be hurt. Let's prepare for that contingency."

Gabe was still hunched over the desk, staring at the computer, the edge of the desk in a death grip in his fingers.

Aiden touched the man's shoulder. "Gabe, let's get her home."

Then Aiden turned to Finn, who nodded, his lips pinched and face a little pale. Who could blame him? His woman was still in the hospital, another would-be victim of Stellman's plots. "We're ready. Let's go."

The ride to the location was made largely in silence. Everyone had their own way of preparing themselves for what was to come . . . and the wait until the action occurred, which was almost more difficult.

Aiden had missed this. Although he loved the work they did at Linear Tactical, loved teaching civilians how to survive in dangerous situations, it wasn't the same as the active missions they'd done together as Green Berets.

The closer they got to their target, the more settled he became. Preparing for action was like muscle memory for him, for all of them. Aiden's senses became more acute, everything more crisp and focused.

He knew what was to come. The moment he stepped out of this truck into the night, prepared to infiltrate the building, he would feel the blood begin to race through his veins. But his mind would stay calm and detached, remote from the adrenaline that would flood his body.

Successfully completing the mission was the priority. It always had been, but this time especially. Aiden forced thoughts of Violet, of what she may have been through, from his mind. In order to be the most efficient, he had to be detached. Failure wasn't an option.

The men in this van, his team, his brothers, would not let that happen.

Gavin held out a fist, almost as if he could hear Aiden's thoughts. Aiden bumped the other man's knuckles the way he had hundreds of times. He looked over at Finn and Zac across from him. Both gave him a brief nod.

Aiden would go in first, get to Violet, to make sure she was out of harm's way if things went sideways. The rest of the team would take down the tangos once Aiden had her safe.

The vehicle pulled to a stop, and they exited into the cover of night.

It was time.

CHAPTER 8

RANDY HAD DECIDED to have some sort of party.

Violet was in the corner of the windowless room. Her wrists were zip-tied and attached to a hook on the wall above her head. Agony burned through her shoulder joints every time she tried to move. Which wasn't often because no other parts of her body seemed to be working right either.

Everything hurt.

And, moreover, help wasn't coming. How could it be when she hadn't been able to keep Aiden's jacket and whatever tracking device had been in it?

The hopelessness was worse than the pain, knowing she'd been so close to helping herself get rescued, then lost it all because she'd been stupid.

Why had she fought?

She was smarter than Randy. She should've figured out a way to keep the jacket that didn't involve a physical altercation she couldn't possibly have won. She should have used her brain to convince him that keeping the jacket was a good idea. Or better yet, *his* good idea.

She should've done that instead of trying to fight, which had gotten her tasered until she couldn't move and given her an intimate knowledge of a level of pain she hadn't even been aware existed. A pain she would do anything not to experience again.

When they'd gotten back to the house, Randy had dragged her back to her room when she couldn't walk herself. Then evidently, he'd gotten a glimpse of himself in the mirror because he'd come back in, grabbed her by the hair from where she'd lain on the floor still naked, and yanked her over into the corner. After securing her arms above her to the wall, he'd grabbed her chin.

"I'll be back for you later. You'll be paying for the damage you did to my face."

His voice wasn't full of his normal bluster. He'd said it quietly, so full of promise that a slimy panic curled its way around her throat, crushing the oxygen out of her.

She had little doubt the "no sex" rule was over.

His friends had shown up a few minutes ago, four of them. They were loud and generally obnoxious, and obviously drugs were involved. She couldn't see them, but hearing them through the thin walls, even from the living room near the front of the house, was no problem.

Maybe Randy would party with them until he passed out and completely forgot about her.

She swallowed a groan as she tried to shift her weight to ease one leg that was falling asleep. The pull on her shoulders was agonizing. She tried to stop the tear before it escaped her eye and down her cheek but couldn't. She refused to cry. Mostly because having to wipe her nose and not being able to do so was the only thing that could make this situation worse.

"Can I have a word with you in the other room,

Randy?" Randy's friends barely lowered their volume as Dillon yelled over them.

"Can't it wait?" Randy whined. "I'm trying to enjoy a little downtime here."

"No, it can't. And tell your friends to keep it down."

Randy and Dillon must have moved into the room right next to the wall she was restrained to, because she could hear them much better even though they were speaking at a lower volume.

"Mr. Stellman gave you specific instructions. No one was to know about this location. Nor was Ms. Collingwood to be removed from here. Now you've done that twice. Mr. Stellman isn't happy."

"Look, I've never even met Stellman. He's never around. What he doesn't know won't hurt him, right?"

"Mr. Stellman doesn't take lightly to people who work for him not following directions. It's how he's run his organization so successfully for so long."

Randy's tone turned cajoling. "C'mon, Dillon. There's no need to tell him about anything. I promise, I won't take the girl out of the house anymore. And I'll get rid of my friends. Don't rat me out."

"Mr. Stellman has stayed on top this long by not allowing his people to do whatever they just feel like. You were given a specific task: escort the women when they were to be at certain places and not allow Ms. Collingwood to escape."

"And I have! Look, man, as soon as I meet Stellman, I swear I'll be on the straight and narrow. I'll be on the straight and narrow *now*."

"You've already met Mr. Stellman, Randy, and he isn't very happy with what he's seen. He likes to check out all his new employees himself to see if they pass muster."

"*What?*"

A phone chirped loudly. Violet twisted her head so she could press her ear closer to the wall.

"What was that?" Randy's voice was loud and fast. "Is that text from Stellman? When did I meet him? Was he at one of the parties? Shit."

"I've got to go."

"Look, don't tell Mr. Stellman I screwed up. I'll do better, okay? I'll get rid of my friends, no more taking the redhead anywhere."

"I won't say anything to Mr. Stellman." Dillon must have moved closer to the door, farther away from her wall. It was harder to hear him. "Just stay here with your friends. Don't go anywhere. We'll talk about it when I get back."

Maybe she should be more reassured with one less criminal in the house, but she wasn't. Maybe the Stellman guy would come here and kill Randy because he couldn't follow the rules.

When the door to her room opened a few minutes later, Violet whimpered and tried to sink back further into the corner. It couldn't be Randy—she could hear him out in the living room.

At her small sound, a beam of light flew into her face. The light after so much darkness caused her to blink and turn away. It immediately shut off.

Before she could even ask who was there, a hand closed over her mouth. She tried to move away, gasping at the pain even as the thought crossed her mind that screaming would probably bring more trouble than help.

"It's me, Firefly."

Aiden?

"You've got to be quiet, okay?"

She nodded under his hand. He let go of her mouth and

reached over her head. A second later she felt the tension in her arms suddenly relax as he cut through the zip tie that had restrained her. Even that tiny movement sent anguish screaming through her shoulder joints, and she sucked in her breath, swallowing her sob.

"I'm sorry, sweetheart."

Before she could ask him why, he pulled her arms from above her head, straight down into her lap.

This time swallowing her sob wasn't an option. All she could do was keep it as low as possible. She felt like her arms were being ripped out of their sockets. His fingers pressed firmly into the balls of the joints, massaging the swollen and aching tendons. The spike of agony flew down her spine, and white dots danced in front of her vision.

"You're doing so great. Breathe with me, Firefly. In. Out."

She couldn't see him but followed his instructions, breathing as his deep, gentle voice told her to. Grimly, she hung on to consciousness as his fingers continued kneading the traumatized tissues for a few more moments until the pain lessened, and she could at least move her shoulders.

"How did you find me?" she finally asked. "Randy took the jacket. Wouldn't let me bring it."

He leaned in and kissed her forehead before reaching behind her ear. She felt the tiny lick of pain of an adhesive being ripped from her skin.

"Oh." It had been on her person all along. The fight for the jacket—and all the pain she'd endured afterward because of it—had been for nothing.

Aiden had kissed her just to put the tracker on her.

To be hurt by that was beyond ridiculous. Aiden had been doing a job. She should be thankful he was so good at it, not act like a teenager who'd been scorned by her crush.

But she was still hurt, stupid as it was.

"We need to get you away from this wall," he whispered.

"Why?"

"I'm not here alone. We just want to make sure you're safe if things get a little more rowdy than we planned." He touched his neck. "Control, this is Shamrock. I've got the package. You're clear to proceed."

"You've really got a whole team here?"

"Absolutely. Now, let's get you away from this wall in case any shots are fired." He stood and held his hand down to assist her.

She tried to stand but her body had taken too much damage today. Too much trauma. Her muscles just wouldn't work. "I can't seem to move. I'm sorry."

He reached down and scooped her into his arms.

"Wait! I'm too heavy."

He kissed her forehead again, keeping her high against his chest as he crossed the room. "Featherweight."

The way he moved so quickly with her, so easily, she almost believed him.

He set her gently on the ground behind him, then pressed something on his neck again. "Control, Shamrock. We're on the south wall. You're clear to breach."

He helped ease her down so she was sitting low on the floor. Then he crouched in front of her, pulling her head against his chest and wrapping his arms around her.

"What's going to happen?" she whispered. "Is it going to be loud?"

"Not if everything goes the way we expect it to. But keep your head down just in case."

His big body was surrounding her on just about every side. Anything that was going to hit her was going to have to go through him first. "What about you? Are you bulletproof or something?"

"My mom always said I had a hard enough head to stop a bullet. Plus I have a Kevlar vest. So we should be okay."

They sat in silence for a few moments. "Maybe at some point after this we could meet each other when I actually have some clothes on. You know, just to try something different."

His deep chuckle was enough to almost make her forget the situation. Make her forget her body had been so abused that she couldn't even make her muscles move at her command. That this man, whose name she wasn't sure she actually knew, had seen her naked multiple times. "That's a deal," he whispered. "And I'm sure Gabe has clothes for you in the van."

The thought of having to walk, or be carried, naked even in front of the good guys sent ice through her veins. She wanted to ask Aiden to help her, but the man was already shielding her body with his own. What more did she really want? But she couldn't be naked again in front of a group of strangers. She couldn't stand it. Her throat started to close, making breathing impossible.

A Paris-Brest with an orange cream rather than traditional praline cream might make for a perfect summer treat. Lighter. More citrusy. Then butterscotch for winter for a more robust flavor . . .

"Hey, Firefly, where'd you go?" A finger trailed up and down her cheek. "It's going to be okay. We're going to get you out of here. Just hang on for a few more minutes, sweetheart, all right?"

His words brought her back. She focused on his voice. On his warmth. "Is Aiden really your name?"

His lips pressed against her forehead again. "Yes." His arms tightened around her. "Here we go."

Not two seconds later, a commotion went up in the other room. Aiden's team was making their move. Ignoring the pain, she brought her arms around Aiden's head. Scientifically, she knew her arms wouldn't do much to save him if bullets began spraying into the room, but she would damn well try just in case.

But bullets never came. As a matter of fact, besides the initial yells from Randy and his friends, there wasn't much commotion at all. Probably less than a minute after Aiden gripped her tightly, he was releasing her.

"Roger that," he spoke into his headset once again, then turned to her. "It's over. We're going to stay here for a few more minutes to make completely sure the house is secure, but it's over."

She wanted to protest as he moved away from her, but she stopped herself. His job was done. He had kept her safe. She should be thankful.

He turned his small flashlight on and set it on the ground, providing them with a little light. He scooted back on his heels and took off his Kevlar vest. A moment later he pulled his long-sleeved shirt off, leaving him in only a black T-shirt.

"Here," he held the shirt out to her, "you can wear this."

She clutched the shirt to her chest, tears filling her eyes. "Thank you," she whispered.

His hand cupped her cheek, and she leaned into it. "From now on, only the people you choose to give the exceptional privilege to, get to see you naked."

A shuddery breath escaped her before she could stop it. He understood. He helped her get the shirt over her head when she couldn't manage herself. Then he smiled at her as he rolled up the sleeves to her wrists.

"Put a belt on this and you might start a new fashion trend."

"SWAT chic." She gave him a smile even though she knew it was shaky. "We might be onto something. It'll be all the rage."

For the first time since all the pain at the truck, Violet felt like she might actually come out of this incident whole.

CHAPTER 9

HER SMILE WAS SO shaky it was all Aiden could do not to pull her into his arms.

But Violet may not ever want a man to hold her in his arms again. A rage, hot and burning, fired through his system. What had happened here may be something she battled for the rest of her life. Hell, how could it not be?

She was clinging to the shirt now that it was on her body. He should've given it to her earlier. It might not have been the most tactically sound plan, but she had needed the emotional protection maybe even more than the physical protection.

It hadn't crossed his mind that the thought of being naked in front of her brother and other people who didn't mean her harm would be just as traumatic as what she'd endured already. It wasn't until her breathing had changed, and her entire body had gone slack that he'd realized the problem. For a second he'd thought she had passed out, but he'd quickly realized she was in the same state she'd been at the auction when he'd first found her—disassociation, her mind pushed beyond what it could handle and protecting itself internally.

If the team hadn't announced it was breaching that very second, he would've given her his shirt right then.

But she'd come back from wherever her mind had gone and then had the courage to make jokes about it with him. He didn't know much about Violet Collingwood, but he was pretty sure she was one of the most amazing people on the planet. He hadn't missed the fact that her arms had come around to protect his head when the team had breached.

What person who had been through what she had over the last week had the presence of mind and selflessness to do something like that? Again, someone amazing.

Gavin's voice came through the communication device in his ear. "Control, this is Redwood. Eagle and I are down in the basement. We've got six women here, and they're all high as a fucking kite."

Aiden wasn't surprised to hear the women Gavin and Finn had found were high. Making them desperate for the next fix was the easiest way for pimps and traffickers to keep their victims in line. He was surprised they hadn't tried it on Violet. Or maybe they had.

"Did anyone give you drugs?" he asked her. "Randy or anyone else you came in contact with?"

"Drugs? No, I don't think so. Not unless they were in the food."

"No, they wouldn't have put crack or heroin in the food."

Her face scrunched up. "Why would they give me crack or heroin?"

"Some of my team just found the other women Randy has been parading around. They're all hooked on whatever he's been giving them. They probably never fought him, right?"

Understanding dawned in her eyes. "The prize," she whispered. "Randy kept threatening not to give them their prize if they didn't do what he wanted."

"Yeah, well the 'prize' was probably low-quality heroin."

"I didn't understand why they wouldn't help me. I thought it was because they didn't speak English and were scared of him."

"I'm sure that's true, too."

She grabbed his arm. "You'll help them, right? You won't leave them behind."

"Nobody's getting left behind." Not this time, damn it. "We're not working here in an official law-enforcement capacity—you can thank your brother for that—but the cops should be arriving any moment now."

"Control, this is Cyclone." Zac. "Ghost and I have all five tangos secured out front. No difficulties. No injuries."

"Except all the shit they're talking is hurting my delicate psyche," Dorian—call sign Ghost—said in jest, although there was probably a lot of truth to the statement.

"Control, this is Kendrick. I'm done with my sweep of the rest of the house and the back. It's all clear. Also, I'm wondering when I can get some sort of cool nickname."

"I think Jackass is available," Finn said.

"This is control, I'm going off coms. Sheriff Nelson is en route," Gabe said.

Aiden knew where Gabe was going. Here. He wanted to see his sister.

She was looking at him. "Can you take me out of this room? Is it safe? I don't think I can bear to be in here any longer."

He was going to tell her that Gabe was coming, that he'd

be here in under a minute.

"Please," she whispered.

He'd be damned if he would make her beg for anything, much less the one thing he'd wanted to do since the moment he'd set foot in this house.

He scooped her up in his arms again, pulling her closer when she forced her traumatized shoulders through the pain of wrapping an arm around his neck and tucked her face into his throat. He made sure the shirt was pulled down enough to adequately cover her.

She didn't look around as he took her through the living room and out the front door. They were only a few steps out the door when Gabriel came rushing up.

The man did not like that Violet was lying so easily in Aiden's arms. Aiden raised an eyebrow. Gabe damn well better not get into it right now. That definitely wasn't what Violet needed. Gabe took a breath, then reached for Violet, touching her but wisely not trying to pull her from Aiden's arm if she wasn't ready.

"Hey, monkey," he murmured, stroking her hair.

Violet pulled her face out of Aiden's neck. "Gabe?"

"I'm here. You're safe. It's all going to be okay."

"Gabe." Her voice was much stronger this time, though she winced as she reached for her brother.

It killed him to let her go, but Aiden didn't try to keep her in his arms. He wasn't surprised she wanted her brother. He handed her to Gabe.

"She was tied up, so she's stiff. Plus our concerns about the Taser were correct. But there shouldn't be any permanent damage."

Gabe crushed her to his chest. "You're alive. You're okay. Thank God."

Aiden backed away to give them privacy as Violet

began to cry into her brother's shoulder. He was sure it wouldn't be the last time she cried over what had happened to her.

Nearby, Dorian, Zac, and Kendrick had five men on their knees with their fingers linked behind their heads. All five of them were talking at once, none of them listening to what the others were saying.

All protesting their innocence. When the wail of sirens became noticeable, they all began talking faster.

Zac walked over to Aiden. "Is Violet okay? Physically, I mean?" Zac knew firsthand what it was like to watch someone you cared about live through trauma.

Aiden shrugged. "Physically, she'll be fine. She's weak right now, but she'll recover—"

Randy caught sight of Aiden and began screaming. "You! Son of a bitch. I should've known you had something to do with this. You were so obsessed with her. Fifty dollars for a kiss? This is entrapment."

Aiden crossed to him. "I'm not a cop, asshole. But you know what? You're damned lucky they're going to be here in under a minute, or I'd be showing you exactly what it feels like to be tasered multiple times."

"Bitch fucking broke my nose," he sneered.

Aiden would gladly hold the man now and let her beat him bloody if she wanted. "Good. I wish she'd gotten in a couple more good blows."

Randy's eyes narrowed, his voice dropping. "You should've heard her cry, Teague. She begged me to stop as I shocked her over and over. And do you know what it was all about? Your damn jacket. She didn't want to give it up." His smile was slimy.

He reached over and grabbed Randy by the collar of his shirt. "*What?*"

"That's right. All sorts of pain just for your jacket. Guess she thought it was important. Or maybe she just has a crush on you. Spineless bitch never fought once except for that damn jacket." He threw his head back and laughed.

Aiden got in one punch to the jaw and was going in for the second when Dorian and Zac grabbed him and dragged him back.

"Cops are coming, Shamrock," Zac said in his ear. "And you won't be happy with yourself later if you beat the shit out of an unarmed man."

"The way he beat the shit out of an unarmed woman? I think I'll be just fine with myself. I won't hit him again." Aiden shook them off, but he had himself under control. He turned to Randy. "But you best pray we don't ever meet again, asshole."

A few seconds later a police car came barreling down the road toward the isolated house. It belonged to Sheriff Nelson, but because he was sheriff of Teton County, he would have no jurisdiction here. Aiden took a few steps back from Randy, mostly to make sure he didn't change his mind and get in a few more punches. A couple to the kidney ought to do enough internal damage to make sure Randy didn't hurt anyone for a long time.

"What the hell is going on here, Mackay?" Sheriff Nelson asked as he slammed the car door.

"Damnedest thing, Sheriff." Zac smiled. "We were all out on a training hike when we heard what sounded like some women calling for help from inside this house. When we took a closer look, we found some women locked in a basement. Also, we found Gabriel Collingwood's sister, Violet."

The sheriff rolled his eyes and shook his head. This wasn't the first time Linear Tactical employees had *happened* to be at the heart of stopping trouble. "That is, in fact, the damnedest thing I've ever heard. Amazing how you boys just happened to be here at the right time. Fremont County PD and ambulance are on their way behind me. Should be here in five minutes."

"I think we're going to need more than one ambulance, Sheriff," Aiden said. "There are six women. All look like long-term trafficking victims who have been dosed heavily with drugs. Violet needs to be checked out also, although I don't think drugs are involved with her."

Randy would need an ambulance too if he decided to run his mouth any more. Thankfully, Gabe and Violet were sitting on the step near the front door, Gabe hovering protectively over his sister. She wouldn't have heard what Randy said.

Why had she fought for the jacket? Had she figured out there was a tracking device and thought that was where it was hidden? Why hadn't he told her the tracker was on her body? The thought of her going through so much pain for no reason ate at him.

"Anybody else hurt? Any questions the locals are going to have?" Sheriff Nelson asked. "I'd rather know up front."

"Nope," Zac said. "Randy and his friends here were the only tangos in the house and didn't give up much of a fight. We're not sure wh—"

The rifle shot rang out from a distance at the same time Randy fell straight forward onto his face. From the crater where the back of his head used to be, there could be no doubt the man was dead.

Time slowed for Aiden as the Linear team did what they'd trained together for years to do: evaluate, fight, and survive. Every single one of them, including Kendrick, drew their secondary weapons and dove for cover.

Aiden looked over to make sure Violet was all right just as Gabriel moved her inside. Good.

The druggies were crying, one guy covered with Randy's blood. Kendrick and Sheriff Nelson were pulling them behind the sheriff's car.

They waited for a second shot—or more—to come from the woods surrounding them, but there was nothing.

Gavin came back on the coms. "What the hell is happening out there, you guys? Gabe just dragged Violet back into the house."

"We've got a shooter in the woods," Zac said.

Aiden wished he had binoculars with him, or even better, night-vision goggles.

"Are we under attack?" Finn asked.

Zac looked over at Dorian, then Aiden to get their opinions. Dorian shook his head and Aiden did the same. This wasn't an attack on them. This was someone making sure Randy didn't talk once he was arrested.

"Negative. Looks like someone was taking out Randy Villarreal. There's been no other shots fired."

"I'm going to go after the shooter," Dorian said. "If we're not the target, then you don't need me. I might be able to track him."

If anybody could, it was Dorian.

Zac nodded. "Be careful."

Dorian was already fading into the night.

"Sheriff, you okay?" Aiden called out.

"What the hell was that?" the older man asked.

"If I had to guess, that was Stellman tying up a loose end. It's what he does."

The big question now was whether he considered Violet to be one. Because if he did, she would never be safe.

CHAPTER 10

THREE WEEKS Later

Almost every Saturday morning, Linear Tactical held open sparring. It was actually Dorian's brainchild. The guy had come across some teenagers in Reddington City getting into trouble, a sort of gang without a cause. They'd been stupid enough to take on Dorian, mistaking his soft-spoken demeanor for weakness.

They hadn't been the first ones to do that, but they were perhaps the youngest. Dorian had beaten the crap out of all of them and dragged them to Linear the next weekend just to give them an outlet for their aggression.

Sparring Saturday had grown from there. Two years later, most of those original kids Dorian had dealt with were in college. It was a whole new group who showed up now. There were still a lot of angsty teenagers who needed an outlet for aggression, but now a lot of adults too.

All the Linear Tactical guys participated in Sparring Saturday whenever they were available. It was an excellent community builder, not only because it was free, but also because it gave anybody who wanted the opportunity a chance to whale on the resident Special Forces guys. They'd had people drive in from clear across the state for an opportunity to get into the ring with one of them. And as long as those people—almost always men—understood that the fight was going to be clean and fair and conducted with proper headgear, Linear welcomed the competition.

Aiden and his Green Beret brothers didn't lose their sparring matches often—they trained too regularly with each other for that to happen—but when they did, they took it gracefully. It was just as important to teach the kids in the audience the concept of good sportsmanship as it was the fighting moves themselves.

Normally, Aiden loved Sparring Saturday. He always did his best to egg on any visitors who were looking for a fight. He and Zac tended to get picked the most by strangers since they weren't as big or muscular as Dorian and Finn. Therefore, strangers assumed, they must be easier to beat.

It generally didn't take long to disabuse them of that misconception. But today Aiden's head just wasn't in the game. Hell, his head hadn't been in the game since he'd handed Violet over to her brother the night they'd gotten her out of that house.

He'd spent untold hours over the past three weeks working with law enforcement to try and bring down anyone he could from the human auction. Sheriff Nelson had immediately realized bigger guns were needed. Aiden had spent a day with the FBI in Idaho Falls before they'd brought in a special task force he'd never heard of called Omega Sector.

It had been a pain in the ass to drive the ninety minutes there a dozen times in the past three weeks, but Aiden was glad he'd done it. The people at Omega Sector knew what they were doing. He'd been assigned to work with an agent named Brandon Han, who might possibly be the smartest person Aiden had ever met. Brandon, along with his team, was determined to bring down these traffickers, as well as Stellman.

All the hours poring over photos and footage Omega Sector had collected over the years was worth it when they had positively identified one of the masked buyers late last week. The arrest of a high-profile business owner in California had been made a few days ago. Hopefully, it was all going to snowball from there. They would sell out each other in order to save themselves.

Aiden wondered if Violet knew about the arrest. Did she know that her courage and pain were counting for something?

Aiden didn't have to be the one to tell her, he just wanted her to know that what she'd been through hadn't been for nothing.

Who was he kidding? Aiden would give just about anything to see her with his own eyes and make sure she was doing all right. Being so close to her in Idaho Falls, knowing Collingwood Technology was nearby, was also hard. Every day he'd had to force himself not to just show up there.

But he had to face the facts. He was a part of her life she was desperately hoping to forget. She didn't hate him, but she didn't want to call him up and relive the good old days when she'd been kidnapped and assaulted either.

But hell if Aiden could get her out of his mind.

There was a big crowd here today, particularly since Finn and Charlie had announced they were engaged. The woman was out of the hospital but still moving a lot slower than her normal whirlwind speed. She was sitting in the small set of bleachers against the east wall of the barn they'd turned into their huge sparring center. Her friend Jordan Reiss had been sitting next to her for a while, before more people from town came in. When it became obvious that people wanted to congratulate Charlie without talking to Jordan, the younger woman had made an excuse and left. It was a damn shame how some of the townspeople treated Jordan. Oh, there was a lot of past baggage there, obviously stuff a few refused to forgive.

Aiden was helping with the fundamentals of a self-defense crash course they offered for free pretty much anytime anyone asked for it.

The course was for any age, men or women. They taught basic knowledge about how to get out of a bear hug, what to do if you were grabbed from behind, and attackers' most vulnerable areas and how to take advantage of them. With each move he taught, Aiden wondered if Gabriel or Kendrick or *somebody* was showing Violet the same.

Was she scared? Did she have nightmares? Did she wake up not knowing where she was and worried that Randy or any of the other people who had molested her were nearby?

Not his business. And that just sucked. Because he very much wanted it to be his business, but that wasn't his move to make.

Aiden had identified as many of the scumbags attending the auction as he could. Omega Sector felt confident they were closing in on Stellman. No one had found any trace of the shooter who had executed Randy, but Violet had told law enforcement that the man she called Dillon—the silent one Aiden had seen at The Barn—had been at the house just minutes before the team had arrived. He had to have been the one who killed Randy.

If they'd been five minutes earlier, they would've gotten him too. They could've taken both him and Randy in alive for questioning and been so much closer to knowing who Stellman really was.

But for now, Aiden's role was over. It was time to get back to his real life. Maybe he would ask Dorian if he could teach the extended wilderness survival class coming up. Dorian was best at it, but being out in the elements would require all Aiden's focus and concentration. Which was exactly what he needed to forget about Violet Collingwood.

"Last call for any sparring matches," Zac yelled. "Anybody here want to take on any of the Linear guys?"

"I would," Gabriel Collingwood said as he walked up to the ring. Aiden hadn't even realized the other man was here. He couldn't stop himself from looking around to see if perhaps Violet was with her brother, but he didn't see her anywhere.

"Collingwood," Gavin said with a big grin on his face. "We are always happy to kick some Navy SEAL ass. I'll go a few rounds with you."

Gabe shook his head. "Nope. I want to fight Teague." Those green eyes so similar to Violet's burned with anger. "You in?"

Aiden walked closer to the ring, tone calm. "You sure getting into the ring is a good idea? If you've got something to say to me, just say it."

"I don't have anything to say. I just have a nice floor to beat you into. Put on your safety gear, Teague."

"Well, aren't you a little ray of pitch black today." Aiden stepped into the ring and fastened on his headgear, then slipped on the padded half gloves used for martial arts fight-ing. Gabe was already putting his on too. If the man needed to blow off a little steam, Aiden could certainly use the outlet too.

At six feet tall and 170 pounds, Aiden was no light-weight, but Gabe had at least four inches on him and big tree-trunk-sized biceps.

Aiden shook his head. "You know, you don't look like a computer genius."

Gabe met him in the middle of the ring, holding out his hands to bump Aiden's and begin the fight. "I don't fight like one either."

As soon as they stepped back from each other, Gabe took his first swing. If Aiden hadn't been expecting it, it would've taken his damn head off. He'd have to stay out of the way of the bigger man's fists as much as possible to keep himself off the floor.

He got in a couple of quick jabs before stepping to the side, out of the way of an uppercut, but Gabe was more ready this time and spun, bringing his elbow back around into Aiden's midsection. Aiden jumped back and swung around in a roundhouse kick, which Gabe blocked.

They went on like that in silent battle, neither getting the upper hand—Gabe too strong, Aiden too fast—for a good five minutes. Neither of them said a word besides a random curse here or there when a blow hit its target.

This could last all damn day. Aiden dropped low and swept Gabe's legs out from under him, dropping him to the mat. Before Aiden could pin him, Gabe rolled and sprang back up.

Aiden shook his head. "So you can move fast when you're not trying to pound the shit out of me."

Gabe swung one of his massive arms at Aiden's chin, a

blow he was barely able to block. "Stay the hell away from my sister, Teague. You are not what she needs."

Aiden flew at Gabe, feigned one way, then slid the other, getting in two solid jabs before the man was able to get his guard up. "I don't know what your problem is, Collingwood, but I haven't seen Violet since the night we got her out."

"Then why the hell has she been in Oak Creek nearly every damn day for the past two weeks?"

Aiden stopped moving to try to process what Gabe was saying—*Violet has been here in town for the past two weeks?* —and took the blow to the face he'd been trying to avoid this whole fight.

Even through the protective gear, Aiden saw stars and fell to the ground.

It only took a moment to regather his senses while he was there. If this had been a real fight, Aiden would've used his foot to take out the side of Gabe's knee. Even if he hadn't already known about the other man's weakness, Gabe had been favoring it just enough to give it away.

But Aiden was reeling more from what Gabe had said than the punch he'd gotten in. "Violet has been here in town?" he said from down on the ground. "Why?"

"She won't tell me. I thought for sure you were behind it." He reached down a hand to help Aiden up, but he ignored it. He was better off staying out of reach of those biceps in case Aiden said something else Gabe didn't like.

"Don't you have a security detail on her?" God, if not, they were going to be fighting for real. Stellman was a threat.

Gabe grimaced. "I do, but she would only accept it if the team was for security only and didn't report back to me what she was doing and who she was doing it with. I've almost fired Kendrick five times because he refuses to tell me anything."

"Maybe we'll have to give that guy a call sign after all." This time when Gabe held out his hand, Aiden accepted his help. Both of them began pulling off their sparring gear. "Rest assured, she hasn't been with me. I've been in Idaho Falls almost every day, working with Omega Sector to identify those traffickers. You know that."

Gabe shrugged. "I didn't know who else she could possibly be seeing in this one-horse town besides you."

Charlie, with the help of Finn, walked over to the ring and raised one eyebrow. "If I tell you Violet has been hanging out with me, Zac's girlfriend Anne, and Finn's sister Wavy, am I going to have to get into the ring and fight you?"

Gabe shook his head. "I don't understand. How do you even know Violet?"

"Anne reached out to her as a physician and someone who had lived through an attack herself. I was basically along to shake the hand of an amazing woman. And because anyone who is trying to take down Stellman is my new bestie."

Gabe still looked confused. "Okay, so you all became chummy. Why has she been out here so much?"

Charlie just shrugged. "When Violet wants you to know, she'll tell you. It's nothing that's harming her or bad for her in any way."

"Oh really, then why has she dropped out of her chemical engineering program?" Gabe's eyebrow looked like it was finding a new home in his hairline. "You don't think that's bad for her? I would understand if she needed time to recover, wanted to take a semester off. But she quit *completely*."

Aiden was starting to understand some of Gabe's concern. Violet making knee-jerk, life-altering choices so soon after her ordeal wasn't good news.

"I didn't know that," he said when Gabe looked at him. "But I promise I haven't been in touch with her."

"Really?"

Aiden rolled his eyes. "What do you want, a pinky promise? Yeah, really." And it was damn well killing him.

Gabe looked sheepish. "Then I guess I should deliver the message Brandon Han asked me to provide. One of the people you ID'd from the auction rolled on Stellman and provided a positive identification. Omega Sector moved in last night and arrested him."

"What the hell, man? You couldn't have led with that?"

Gabe just shrugged. "And miss the chance to pound on you? Where's the fun in that? It's the whole reason I volunteered to give the message rather than let Han call you."

Aiden sat down on the edge of the mat. "You're an asshole, Collingwood."

Gabe just shrugged again.

Aiden should be pissed. He should take another swing at Gabe, but all he could feel was relief. Stellman's arrest meant Violet was safe.

"Thank God," Charlie muttered. Finn came over and put his arm around her. They would all sleep better knowing that bastard was out of their lives.

"After everything," Finn said, "it almost feels too easy."

Charlie smacked him on the arm. "It wasn't fucking easy for me or Violet."

Finn pulled the tiny blond woman closer and kissed the top of her head. "No, you're right. Easy is the wrong word. Nothing about any of this has been easy."

"Convenient," Gabe said. "That's the word you're

looking for. It seems too convenient. But Omega Sector is pretty positive that this is Stellman. He was caught red-handed in an arms deal."

Aiden didn't care if they had caught the guy jaywalking. He just wanted Stellman off the streets so Violet would be safe.

"Then let's not look a gift horse in the mouth. Contrary to my life story, not everything has to be done the hardest way possible." Finn walked over and slapped Aiden on the back. "Looks like Shamrock's string of good luck lives on."

Aiden would take it.

CHAPTER 11

VIOLET STOOD ACROSS THE STREET, staring at Aiden's house. He was a single man living alone, and he had a *house*. Granted, it wasn't very big, probably just two or three bedrooms. But it was a house.

She'd lived in downtown Idaho Falls since she was fifteen, when her parents had died. Gabe had moved the two of them into the condo above the Collingwood Technology—CT—offices so he could be close by even though he had to be at work so much. The living space had been fine—luxurious even—but it had never been a house with a little porch like the one she was looking at now. And she'd never had a yard.

Everybody in the town of Oak Creek had a yard. Maybe that was true for all of Wyoming, or maybe just here, but these people loved their wide-open spaces. Violet was finding that she loved those spaces too.

That definitely didn't mean she knew what she was doing. Not only with standing in front of Aiden's house, but also with the choices she'd been making over the past three weeks.

Gabe was worried about her quitting school, spending so much time in a new town. He thought she was being situationally reactive and maybe immature. She couldn't blame him. Especially since she hadn't given him any details.

But these decisions weren't really about being mature. Gabe should know that. Violet was the oldest twenty-two-year-old in the history of the world. She'd never been immature, and she wasn't starting now. But she wasn't sure her brother would see it that way.

This wasn't about hurting him or making poor decisions based on a trauma.

This was about refusing to be passive in her own life any longer.

The past three weeks had been filled with changes and growth. She'd spent hours talking about what had happened to the therapist Gabe had insisted on. It had felt good to express the anger, fear, and helplessness she'd felt.

Talking hadn't taken away all her anxiety—she still couldn't sleep without a night-light, and she broke out in a cold sweat at the thought of ever walking to her car alone again. But therapy did help. She felt stronger and more capable. And she wanted to live life on her own terms.

If there was one thing being held captive had taught her, it was that no one was guaranteed a tomorrow.

That knowledge gave her the courage she needed to finally take the steps across the street to his door. He had been on her mind for three weeks. Even though she'd been spending a lot of time in Oak Creek, she hadn't seen him like she'd hoped.

So now she was taking matters into her own hands. She knocked on the door of the man whose kiss she hadn't been able to get out of her thoughts.

To her surprise, he opened it immediately.

"I was wondering if you were going to actually come over." He leaned against the doorway and smiled casually at her. "I was hoping you would."

She couldn't stop looking at him. She'd already known he was handsome. But now when she was looking at him with no filter of fear or shame clouding her judgment, he seemed so much more than that.

His face was rugged, stubble covering his square jaw but not hiding the handsome features beneath it. His eyes, a soft brown like melted honey, were flecked with green and gold throughout.

He wasn't big and muscular like Gabe. His was a lean, concealed strength. Unlike her brother, Aiden would be able to fit in wherever he wanted to and not stand out.

But he was definitely a warrior. The way his eyes took in everything about her, the intelligence and awareness . . . Even if she hadn't seen him move with lethal grace, she'd know it by looking at him now.

And it was sexy.

Damn her pale skin, there was no hiding the flush that came over her cheeks. She grimaced. "I'm not taking up a job as a stalker, in case you're worried about that."

He crossed his arms as he continued to lean against the doorframe. "You aren't one of the hundreds of women who have applied to stalk me, so I figured it was safe. Want to come inside?"

"How did you know I was out here?"

"Mrs. Mazille down the street. She's married to the librarian. When you didn't move along after a minute or two, she performed her neighborly duty and contacted me. Texted me, actually. Happens a lot."

Violet raised an eyebrow. "Because of all the women skulking around?"

The corners of his mouth turned up. "Mrs. Mazille takes the concept of a neighborhood watch very seriously. I was in the army for more than ten years and can tell you that she has the concept of covert surveillance down better than anyone in the military. They should recruit her to train troops."

Aiden's affection for the older woman was evident. "I guess I better come inside then before she comes down here to rescue you from the clutches of an evil female."

He gripped her arm lightly and ushered her inside. "You say that in jest, but she just might. Get in here."

Violet laughed, the sound surprising her a little. It had been a long time since she'd laughed out loud.

He touched her arm, leading her into his kitchen. "That's a nice sound, you laughing."

"I was just realizing that I haven't done it much lately. Since . . ." She shrugged. "Not that things have been bad. I mean, all things considered, I'm in pretty good shape."

"I'm glad to hear that. I've been thinking about you. And I hear you've been around Oak Creek quite a bit. At least that's what Gabe told me when he stopped by Linear yesterday."

Oh crap. "Um, yeah, I haven't really been talking over my plans with him. He can be overbearing. Sorry if he caused you any trouble."

"I can handle your brother. But I know he's concerned about you. He said you dropped out of your engineering program."

This was not the conversation she wanted to have with Aiden. She didn't want to explain the changes she'd made in her life or the new direction her career was heading. None of that had to do with why she was here.

She was here because she wanted to have sex. With Aiden.

But evidently, thanks to her brother, she first needed to convince Aiden she wasn't having some sort of nervous breakdown.

"I brought you something." She held out the box that contained the glacé petit four pastries. Tiny versions of some of her best concoctions.

He opened the box and literally licked his lips. "Those look amazing. Mind if I eat a few now?"

She smiled. "Be my guest."

He took a bite and sighed in bliss, just the response she loved to see. "These are wonderful. I don't even want to know where you bought them, because if I do, I'll be showing up there every day, and soon I'll be too fat to move." Almost reluctantly, he held the box out toward her. "Do you want one?"

"No, I'm good. Thanks."

He finished off a few more, licking his fingers, after putting the box down on the counter. She had to force herself not to offer to do it for him. "So, tell me about deciding not to finish your engineering degree."

"Anne Griffin, Charlie Devereux, and Wavy Bollinger all showed up at my place in Idaho Falls about a week after I got home."

He nodded. "I heard about that. I think your brother is calling them the terror triplets."

Violet laughed again. "Let's just say Gabe likes to be in control of everything. Maybe it comes from his Navy SEAL training. Or maybe from being a CEO. But he likes to call the shots." She studied Aiden for a second. "Were you a SEAL too?"

He shook his head. "No. The Linear guys and I were all

army. Special Forces. But actually I did work a couple of missions with your brother before he got out of the navy."

Special Forces. No surprise there. "Charlie, Anne, and Wavy have been godsends. Charlie because of understanding the physical pain I've been through, although what I went through was nothing compared to what she did. Anne because she's so much more like me in temperament. Plus," Violet swallowed hard, fighting to get the words out, refusing to let the thought of it all take over now, "Anne was attacked once. I guess you know that. So she understood some of the other elements of what I've been going through."

Aiden nodded.

She finally shrugged. "And Wavy . . ."

"Wavy is Wavy. You can't help but smile around her," he finished for her.

"Exactly. I've never really been one to have a lot of girlfriends. I spent most of my time at school or working. But having them around has really helped me."

"And that's why you've been in Oak Creek? Because you were hanging out with them?"

Violet grimaced. Damn it, this talk was not taking them down the right path. The *sex* path.

What was she going to do, tell him the whole story? About how her parents had died in a car accident that had pretty much been her fault? That her brother had left a career he loved in the navy to take over the company and raise her?

She didn't know how to tell Aiden that her brother, only in his mid-twenties himself, hadn't known what to do with the traumatized teenage girl she'd been after her parents' death, so he'd encouraged the parts of her that had made sense to *him*: her gift for math and science.

Or how, even though that hadn't been what really interested her, she'd acquiesced her whole life.

She'd acquiesced when she'd agreed to study engineering instead of going to culinary school like she wanted. She'd acquiesced when she'd started working at CT at sixteen, as Gabe and Edward Appleton—her parents' good friend who had helped with the company after their death—had wanted. It wasn't like Gabe had been forcing her. Everybody knew how good she was in research and development even as a teenager. She'd had two scientist parents who had passed down their intelligence and analytic abilities to her. Not using those gifts would have been a waste.

How many times had she heard that?

Maybe it was true. But she couldn't do it anymore. At least not right now. She was done acquiescing.

Done being passive.

But none of that information was going to get her what she wanted with Aiden.

So she just told him the very basics to get it out of the way.

"I bought a shop in downtown Oak Creek, and I'm going to open a bakery," she blurted out.

His poker face was good, she would give him that. If it hadn't been for the slightest widening of those hazel eyes, she would've thought he'd already known. "A bakery?"

"It's what I've always wanted to do as a career. But I let myself get talked into going the engineering route." She pointed to the box of pastries.

"You made those?" Now he couldn't hide the surprise in his eyes.

"Yes. My own recipes." Maybe at some point she'd be willing to share that it was some of the same recipes that had kept her sane during her abduction. "I love coming up with new recipes. You'd be surprised how similar science and baking are. Both require such exactness in order to be successful."

He took out another chocolate pastry and ate the entire thing in one bite. "This is amazing."

His mouth was so full of food, it was difficult to understand him. But Violet wasn't offended. This was how she wanted people to feel about her food. "I always thought that one day I would open a bakery. But it was always just that . . . *one day*. I guess now I realize that we're not all guaranteed one day. So I decided to make *now* that day."

She hadn't realized until right this minute how much Aiden's support would mean to her. Not that she wasn't going to open the bakery if he told her it was stupid, but she wanted him to understand. He'd been such a crucial part of her survival. He'd been such an encouragement to be strong. She wanted him to understand that this was a continuation of that, of finding her strength, finally.

He popped another pastry into his mouth. "I don't know how good of an engineer you are, but if you are anywhere near as good as you are a baker, your brother and the rest of Collingwood Technology are going to be crying about losing you."

"You don't think it's stupid?"

"Well, to be honest . . ."

She could feel her heart clench. She braced herself for his words. *No more acquiescing. No more passivity.*

He shrugged. "I'm going to need more samples to be sure. You know, three or four a day for the next year or so. All your different flavors. Then I can let you know for sure if it's a smart idea or not."

She smacked his arm, taking the opportunity to stand closer to him at the counter. "I'm glad you like them."

"*Like* is definitely too weak a word. Those things are sinful."

Sinful. She very much enjoyed the sound of that.

She eased a little bit closer, happy when he didn't move away. Should she touch his arm? Step closer? Let him make a move?

She was so not good at this seduction stuff.

"I came over today to tell you about the bakery," she whispered. "But also to ask you something."

He smiled. "Sure. Anything. What's on your mind?"

"That first night, when we were in the back room together, I know it was all part of a mission for you, a rescue operation . . . But I was wondering if any of what you said that night was true."

His eyes dropped to her lips, then popped back up. "Which parts exactly?" His voice was deeper than it had been a moment ago.

"The part where you said I was sexy."

"Firefly . . ."

"I get that the situation was bad, and you were acting. I understand that. I was just wondering if any of it was true for you."

He eased back slightly. "That's not as easy a question to answer as you might think. Thinking about you in that situation is definitely not a turn-on."

"No, of course not. Not for me either. I guess what I'm asking is if you're attracted to me *now*. If you kissed me that second night only to put the tracker on me, or if you felt something. If you feel something now."

His eyes drooped, and he leaned just the slightest bit closer. She remembered the feel of his lips on hers. She wanted that again. And with nothing hanging over them this time.

She closed her eyes and just said it. "I want you, Aiden. It's not out of hero worship or anything like that. I want you because I refuse to give Randy or any of those other people any other part of me. I came here because I wanted to see if our connection was real." She kept her eyes closed so she could get the words out. "Because I'd like to . . . have sex with you."

She let out a breath. It felt good to say what she wanted, that she wanted him and what the two of them had felt together.

When he didn't respond she opened her eyes—and immediately wanted to close them again. She wanted to suck back all the words she'd just spoken. Because although Aiden hadn't moved, there was suddenly a huge chasm between them. She could feel it, full and obvious.

She'd come here to ask him if he had really wanted her, and now she had her answer.

A resounding no.

He cleared his throat. "Violet, you're a beautiful, intelligent, amazing woman."

She took a step back but forced herself to keep her smile plastered on her face. "And a fabulous baker, don't forget that."

He scrubbed a hand over his eyes. "I'm not trying to say I don't want you . . ."

"You're just saying the situation was already weird enough without me coming in here and hitting on you."

Now he let out a sigh. "No. I mean, yes, our situation is weird but . . . you need time. I mean, I'm glad you're opening your bakery because that seems to be something you're really passionate about. But be careful about making decisions that you might regret long-term."

Oh, she already knew she was going to regret long-term

coming in here and telling him she wanted to sleep with him. It was time to go. "You know, you're right. I shouldn't have come in here like this."

"Firefly . . ."

No. And she didn't want to hear him call her that in his sexy voice that had meant so much to her.

She wasn't going to be mad at him, of course. He had every right to be weirded out at the thought of being intimate with her.

But she sure as heck wasn't going to sit around and discuss it with him anymore.

"The five million items on my new-business to-do list are calling, so I'm going to go. I promise I'll still send some goodies to the Linear office. I expect you soldier types need lots of carbohydrates to keep up your rescuing skills." Gabriel had told her about the men who had helped him get her out, Aiden's partners.

She grabbed her purse—a bigger bag than she normally carried, one she'd stuffed a toothbrush and deodorant in because she'd been stuck in the delusion that she might be spending the night with Aiden—and headed toward the door.

She would not cry. Not about this. He wasn't trying to hurt her feelings, he was just being honest.

If she wasn't acquiescing anymore, she shouldn't want anyone else to either. Not for any reason.

"Violet, wait. I'm sorry. I'm not trying to . . ."

She turned around and gave him a smile. She needed to make this right before she left, or things might always be awkward between them. That wouldn't be a problem in a city the size of Idaho Falls, but in a small town like Oak Creek? It wasn't how she wanted to start her new life here.

"Aiden. It's fine, I promise. There's nothing else that

needs to be said about it." She reached up and mock-punched his shoulder, then wanted to take the movement back because how stupid and lame was that?

"And look," she said quickly, words running over each other, "in case all the baked goods I'll be throwing your way don't make it clear, thank you for what you did. For getting me out and going way above and beyond even your Special Forces duties. For figuring out I was in trouble. For being persistent."

He grabbed her by her upper arms, stilling her frantic words and movements.

Breathe with me, Firefly.

He didn't say it, of course. But she could almost hear it as if he had. They stayed that way until they were both breathing in tandem. In sync.

Finally, he reached up and tucked a strand of hair behind her ear, looking like he wanted to say something. She waited, her heart bubbling up again, hoping he would tell her that he wanted her too. That she'd just caught him off guard. That he wasn't sure this was a good idea, but hell, who cared?

But finally, he just dropped his hand. "Any time."

It took her a second to even remember what she'd said.

Thank you for what you did.

Any time.

And for *anybody*. That's the variable she'd failed to factor in. What Aiden had done for her, the words he'd said, the way he'd acted—even that kiss they'd shared—he would've done for any woman in need. Violet had just happened to be that person.

She had just been a job.

She gave him a nod, her heart cracking a little, although it shouldn't be. "Thanks again, Shamrock. See you around."

CHAPTER 12

VIOLET LOOKED around the small building on Oak Creek's main street. It wasn't huge, just enough space in the front for three small two-top tables and a little cozy sitting area with a couch and a couple of chairs near the front window. The kitchen area in the back was bigger but still not huge.

Fancy Pants Bakery. And it was hers.

She had been working from morning until night for the past five days to prepare for the grand opening scheduled ten days from now. She had crews who'd been working with her, but she had wanted to be involved in as much of the process as possible, even when that meant grabbing a paintbrush or even helping with wiring—something she understood the basics of due to her engineering background.

But most of the time she spent on the recipes. The men and women working in the bakery didn't mind her poking and prodding in their business because she used them as guinea pigs for her concoctions. They seemed willing to provide her their opinions as long as she kept feeding them.

She wanted to make sure she had the most fantastic offerings possible the first week she was open. So after working all day, she stayed up well into the night reworking recipes, sometimes in her mind, sometimes on paper, sometimes back down in the bakery kitchen, since she was, ironically, living in the small studio apartment right over her shop. Some things didn't change.

Not that working herself into exhaustion had anything to do with trying to keep her mind off Aiden, of course. Not at all. It was just what a new small business owner had to do to make things work.

Right.

Kendrick was still around during most days, even though Stellman had been arrested. He didn't really interact with her or the work crews. Sometimes he spent big chunks of the day parked out front in his car working on his computer, but his dark eyes kept watch over everything. Another security team watched the building at night, and Gabriel had made sure that the security system for both the bakery and her apartment rivaled that of Fort Knox.

Telling her brother that she wasn't coming back to CT had been hard. She loved Gabe and didn't want to disappoint him. For a long time he'd been the only parental figure she'd had.

He hadn't been out here to see the place yet, at her request, but she knew Kendrick reported back details now that she'd freed him from his promise not to report anything non-security related. She and Gabe texted nearly every day, though he was trying to give her space. Although it wouldn't be long before he showed up in person. She had no doubt about that.

But even with the hard and the tired and the not

thinking about Aiden, this felt right. Doing this made her happy. Moreover, it ignited her passion.

She would finish her chemical engineering degree—she only needed two more classes to complete her bachelor's, and not doing so would be a waste. But she wouldn't be going on to the master's program like she'd planned. Or like Gabe and Edward had planned and she'd acquiesced to. And she wouldn't be working for them as an engineer.

Gabriel was hoping this whole thing would blow over and she would change her mind and come back. Edward was even more adamant, with near-daily emails to entice her back to her research.

This wasn't something she was going to just walk away from. But only time would prove that to her brother and Edward.

She hadn't quite been able to force herself to go back to the culinary classes she'd been leaving the night she'd been kidnapped. She wasn't sure she'd ever be able to set foot in that parking garage—maybe *any* parking garage—again. Plus, although she'd loved those classes, their purpose had really been as a creative outlet since it was the only kitchen work she'd done. Now she had plenty of kitchen work to thrill her soul.

The Fancy Pants name was hers. She spun around and looked once again. The crews were gone for the day. Even her baking couldn't keep them here past five o'clock on a Friday. They all had places to be. Some had even been talking about dates and going out to the local bar called The Eagle's Nest.

Dates. That only served to remind her what a fool she'd made of herself with Aiden. She didn't think she'd be asking for any more dates anytime soon. Heck, she hadn't even been trying to get him to date her, just to sleep with her, and he hadn't even wanted that.

It was all so cringeworthy.

The front door chimed, and she spun, expecting Kendrick or one of the security team members. But it was two of the three terror triplets: Anne and Charlie.

"That is not the face of a woman excited about opening her own fabulous bakery," Charlie said, tucking a strand of her blond hair behind her ear as she looked around. "But, seriously Vi, this place looks better every time I see it."

"Are you having second thoughts?" Anne asked, her voice as always much more soft-spoken than Charlie's.

"Of course she's not having second thoughts!" Charlie said. "She can't. I plan to be pregnant in the next few months, and this place will be my primary source of carbs."

"I'm fine. Everything is a little overwhelming, but in a good way, you know?" She smiled at Anne, then turned to Charlie. "And don't you think maybe you should actually marry Finn before starting to pop out babies? Not that I mind you eating all my concoctions."

Charlie let out a dramatic sigh and plopped onto one of the couches framing the front area of the bakery that Violet hoped would become a neighborhood gathering area. "Finn is so worried about hurting me, I can barely get him to touch me these days. I swear, before the attack it was all"—her voice deepened in an imitation of her fiancé's—" 'As soon as we get home that skirt's going to be around your waist, princess,' and 'There's a desk and the Linear office is empty? Let me bend you over that right now.' " Charlie's eyes took on a dreamy look before she sat up straighter and narrowed them. "But lately it's been all sweet kisses and breakfast in bed."

"You did almost die, Charlie. Cut the man some slack

for wanting to take care of you." Anne laughed. "And you're embarrassing Violet. So keep your dirty talk to yourself."

"Don't mind me." Charlie waved a hand around in front of her. "I get a little uncouth when I'm not getting what I want. Especially when what I want is around me all the time, but I can't get him to be hard and dirty enough with me."

Violet couldn't help the flush that crept over her face, but it wasn't just embarrassment that was causing the color. "I want hard and dirty too." The words blurted past her lips before she could stop them.

Charlie and Anne looked at each other with eyebrows raised before turning back to her.

"Nothing wrong with that," Anne said, scooping an arm around her and leading her over to the couch. "I mean, I'm not quite as bad as nympho here, but hot sex is never a bad thing. If you're ready for it, Violet, only if you're ready."

Charlie grabbed Violet's hand and pulled her down so she was sitting in between them. "You know to take me with a grain of salt, right? I'm just talking a lot of smack. It's easy for me to say all this because what I went through didn't have any sort of sexual component at all. So I don't want you to feel like you have to jump on the *hard and dirty* bandwagon just because I'm running my mouth."

Violet sighed. These two women had encouraged her more over the past month than anyone had her whole life. She might as well tell them the whole story.

"Last Sunday I went to Aiden's house. I told him I wanted to have sex with him. But he turned me down." She pushed the words out in a rush.

"Did he say why?" Anne asked.

Violet shrugged. "He just said he didn't want me."

Charlie let out a string of obscenities Violet had never heard together at one time.

Anne ignored her. "Did he say those actual words? Did he *say* he didn't want you?"

"I have a gun," Charlie muttered. "If someone distracts Dorian, we can kill Aiden and hide the body where no one will ever find it."

Anne rolled her eyes. "Charlie . . ."

"What? I'm just saying that Dorian can find nearly anything in the woods, so somebody's got to distract him so we can get the body out of town."

Anne grabbed Violet's hands, turning her away from the quite violent Charlie. "Seriously, did Aiden say he didn't want you? That he wasn't interested?"

Not in those exact words, maybe. "No, but he very definitely didn't say yes either. I just don't think he's attracted to me."

Charlie and Anne leaned forward and looked at each other again.

Charlie took Violet's hand now. "Hey, I'm obviously not the flowers-and-romance type. But all kidding aside, I saw Aiden the night after he met you when he couldn't get you out. He was crushed. Completely devastated."

Violet closed her eyes. "I believe it. But that's just who Aiden is. It didn't really have anything to do with *me*."

"To a degree, maybe," Charlie said, chewing on her lip. "But it was definitely personal."

She just shrugged. It was a moot point now anyways. There was no way she was going to ever approach him about sex—particularly hard and dirty sex—ever again.

Anne nudged Violet's shoulder with her own. "You have to understand about the delicate psyches of these Linear Tactical guys. Of all Special Forces guys, probably."

Charlie snorted. "Delicate psyches? These are some of the strongest and most highly trained people in the entire world."

Anne laughed softly. "I know. And you put them in a place where they have to survive—no food, no sleep, world on fire, torture every three minutes—and they'll come out with flying colors. But put someone they care about in that same situation? Make it so they can't immediately swoop in and be the hero? They are not quite as equipped to handle that. If I had to guess, the same problem Charlie is having with Finn is what's happening with you and Aiden. I know it's not that either of them don't want the two of you, they just want to make sure you're okay."

Charlie sighed and stood up. "She's right. I'm letting Finn get away with it right now because he needs it. He needs to coddle me and show his sweet and tender side. And hell, I'll deny it, but honestly I need it too."

Violet let out a sigh, laying her head back against the couch. "I appreciate what you guys are saying, but my situation with Aiden is not the same as yours with Finn, Charlie. Finn loves you. Aiden doesn't really know me at all and seems pretty content to leave me parked in the friend zone."

Anne shook her head, then smiled before standing up also. She turned to Charlie. "Call Wavy and Riley. I think I know exactly what we need tonight."

Charlie began clapping her hands. "Please, please, please tell me this involves Electric Smurfs."

Anne laughed. "Not for you because you're still on medication. But for everybody else, I think definitely."

"Fine," Charlie pouted. "I'll be the designated driver."

"I'm almost afraid to ask what an Electric Smurf is," Violet said. "But it sounds like the start of bad decision-making."

"Oh, believe me," Anne said, "it most definitely is. Charlie and I have been remiss in our duties as your friends. It's time for you to have a proper welcome to Oak Creek."

"With a girls' night out," Charlie continued. "I don't even think you've been to The Eagle's Nest yet."

"No, I haven't and some of the crew working here were mentioning it. But you know we don't have to go to the bar if you don't want to. We can just buy a couple bottles of wine and hang out here. That would be nice."

Charlie winked at her. "That *would* be nice. And I promise we'll do that sometime. Maybe to celebrate your grand opening."

Anne was grinning bigger than Violet had ever seen her. She wouldn't have thought the rather shy doctor could get such an evil gleam in her eye. "Another night for the wine and talking. Tonight we've got a different goal in mind. We're going to find someone interested in helping you with your *hard and dirty* problem."

Five hours later, walking into The Eagle's Nest, Violet was sure she had made the worst kind of mistake by agreeing to this.

She was surrounded by friendly women, four of them, all of whom were excited about finding her a man if she wanted one. Or just having a blast if she didn't.

The jokes about *hard and dirty* had abounded as they all got ready at Finn's house, since it was the biggest. Charlie had kicked out her fiancé and his sweet son, Ethan, sending them to hang out with Finn's mom.

And then the women had gone to work on Violet. By the time they were done, she hardly recognized herself.

"Violet's got that same deer-in-the-headlights look you did when we got you ready for your first date with Zac," Riley had said, laughing.

"You two are a little overwhelming for those of us who haven't spent as much time doing girly stuff." Anne bumped hips with Violet as she stared into the mirror, unable to believe she was actually looking at herself. "But you look fantastic."

Her auburn hair had been lightly curled and fell past her shoulders in soft waves. The makeup they'd put on her —dark eyeliner and eye shadow that she'd never be able to replicate—made her eyes look big and bright. The red on her lips was not a color she would've ever chosen for herself, but everyone swore it worked.

But it was the black bustier they'd put her in that was going to draw the most attention. It had already caused Wavy's and Riley's eyes to bug out of their heads.

"I knew it!" screamed Riley, doing some crazy dance in the middle of the floor.

Violet could only stare. "Knew what?"

"Knew that was going to look wicked good on you. Those curves you have . . . so much more exciting than stick-figure me." Riley sighed.

"Holy hell, I wish I had boobs like yours," Wavy said as she cinched the waist of the bustier tighter, pressing Violet's breasts up even further. Paired with jeans, it was the perfect girls'-night-out wear, or so the women had decreed.

"You don't think this is too revealing?" she asked the other women. All of them were older than her, Wavy and Riley by a couple years, Charlie and Anne by at least another five. But Violet felt like she was the only voice of reason in the room. "It's a little risqué, don't you think?"

" 'Damn sexy' are the words I would use," Charlie said,

coming over to kiss her on the cheek. The petite woman looked fantastic herself in a short skirt and halter top.

"You look great, Violet," Anne said in her soft voice. "The first time Riley and Wavy got their hands on me, I was pretty skeptical too. But the way Zac nearly swallowed his own tongue when he saw me made it worth it."

"But I'm not going on a date."

Riley wagged her eyebrows. "You may not *start* on a date, but you may have one by the time the night is done. Hard and dirty, remember?"

She'd wanted that from Aiden, but would it be the same with someone else?

Charlie drove them to The Eagle's Nest at about ten p.m. The closer they got, the edgier Violet became.

"You okay?" Charlie whispered as they got out of the car. Riley and Wavy ran on ahead, ready to get started. "You look great, but you know you don't have to do this if you don't want to. If this is too much, we can still go grab those bottles of wine and head back to the bakery."

"I'm not worried, as in, afraid I'll get abducted or anything like that. Knowing Stellman is behind bars helps. But I don't know if I want to do anything with some random stranger."

"Don't worry about it." Anne linked arms with her. "Just enjoy the line dancing and the Electric Smurfs and having a good time. If you see a guy who catches your eye and you think you want to have some fun, we'll let you know if you're picking a good one. Certainly, among the four of us, we know every single man in this town."

Violet couldn't even think about men right now, not when every time she glanced down all she could see were the pale tops of her breasts. They were more than adequately covered, but it still wasn't what she was used to.

"I don't really know how to dance. And even if I did, I don't think anyone will want to dance with me."

Her friends pulled her forward. "It's line dancing," Charlie said. "You don't have to have a partner."

"Plus, finding a partner isn't going to be a problem." Anne squeezed her arm. "You just wait and see."

CHAPTER 13

AIDEN SAT on his back porch, sipping a beer. Alone.

Who had two thumbs and was a complete idiot? This guy.

It wasn't the first time he'd thought that since mishandling the Violet situation so badly a few days ago. It wouldn't be the last.

When Zac Mackay had approached him about being part of Linear Tactical a little over four years ago, Aiden had immediately agreed. The fact that they were going to open the facility in Zac and Finn's tiny hometown in the middle of Nowhere, Wyoming, had given Aiden a little bit of pause.

Aiden was a city boy, born and raised in Seattle. To try to offset the change to Wyoming, he'd bought a place in the town proper—such as Oak Creek was—so he could be closer to entertainment. To nightlife and action.

The fact that the *action* had ended up being a lot of kids riding their bikes, an occasional town-wide picnic, and Mrs. Mazille watching over the neighborhood like a hawk had bothered Aiden much less than he would've thought.

Living *downtown* also meant he was two blocks from what would soon be the new Fancy Pants Bakery. He'd been two blocks away all week from walking over to Violet and explaining exactly what an idiot he had been when she'd come to his house.

Maybe turning her down, at least in that second, had been the right thing to do. The noble thing to do. He took another sip of his beer.

He was still a fucking idiot.

Mostly because he let her get out of his house without making the most important point clear.

Yes.

Yes, what he'd said about her being sexy had all been true. Yes, that kiss had been much more than just an opportunity for him to put a tracker on her. He thought about it nearly every damn day.

And yes, he wanted to have sex with her. Yes. *So much yes.*

It had taken every ounce of mental fortitude he had to say no. But before he could gather the presence of mind to explain exactly what he'd meant by no, sweet Violet's feelings had been hurt. She'd been on her way out the door, thinking he didn't want her.

That he didn't want to lift her up on that kitchen counter, spread her legs, and use his mouth on her until she was screaming his name.

That he hadn't thought about taking her on his couch, in his bed, against his front door.

That he—God save him, because he was probably going to hell—hadn't been able to stop thinking about her lush, naked curves. And how he wanted to see them again, this time with no backdrop of terror around them.

All she heard was *no.*

Another sip of his beer. Cheers to the idiot.

A fist pounding on his front door had Aiden out of his seat. He opened it, only mildly surprised to find Finn and Zac there. Only they would show up at nearly midnight without calling.

"Got another couple of those?" Zac asked, pointing at the beer. "I think we're going to need them."

Aiden left the door open and the other two men came inside behind him. They walked into the kitchen, and he grabbed two more beers, handing them to his friends. "Did you both get kicked out or something?"

Finn shook his head. "I was hanging out with Ethan and my mom when I got called in for backup. So he's going to spend the night with her tonight."

"Trouble?" Aiden asked becoming more alert.

"Of the worst kind," Zac said, then took a long drag of his beer.

For there to be trouble *of the worst kind*, his friends looked awfully relaxed, sitting on his kitchen-island barstools.

Zac glanced over at Finn. "What should we give them, another fifteen or twenty minutes?"

Finn shrugged. "Last report was that things were getting pretty dangerous. Oh, and that it was all my fault, because, quote, 'I was being sweeter than Jesus and keeping it in my pants way too much.' "

Aiden nearly spewed his beer.

"I thought Charlie wasn't drinking," Zac said.

Finn sighed. "She isn't. But evidently, she feels like this is a good opportunity to express her discontent."

Realization dawning, Aiden couldn't help but laugh at his friends' faces. "What, did Anne and Charlie decide to hang out together and talk shit about you guys?"

Zac took another chug of beer. "Not only that, but Electric Smurfs are involved. So we're headed over to The Eagle's Nest in just a few minutes to make sure things don't get out of hand. Especially since Baby had texted Finn a few minutes ago and told him that just about every guy in town is there, and the gals are in rare form."

Aiden laughed again. This just kept getting better. "Your brother won't let anything happen to them."

Finn nodded. "Oh, I know Baby will watch out for them. I'm not really worried about it. I just want to be there when the fireworks really start."

"Fireworks? And how much trouble can Charlie and Anne get in, especially if Charlie is not even drinking?"

Finn just smiled. "Oh, it's not just our women." He hooked a thumb at Zac. "Evidently, it's a whole girls' night out. Wavy, Riley, Electric Smurfs . . . the whole posse."

"I guess we should get going." Zac finished his beer as he stood up. "I know how the doc gets once she gets her hands on those blue shots."

Aiden stretched his leg out on his stool. "I'm a little bit glad right now that I don't have a woman I have to go fish out of trouble. Definitely less complicated."

A look passed between his two friends. And a smile. Aiden's eyes narrowed at that. He'd spent too much time in the army studying nonverbal communication not to realize what had been happening. This entire little drive-by had been a setup. All he could do now was wait for the blow.

He didn't have to wait long.

"Yep, Shamrock, you're definitely the lucky one with no complications." Finn stood slowly, throwing his beer bottle in Aiden's recycling bin. "I'm going to walk over to The Eagle's Nest. Dance with my fiancée. And hopefully stop my brother from picking up the town's new baker. Word on the street is that a hot young redhead is looking for a good time."

What the fuck?

Violet?

Looking for a *good time?*

Aiden stood up so fast he knocked his stool over. Both his friends just grinned.

Zac slapped Finn on the back. "Time for the fireworks."

Aiden had walked into some of the most dangerous situations on the planet. Situations where he couldn't necessarily tell the bad guys from the good guys. Situations where there were no good guys at all. Situations where he was convinced he and his team would never get out alive.

None of those held a candle to the one he walked into at The Eagle's Nest.

Girls' night out, where the *girls* were very definitely *women* and on the prowl . . . He was in a place where a smart man feared for his life.

Aiden had not been able to take his eyes off Violet from the moment he'd walked into the bar. And everyone in here knew it. Except her.

His friends had played him, and he had walked right into it. Baby Bollinger wasn't hitting on Violet. Nobody was hitting on her. Not because she wasn't attractive enough— God knew Aiden's pants had been too tight from the moment he'd stepped foot in the bar and seen her in that . . . *thing* she was wearing that ratcheted her curves from gorgeous to mind-meltingly hot. Damn near every eligible male in the room was staring at her.

But because the town's new pastry genius was drunk as a skunk.

Most of the men in Oak Creek had too much respect for women in general to try to pick one up when she was this intoxicated—and they would stop the few dishonorable enough to make the attempt.

Of course, that was all based on the assumption they could get through that thick ring of friends surrounding Violet.

Aiden had seen military compounds more vulnerable than Violet currently was. She might be in danger of vomiting up the copious amounts of blue liquor she'd been drinking or passing out, but there was no danger of anyone taking advantage of Violet Collingwood.

And damned if this wasn't one of the reasons Aiden had come to love this town so much. Even when it drove him crazy that the nearest movie theater was more than thirty miles away.

Oak Creek took care of their own. Even when their own was brand new.

"I see that Zac and Finn are smart enough not to be sitting here with you." Gavin, another of the Linear partners who tended to do a lot of work out of town, sat down on the stool beside Aiden.

"Those bastards set me up. They knew I'd come running here as soon as I heard Violet might be in trouble." His eyes never left her out on the dance floor. She was laughing, face flushed.

Beautiful.

Aiden had switched to water as soon as he arrived, but Gavin took a sip of his whiskey. "They told you she'd be in trouble, or that she might find someone she'd enjoy getting to know better?"

"Nobody better damn well try anything with her when she's in this state. You included."

What the hell was he saying? Gavin Zimmerman was the most honorable guy he'd ever met. Hell, they'd nick-named him Redwood in the army because the guy was so fucking upstanding.

But Gavin just laughed and slapped him on the shoulder. "Nobody's going to touch her. You know that. At least not tonight."

His hand tightened around his glass of water. "What are you saying? That they're going to wait for the next time she gets drunk?"

"No, brother, I'm just saying she's a young, attractive, unattached woman. Who can bake well enough to make a man beg—if he wasn't doing that already just by looking at her, for crying out loud. I doubt she's going to find it very difficult to find suitors. Or if she's not interested in some-thing serious, even more guys will be willing to show her some fun."

Over his dead body. "If she wants fun, I'm going to be the one to show it to her."

Gavin smiled and took another sip of his drink. "And that's why Cyclone and Eagle got you out here tonight. Not to take care of Charlie and Anne. Hell, Aiden, each of those men would trust his woman with his life. They definitely trusted their women to take care of a gal who might be a little bit fragile."

Aiden ripped his eyes away from Violet to glare at Gavin, but the other man didn't let up.

"It was *you* who needed to get shaken up a bit. Every-body's tired of walking on eggshells around you at the office. You've been a mess all week." They both turned back to the dancing women. "It looks like Violet's trying to put the past behind her, where it belongs. Maybe you should try that too."

Aiden rubbed his fingers over his eyes. Unfortunately, it wasn't that easy. It wasn't like she was going to give him another chance after the way he had rejected her.

The disco song about raining men ended, and a slower song took its place. The group of women groaned in disappointment and began moving off the dance floor. As soon as Aiden saw Finn and Zac moving toward Charlie and Anne, he stood.

The pack was broken. He knew exactly what that meant, and he wasn't about to allow it to happen.

He made it over to Violet, barely reaching her before two other men did.

He touched her on the shoulder. Her bare, sexy shoulder. "Dance with me, Firefly."

Those green eyes got big. "Aiden? What are you doing here? It's girls' night out."

He smiled. "Believe it or not, they let a few guys in here too. Would you dance with me?"

She nodded, and he didn't even try to hide his sigh of relief as he pulled her into his arms. The other two men faded back now that she hadn't rejected Aiden.

That's right, assholes, get lost.

He had Violet in his arms and no plans to let any other man near her.

They'd barely started swaying before Finn and Charlie were beside them, Charlie obviously maneuvering her fiancé closer so she could talk to Violet.

"You okay, Vi?" Charlie asked, shooting Aiden a dirty look. "There are plenty of other guys who want to dance with you. Or you don't have to dance at all."

Aiden forced himself not to tighten his arms around

Violet. Charlie was right. She could do what she wanted. And he had nobody to blame at all if she walked away.

But she didn't.

"No," Violet told her friend. "I'm okay. I want to talk to superhero man anyway. I've got stuff to say to him."

Charlie winked. "Got it, warrior woman. Just remember you're pretty sloshed, okay?"

"I got this. I'm totally in the control of myself." It would've been almost believable if the words weren't slurred.

Charlie met Aiden's eyes, and he gave her a nod. She was passing custody of her friend over to him. He didn't take that responsibility lightly.

And he wouldn't take for granted the fact that she was pressed close to him, her hands holding on to his shoulders as he maneuvered them toward a less crowded part of the dance floor.

"I've got something to say to you, Mr. Man." Her eyes narrowed as she looked up at him, the heels she was wearing making her only a few inches shorter than him.

"That I'm an idiot?"

She pondered that. "You think you're an idiot because you're dancing with me?"

He trailed his hand up her right arm until it reached her shoulder. He pulled her hand down, cradling it in his, holding it between their torsos. He swayed gently back and forth, afraid anything else might cause her to topple over.

"No, Firefly, I'm an idiot because I haven't been dancing with you all week. Because I've definitely been thinking about you all week."

She studied him, then wiggled one finger out of his grasp so she could poke him in the chest. "Listen, buddy, just because I'm drunk doesn't mean I'm going to get into your pants."

He swallowed his bark of laughter. "No, I would never presume such a thing."

She narrowed her eyes like she knew there was something off with the conversation but couldn't figure out what it was. Then she sighed.

"Look at you with your stubble on your perfect Adonis jaw." The fingers from her free hand came up and tapped him on the cheek. Her voice lowered in an imitation of his. " 'I don't have time to shave daily, I'm too busy rescuing all the damsels in distress.' "

He swallowed his laughter again. *This woman* with her adorable, scrunched-up face. God, he wanted to kiss her more than he wanted his next breath, even knowing he'd have a gaggle of women beating him with their purses if he did.

So he shrugged. "I sometimes take a razor with me on missions, so I can shave in between taking out bad guys."

She nodded seriously, like she believed that was the truth. "Can I ask you a question?"

The music changed but remained slow, so he kept her snug against him with his arm around her waist. "Sure. Anything."

"Do you think my boobs look good in this bustier?"

Eyes up, asshole. And do not swallow your tongue. He had to clear his throat to even get words out. "Is that what it's called? A bustier?"

"Yeah. Riley and Wavy picked it out for me."

"Well, yes, your . . . breasts look fantastic in it." And then, because damn it all, he wasn't a fucking saint, he lowered his head to her ear and whispered. "But, if memory serves, and believe me my memory is very, very good when it comes to you, your breasts look absolutely gorgeous in nothing at all."

He eased back to find those green eyes staring up at him, studying him like he was a puzzle she couldn't quite solve. "I thought you didn't like my breasts."

He pulled her just a little bit closer. "Why don't we have this conversation when the room isn't spinning quite so much for you, okay? But suffice to say, I think your breasts, and every other piece of you, are darn near perfect."

She sighed and pressed herself up against him. "Aiden, will you take me home? I really want hard and dirty sex with *you*."

He closed his eyes, praying for control. Reminding himself that she was drunk. Trying to ignore the fact that he was going to have the impression of his zipper on his cock for a week after hearing the words *hard* and *dirty* come out of that sweet mouth.

And, oh God, he didn't want her to feel like he was rejecting her again when he had to say no.

"Firefly . . ."

She laid her head on his chest. "But not tonight, okay? Because I might have had one too many drinks."

Thank God. "I think that's probably a good idea."

"But next time. Promise? Next time I ask for hard and dirty sex, you have to give it to me. Cross your heart like you did when you rescued me."

Aiden took his finger and crossed it over his chest.

That was the easiest promise he'd ever made.

CHAPTER 14

VIOLET DIDN'T EVEN HAVE to open her eyes to know she was never, *ever* going to drink anything blue ever again ever. Nothing that color was meant to be ingested. And she was darned fortunate it hadn't come back up the same way it'd gone down.

She only had a cloudy memory of the night before, and it just got more hazy as the night went on. She remembered Riley and Wavy getting her dressed up. She remembered walking into the bar feeling a little self-conscious at the beginning, then more and more confident as guy after guy had asked her to dance.

She hadn't danced with them. She had only danced with her friends . . .

Until Aiden.

Her eyes flew open and then she snapped them back shut with a groan at the brightest light in the history of the world shining in through the window. As if the sun had nothing better to do than cheerfully shine on this fine Saturday morning.

Aiden.

He'd shown up. And they had danced. And then she'd said . . .

Oh God.

She tried to push the memories out of her head, but she couldn't. Every single ridiculous sentence she'd said to him was running through her mind in Technicolor.

Do you think my boobs look good?

Promise you'll have hard and dirty sex with me.

And then lying . . . in the grass?

That was the last thing she remembered. Aiden had agreed to walk her home, all of her friends hugging her and telling her to just go straight to her apartment, take two Advil, and drink a full glass of water.

But walking from The Eagle's Nest to her place, she'd somehow decided she wanted to go lie in the grass. Specifically, in the lawn at Aiden's house. She'd told him how she never had a yard growing up, and didn't have one now, and how a gal sometimes just needed to lie in the grass late at night in her bustier, when her boobs looked good.

Oh sweet baby Jesus.

She didn't remember a single thing after that.

She cracked open an eye again, cringing when she realized she wasn't at her apartment. She was lying alone in a bed much bigger than hers.

She forced the second eye open and took a better look around. The other half of the bed was still completely made. Evidently, she had been sleeping here alone all night. Considering she couldn't remember any of it, that was probably a good thing. And at least she'd been passed out enough to not have to worry about being in the dark on her own. She'd yet to conquer that ridiculous fear since the kidnapping. She couldn't stand being in the dark.

She pulled up the covers and peeked underneath. Her

bustier was gone, replaced by a large white T-shirt. But her jeans still covered her legs.

She looked to the other side of the bed and found her phone and a glass of water on the nightstand. She gulped down the water in an attempt to wash out whatever had died in her mouth and then grabbed her phone. There was a message from Charlie.

Aiden called and said you passed out in his yard. He let me know he was going to put you to bed at his place but swore on his life he wouldn't be sleeping anywhere near you. Call me when you feel alive tomorrow.

Violet weighed the pros and cons of hiding under the covers and never coming back out. Or sneaking out the front door and moving back out of the state. Or spending all her time and energy for the rest of her life working on a time machine so she could go back and not say the words *boob*, *hard*, or *dirty* to Aiden Teague while in a drunken stupor.

It didn't seem fair that none of those were viable options.

"Are you going to lie in bed for the rest of the day?"

She turned her head toward Aiden, who was standing in the doorway. "I was actually trying to figure out if it was possible to stay here for the rest of my *life*."

He chuckled. "Do you feel that bad? Those Smurf bastards will get you every time."

She threw an arm over her eyes. "They should have warnings on those things. Ugh, I'll never be drinking *any* alcohol ever again."

"I don't suppose you feel like eating any food?" He arched a brow.

She couldn't even stop the retching sound she made.

He laughed again. "Then how about a little coffee? Maybe by dinnertime you'll feel a bit more like eating."

Dinnertime? Oh crap. "What time is it now?"

"Almost noon."

She groaned again. "Okay, coffee."

"I'll be downstairs on the back porch. You're welcome to use the shower or tub or whatever you want. Just come down when you're ready. I thought maybe we could talk."

Talk. Hadn't they talked enough?

She wanted to dive back under the covers but just nodded. Once he left, she dragged herself to the bathroom, stripped off her clothes, and stepped into the shower. Twenty minutes later, she at least felt human again. She brushed her teeth as best she could with toothpaste and her finger, and wrapped her hair up into a wet, messy bun.

She put her jeans and his T-shirt back on. Because there was no way she could face him in that bustier.

She made her way downstairs and into the kitchen, pouring the strong brew into a mug that had been set by the coffee maker. She stopped before she got to the door leading out to the porch, studying him through the glass. He was sitting at the small table, long legs stretched out in front of him, reading something on his electronic tablet. He had on jeans and a white T-shirt that had probably come from the same package as the one she was currently borrowing. He had a plate of fruit—grapes and melons and berries—set out in the center of the table. Every once in a while, he would absently grab a piece and toss it into his mouth.

God, he was gorgeous. So much more a *man* than any of the guys in her engineering classes or the ones she'd worked with at CT. And it wasn't just Aiden's age. Yeah, he was a decade older than her, but the difference between him and the other guys was much more than just about age.

It was about experience, awareness, and danger. She hadn't been wrong in thinking he was dangerous that first night she'd seen him. He wasn't dangerous to *her*, but he was still dangerous.

And she wanted him. She couldn't stop herself from staring at him. The stubble on his cheeks was even more pronounced, probably because he hadn't been able to get to his bathroom to shave . . . And wait, had she made some joke about his five-o'clock shadow last night?

She let out a distressed squeak. Things just kept getting worse and worse.

The sound alerted him to her presence. He turned and gave her a smile, reaching over to open the French door. "Want to come out here with that coffee?"

"Honestly, no."

"Oh." He looked at the fruit, then back at her. "Do you not want to be outside? I can bring everything inside."

She shook her head and walked out, sitting down across from him. "No, it's not the outside that's the problem. It's my big drunken mouth last night that's the problem. I'm such an idiot. Believe me, that was my first time getting drunk, and it will probably be my last." She took a sip of her coffee, then grabbed a strawberry and bit into it, not looking at him.

She could feel his eyes on her as she continued to eat the fruit. "First time drunk, huh? Well, as someone who has a bit more experience in that area, believe me when I say we all promise never to drink again the morning after."

"So you know what this feels like?" She wouldn't wish this on her worst enemy.

He just grinned. "We've all had our own version of a girls' night out. Believe me, I've gotten in trouble with the Linear guys all over the world. You could do much worse than getting drunk at The Eagle's Nest in Oak Creek. Ask one of the guys to tell you about Krakow and how our commanding officer had to come bail us out when we ended up in the custody of the local magistrate."

She couldn't help but laugh at that as she grabbed another strawberry. "I guess I should be thankful I didn't wind up in a jail cell. I've never been a big one for partying, and, believe me, the way I feel now definitely does not change my stance on that. But it was fun, I guess. At least at the time."

"Good. I'm glad you had a good time."

She finally forced herself to look at him. "But it was fun in a different way than I thought it would be. Not because of the alcohol, but because of the people. I'm not even sure what I mean by that."

"No, I get it. It was fun because you were part of a community. Your tribe. It might not have been safe doing something like that in a big city, but here everyone is looking out for each other."

She took another sip of the coffee and grabbed a little more fruit from the plate, feeling better, at least physically. And he was right about last night.

"Yeah, almost like a big, extended family. I guess I dove in headfirst with that here."

"Sometimes headfirst is the best way to go."

Violet sighed. She could keep stuffing fruit into her mouth and drinking her coffee, but it wasn't going to change what she'd said last night. She was tempted to ignore it, maybe even pretend like she had no recollection of the absurd things she'd told him. But it was always going to be between them. She might as well get *the talk* over with.

And yet she still sat there popping grapes into her mouth, one after another.

"Want me to go get some more?" he asked after she'd eaten the last one.

"I'm sorry for all that crazy stuff I said last night." The words came out slightly mangled by the six grapes she was still chewing.

What was wrong with her? She had a relatively high IQ. Why could she not seem to have any sort of intelligent conversation with this man?

Thankfully, he just waited as she swallowed the last of the grapes. "I was drunk last night—you may have noticed —so there's no reason to pay any attention to anything I said."

He studied her from across the table. "Do you even remember what you said last night?"

She closed her eyes. "Unfortunately, damn near every word. I haven't referred to my breasts as *boobs* since I was . . . well, I don't think I've *ever* referred to my breasts as boobs."

All of a sudden, she was overtly aware that her breasts or boobs or whatever anybody wanted to call them were bare under that white T-shirt. The bustier hadn't allowed for a bra, so she didn't have one now. She crossed her arms over her chest, wincing when Aiden's eyes followed her actions. He had to know she didn't have a bra on too, considering he was the one who'd peeled her out of her outfit last night.

"Anyway," she finally forced out, "I didn't mean any of that stuff I said."

He crossed his arms over his chest, leaning back in his chair. "Is that so? In my experience, I've found drunk people, children, and leggings always tell the truth."

She couldn't help but snicker at that and relax a little bit. This didn't have to be so bad. "As much as I'm tempted to get that on a cross-stitch pillow, what I'm trying to say is I didn't mean to make you uncomfortable. *Again.* I'm sorry you had to babysit me, and just know that I don't expect you to actually . . . keep your promise."

He didn't say anything, just shifted his legs so that they were stretched out on either side of hers. Him touching her, even casually, was not helping her with this conversation.

"And which promise was that?" he asked.

Oh please God don't make her say the words out loud. Not when they were sitting here in the beautiful Wyoming sunshine like normal, happy friends. This was going to throw things directly into awkward.

"The one where, you know . . ." She couldn't force the words out. She wanted to melt into the porch.

"The one where I promised to fuck you hard and dirty next time you wanted it?"

His long legs on either side of hers closed, trapping her legs between his. He leaned forward, propping his forearms on his knees, and trailed his fingers up and down her thighs.

Violet forgot how to breathe. "Yep, that's the one," she finally managed to push past her lips.

"Maybe I'm not interested in being released from that promise." His fingers were still touching her legs.

"But last week you said you weren't . . ."

"Last weekend when we talked, I handled things poorly. You shouldn't be apologizing to me, I should be apologizing to you."

"I don't understand."

He reached up and played with a piece of her hair that had fallen from her haphazard bun. "You've been through a trauma, Firefly. That changes a person, sometimes for the better, sometimes for the worse, but usually both. I think what you're doing with the bakery is fantastic. Maybe not for my waistline, but definitely for you, since it seems like it's what you want."

She nodded. "It is."

"Good. When you showed up here last week, I was caught off guard. So when you told me you wanted *me*, I lumped in what you were saying with the effects of trauma. I didn't handle it well." His lips pressed together in a slight grimace.

She eased back from him. What exactly was he saying? The last thing she wanted was for him to do something with her because he felt sorry for her or guilty or something. "I don't need to be *handled*. And I don't need to be pitied either."

His fingers tugged on the strand of hair. "Pity is the very last thing I've ever felt for you."

"Good. Because I'm a normal woman with a normal woman's desires. The question I asked you was simple. Do you want me or not?"

"But it's not actually that simple."

She threw up her hands. "But it *is*, Aiden. Just answer the damn question. Do you want me or not?"

She didn't want him to pity her. If he wasn't attracted to her, then fine. She was a big girl, she could handle it.

Before she could even process what was happening, he'd lifted her off her chair and onto his, her legs straddling his. His fingers bit into her hips and ass as he pulled her down hard, rubbing her very deliberately against him.

"You want the simple answer: *yes*. Fucking yes, I want you."

The hardness pressing between her legs could leave no doubt about that.

His fingers slid up her back and threaded into her hair, forcing her head closer to his. "It is that simple," he continued, "and yet it's not. I didn't explain it well last weekend, so let me explain it now."

"Is it because you see me as damaged? Because of what they did to me?"

She was surprised at her own words. Those thoughts had been buried so deep inside her she hadn't even been aware it was something she feared. But now that the words were out she realized they very much were.

Aiden had seen her at her lowest. He had seen her when she was trapped and helpless and being treated as if she were less than human. How could that not affect how he saw her now?

He pulled her face closer. "No. The only people I will ever think of as damaged in that situation were those bastards who treated you like that, Randy and those assholes buying people at the auction. I have never thought of you as less than absolutely courageous."

She just shrugged.

His fingers gentled in her hair, and his voice thickened. "I left you behind. You suffered so much more because I couldn't get you out that first night."

"*What?* No. You tried." She grabbed his face in her hands. She already knew what had happened the night at The Barn and how he'd been willing to blow his undercover status to get her away from Randy and Dillon.

He shook his head. "Leave no fallen comrade behind. That's part of the army warrior creed. And I failed miserably."

Those hazel eyes held such anguish her heart might shatter. She'd never once considered that he'd paid a price in all this too. "Aiden, I—"

He held a finger up to her lips. "That's not for you to worry about, and it's not what's important. What I bungled saying last weekend was that our situation is complicated because yes, I want you. But I want to take this as slow and easy as you need. You've got nothing to prove, and there's no need to rush."

"But—"

"I'm here. I made you a promise last night, and believe me, I have no problem keeping it. Whatever type of sex you want—hard, dirty, slow, easy—I'm more than up for it."

"But . . ." She could hear the word even if he wasn't saying it.

He sighed and pressed his forehead to hers. "But . . . do it because you want to, not because you think you have to. Not because you're forcing yourself. Because as much as I'm willing to have sex with you, I'm also willing to just hang out, if you want. Go on dates, picnics, dancing . . . do things that fill up your memories with good stuff until it pushes out the thoughts of what they did to you. And those things don't have to be sex."

Oh.

"Because you're amazing and beautiful and spending time with you would be my pleasure. Then when you're ready, we can add the sex. It doesn't have to be now. Your kidnapping has already been the catalyst for a lot of changes in your life. And that's fine. But I just want to make sure *you're sure* before you jump into bed with me."

Violet leaned back so she could look at Aiden more clearly. He was a good, honorable man. She'd known that, sensed it from the moment she'd first met him in the damn Barn. He'd done nothing but take care of her and help her in any way he was able to from the moment he'd seen her at The Barn until last night, when he'd slipped her into one of his T-shirts and left her sleeping in his bed.

Aiden Teague was one of the good guys.

What she wanted to know was whether she could find the bad boy inside that good man.

Because while she appreciated what he was offering, and she really did plan to take him up on the dancing, picnics, and dates, he didn't quite seem to grasp that she knew what she wanted.

No more being passive. No more agreeing to what might in fact be good for her but wasn't what she really wanted.

"You respect me," she said gently.

The relief flashed and those hazel eyes. "Yes. I have nothing *but* respect for you."

"Thank you," she whispered, trailing her fingers through his thick hair. "And thank you for getting me home safely last night. And like I said before, thank you for getting me out of that hellhole a month ago, for figuring out that I was in trouble when to anyone else it just looked like a normal part of that situation."

His brows furrowed. "You're welcome for all those things. But there's no need—"

She put her finger up to his lips. "I just wanted to say it one more time to make sure I'd been clear. Because now I'm done saying thank you. And I think you better take me inside. Otherwise, Mrs. Mazille and her neighborhood watch might get quite an eyeful with what I'm planning to do to you."

CHAPTER 15

THERE WAS ONLY SO MUCH a man could take. A line where he snapped. A great deal of his Special Forces training had been spent learning how to push that line as far back as possible.

But when Violet's fingers reached for the hem of the T-shirt covering her body and began pulling it off, Aiden found his line very clearly.

He'd given her every possible out. She was young—so impossibly young, for God's sake she'd just woken up hungover *for the first time*—and he'd been trying to do the right thing, trying to explain he'd take it slow.

But now she'd made her choice. He hadn't been lying when he said he respected her. But respect didn't necessarily mean keeping his distance. Respect also involved agreeing that she knew her mind better than anyone else did. If she wanted him, he wasn't going to say no.

He wrapped his hands under that lush ass that had kept him hard for more hours than he could count and stood, bringing her up with him. Her arms wrapped around his neck and her legs looped around his waist. He couldn't wait one more second, even if Mrs. Mazille had somehow figured out how to peer into his back porch from down the street. He kissed Violet.

It was the opposite in every possible way from the kiss they'd shared at the auction. That kiss had been so much more than just an excuse to slip the tracker on her, but it had been laden with the ugliness of the situation. She'd been frightened, hurt, and trapped, and even though she'd known Aiden wasn't one of the bad guys, she hadn't truly had the ability to withhold her permission.

He had never in his life kissed or touched a woman who hadn't given her explicit consent. His partners had not only been consensual, but enthusiastic. Except for Violet, in that situation.

She hadn't tried to get away from him, but she hadn't had much choice in what was happening to her at the time.

So feeling her lips latch on to his own with such passion now eased something in Aiden he hadn't even been aware was hurting. The fear that maybe somewhere inside her mind, she would associate him with her abusers.

But not now, not here. Here the playing field was equal. They were both free to search and take and do whatever felt right and good.

And, holy Jesus, her lips felt right and good.

He held her with one arm and opened the door inside with the other. He was only a step into his living room when her lips wrapped around his tongue and began sucking. That sent his mind to other places he would like those lips wrapped around.

He slammed her back against the wall next to the door. There was no way in hell he was going to make it all the way upstairs if she kept that up.

"I hope you meant it about hard and dirty," he said

against her mouth. "Because that's just about all I'm capable of right now."

He thrust against her core, rubbing her through their jeans, loving the way she gasped.

"You do this to me, Firefly. You make me forget that I've been trained to have more self-control than ninety-nine percent of the people on the planet. Your lips, your body, your curves . . . they make me forget I even know what the word control means." His voice was thick with the need coursing through his body.

She squirmed against him. "Yes. Oh God, yes." Her arms and legs wrapped tighter around him.

He cupped her face, using his body to keep her pressed up against the wall, running his tongue over her bottom lip, then into her mouth as she opened for him. The noises she was making in the back of her throat were going to drive him over the edge.

He brought his hands down to her thighs and eased them from around his waist, smiling at her whimper of distress. "Just to get these clothes off, sweetheart. We both have too many clothes on."

She nodded with grand exuberance at that plan, and he grabbed the hem of his T-shirt first, snatching it over his chest, smiling as she stared, then ran her fingers over his torso. He didn't think much about his physique. He kept himself in shape because his job—first in the army, then at Linear—always demanded top physical form, and he regularly pushed his body hard.

But now, watching those emerald-green eyes prowl over him like she wanted to lick every inch, Aiden was damned glad for the good physical shape he maintained.

"Can we take your shirt off too?" he asked, voice much deeper than he'd intended.

Consent didn't get much more explicit than her "Hell, yes." She ripped her shirt off her body, and it joined his on the floor.

Now it was his turn to stare. He almost brought his hand up to his mouth to make sure he wasn't drooling.

"You're looking at me as if you haven't seen me naked twice already." She grimaced.

That was so totally different than this. So totally different than her willingly baring herself to him. "You're so much more gorgeous without any fear."

But there was still just the slightest bit of concern in her eyes. Not enough that she wanted to stop, but enough that he knew it was time to slow things way down.

And he trailed the finger from her cheek and down her neck to those gorgeous breasts. He smiled as he trailed the finger over one hardened nipple, then the other, watching her eyes flare with desire.

"I was thinking maybe this first time we could switch to slow and lazy. Certainly hard and dirty has its perks, but slow and lazy"—he bent down and took one breast in his mouth, twirling his tongue around the flesh until she was clutching her fingers into his hair—"has a lot more going for it, in my opinion."

He switched over to the other breast, nipping just enough to have her gasping and jerking him closer.

"There are things I'm going to do to you that require a bed and multiple hours to do properly."

She let out a tiny kitten mewl. It was the sexiest thing Aiden had ever heard.

He lifted his head up from her breast and leaned his forehead against hers. "Of course, if you keep making sounds like that, you're definitely going to get fucked right up against this wall."

She smiled, and it was one hundred percent confident woman. "Both hard and dirty and slow and easy sound good to me."

He smiled. This woman was going to be the death of him with her unique blend of sexy confidence and youthful shyness. "I think we might need a mix. How about *slow* and dirty?"

Her hips rubbing against him were once more almost his undoing. He needed to get her up to the bed or they'd never get there at all. He swung her up in his arms.

"Aiden," she croaked in surprise. "You can't carry me all the way upstairs. I weigh too much."

He didn't even try to stop his eye roll. "Watch me." He had regularly carried more than what she weighed for miles in training exercises. "I don't like you insinuating that you're overweight. Unless . . . you're insinuating that I'm just weak." He arched a brow.

Now she rolled her eyes. "I'm not fat. I know that. But I'm not thin either. I'm at that point where you can definitely tell I'm a baker."

He was up the stairs and laying her on the bed before he answered. He peeled her jeans down her generous hips, kissing and nipping as he went.

"First," he whispered as he trailed kisses down her thighs, "never trust a skinny cook."

She giggled at that, a sound he would never get tired of hearing. He dragged her jeans the rest of the way off, dropping them to the side, then reached up and slid her sky-blue panties off too.

He just stared down at her, the breath sucked out of his body.

That gorgeous auburn hair was falling from its bun all

around her in beautiful disarray. Her smooth, pale skin was reddened where his unshaven jaw had rubbed against her—and where her own desire was making her blush.

Those hooded green eyes peered out at him through thick lashes. And her soft pink lips were swollen from his kisses.

And that body. He couldn't stop staring at it. The curves. She was so soft everywhere he was hard.

"Firefly." His voice was so guttural he almost didn't recognize it. This woman absolutely wrecked him. It was terrifying.

Whatever self-consciousness she might have felt slid away under his hungry gaze. The smile she gave him was all confidence. "Do you know that the light in a firefly is caused by a chemical reaction happening in its body?"

Aiden smiled and grabbed her ankle, spreading her legs apart, kissing his way up her calf, reaching the place under her knee that made her breath come out in a hiss.

"Is that so?" he said against her skin before switching over to the other knee. "Maybe we should see if we can get a chemical reaction happening in *your* body."

He held her legs open wider, making room for his shoulders as he kissed his way up her thighs straight to her core.

Her hiss became a moan as he took his time licking, sucking, laving, discovering what made her squirm, gasp, beg.

Slow and dirty was definitely what they both needed.

He loved the way her back arched off the bed and she clutched his head closer as the first orgasm hit her. He didn't give her much time to come down from it before his fingers joined his mouth to drive her back up for another.

As he kept her pinned to the bed and feasted on her, his

name left her lips in a hoarse cry that was the most beautiful thing he'd ever heard.

Her legs were limp and shaking as she pulled up on his hair. "I want you inside me," she whispered. "Now."

"Yes, ma'am." Pulling off his jeans, he grabbed a condom out of his nightstand and made quick work of it. He bent down to nibble on one erect nipple, then the other, before sucking them deep into his mouth.

Then he leaned back and ran one hand from her ass up her inner thigh to the crease of her knee, opening her and positioning himself at her entrance.

Sweat was gathering at his forehead, the need to drive into her wet heat robbing him of damn near all reasonable thought.

But he had to make sure. His eyes met hers, trying to communicate the words he couldn't articulate.

"Yes," she said, her hand reaching his waist and clasping him toward her. "I want you. Now."

He slid in slowly—forcing himself to go *so goddamned slowly*—hissing as the heat of her surrounded him, clutching him inch by inch until he was embedded deep within her.

He stilled inside her, giving her time to adjust. Then he released her leg, wrapping it around the back of his thigh, and held his weight on both arms, propping his forehead against hers.

He began to move. First short, shallow strokes, then longer, deeper ones.

She let out a soft keen as he withdrew almost completely, lifting her hips against him, clutching at his back with her fingertips. He couldn't hold back his groan as he thrust in to the hilt, withdrawing again before plunging back into her with a hard drive.

But it was those green eyes looking at him with a mixture of trust and wonder, her voice calling his name over and over, that sent him spiraling over the precipice.

It was her name he called as he fell.

CHAPTER 16

AIDEN DIDN'T LET her out of bed for the rest of the weekend. She texted Charlie and Anne to let them know she was fine—promising to never drink anything again, much less Electric Smurfs—and that she would talk to them soon. She conveniently left out that Aiden was currently lying on top of her, threatening to turn her facedown, tie her to the bedposts, and have his wicked way with her if she didn't put away the phone.

As if *that* was some kind of scary threat.

When she explained that her friends might come looking for her if she didn't check in, and then they'd have to explain why she'd been here the whole time, he'd reluctantly let her finish her texts with no more interference.

Then he'd proceeded to flip her facedown on the bed and have his wicked way with her anyway. No tying necessary.

But now she was back at work and needed to push all thoughts of Aiden out of her head. She had a bakery that was opening in one week. The crews may be done and all the painting and wiring and plumbing complete, but there was still so much to do.

She needed a full-time employee. She wasn't Wonder Woman.

She'd been thinking a lot about the women who'd been in the human trafficking ring, prisoners of Randy, Dillon, and that Stellman guy she'd never met. She would talk with the people she'd met at Omega Sector. If any of the women were still in the country, maybe they needed a job. It might take a while to work out the details, but she'd keep trying.

But still, Violet needed an employee now, not weeks from now.

She'd had the help-wanted sign in the shop window since a day after she leased the place. So far she'd only had two teenagers and a mom with three young children who just wanted to get out of the house apply for the positions.

Violet had no problem hiring any of the three of them, but none of them could work the shifts when she needed them the most, early and midmorning during the week.

If the number of people who had come by just to check things out was anything to go by, Violet definitely wouldn't be able to handle everything herself. She wouldn't be able to handle it herself even if it was *half* the amount of business she was hoping for.

Violet needed a right-hand man. Charlie had offered to help out since evidently the bar where she'd been working had burned to the ground about a month ago. But Hurricane Charlie still admitted she wasn't back to one hundred percent after what she'd been through. And as much as Charlie didn't like it, an hour or two was as much as she could work at one time.

Violet looked up from where she was organizing coffee cups behind the service bar as a young woman walked by.

Again. She'd already passed the shop window two other times that Violet had seen. Maybe she was lost, although in a town the size of Oak Creek that seemed near impossible.

But when Violet looked up again five minutes later, the woman was outside once again. This time, after standing frozen in front of the door for nearly a full minute, she actually came inside.

She was young, maybe just a year or two older than Violet, tall, with long straight brown hair pulled back in a neat ponytail.

"Hi," Violet said. "You're welcome to come in and try one of the pastries I set out on the table, but we don't actually open for another week."

The woman nodded curtly. "Actually, I'm here about the job." She said it with a cringe, like she expected Violet to yell at her or something.

"Oh, are you from out of town? I ask because I saw you walking up and down the sidewalk a few times and thought you might be lost." She smiled to try to put the woman at ease.

Her arms crossed low over her stomach. "No, I've lived in Oak Creek most of my life, um, except for a few years while I was . . . away. Charlie's my roommate, or at least she is until she and Finn get married in a few months, and she suggested I stop by and talk to you about the job."

Realization dawned. "You're Jordan?" Charlie talked about her roommate all the time, but Violet had never met her. She never went out with Charlie, and this was the first time Violet had seen her in town.

And she was here for a job? This could be the answer to her biggest problem.

The woman flinched once more. "Uh, yeah. That's me." She wasn't exactly a fountain of information. Maybe she was uncomfortable around new people. Violet definitely understood that. "Charlie said she tried to get you to go out with us on Friday night, but you wouldn't go."

Jordan walked farther into the shop, still looking like she might make a run for it at any moment. "No, I'm not big on . . . bars and crowds."

Violet rolled her eyes. "You're speaking my language. And after what we were drinking, you should probably consider yourself fortunate that you made the more mature choice to stay home."

A look of longing passed through the woman's big gray eyes before almost immediately disappearing. She looked away and began to study the shop. When she turned back to Violet, her wary expression was back in place.

"Well," Violet smiled, "I'm glad you came in, because I really need to hire someone. Can you work mornings?"

"Yep, I can pretty much work any time you need me."

Violet barely refrained from jumping for joy. Charlie always spoke so highly of Jordan. She would definitely recommend her. "I can't believe Charlie didn't tell me she was sending you here."

"Actually, I kind of insinuated to Charlie that I wasn't interested in the job. Because I wanted to come here and talk to you myself, so that you wouldn't feel pressured because Charlie is both your friend and mine."

"Pressure about what?"

"You might not want to hire me, and I don't want that to be awkward for you and Charlie if that ends up being the case. It's better for her to think I didn't even apply to begin with."

"Oh. Why would I not want to hire you?"

"My last name is Reiss. I'm Jordan Reiss. Does that mean anything to you?"

"No." Was she like a celebrity or something? "I just moved here, so I don't know everyone. Should I know you?"

Jordan let out a sigh and rubbed her eyes. "No, I guess not. Look, I'm a convicted felon. Let's just get that out of the way. I'm not sure that you want to hire somebody with a record."

Violet was torn. Charlie hadn't mentioned any of this. On the one hand, no, she really didn't want to hire somebody who was a criminal. On the other hand, Charlie wouldn't be suggesting Jordan apply for the job—wouldn't be *living* in the same house as the other woman—if she was dangerous or untrustworthy, right?

"What were you in jail for?" Violet finally asked. Was that rude? She wasn't sure.

"Vehicular manslaughter. I fell asleep behind the wheel six years ago when I was eighteen and ran into another car. The lady driving and her toddler son were killed."

"Oh my God." She covered her mouth with her hand. How horrible for everyone, even Jordan.

Jordan cleared her throat a little hoarsely. "And you should know it was Zac Mackay's family that I killed. He seems to have forgiven me, but a lot of people in this town hate me. So I may not be a good prospective employee for you. If you don't want to hire me, I understand. And I don't want it to be awkward between you and Charlie."

Jordan looked like she was one point five seconds from turning and running out the door.

"Have you ever done any baking?" Violet asked quickly.

She shrugged. "I worked in the kitchen a lot in prison, so I know my way around. And I know how to clean. And I work hard."

"Can you give me just a second?" She held up a finger. Before this conversation went any further, she needed to text Anne. She couldn't hire Jordan if Anne had a problem with it. Zac was her boyfriend.

Jordan nodded stiffly. "But listen, if you're going to call the sheriff, that's not necessary. You can just tell me to leave, and I will."

"Why would I call the sheriff?"

Jordan rubbed her hands up and down her arms. "Let's just say it's happened before."

That seemed a bit extreme. Jordan certainly didn't look dangerous. And while she was a convicted felon, it wasn't like she'd gone to jail for some violent crime. "I'm not calling the sheriff. Please help yourself to a pastry. I'll be right back."

Jordan was at least heading toward the table with the pastries rather than the door as Violet grabbed her phone out of her purse and stepped through the back door into the kitchen.

She quickly texted Anne, hoping the doctor wasn't too busy to respond right away.

I have Jordan Rice here applying for a job. She told me what happen with Zac's family, and I wanted to make sure it was okay with you before I possibly hired her.

Anne's response came back almost immediately. *Jordan Reiss. But yes, definitely hire. She's honest and hardworking and sometimes the people in this town piss me off.*

Violet laughed. That was as feisty as she'd ever seen her quiet friend be. She typed a smiley emoji and put her phone away.

Okay. It looked like she and Jordan might be able to help each other out.

She walked back to the front to find Jordan chewing on a pastry. "These are really good."

"I'm glad you think so. Want to learn how to help me make them?" She grinned and wagged her eyebrows.

Jordan took a step closer as if she couldn't help herself. "Are you offering me a job?"

"I had to check with Anne Griffin first. She's my friend, and if she had a problem with you being here, that would've been a problem for me too. But she doesn't. She gives you a glowing recommendation."

"The doc has always been nice to me. She's just a good lady in general. Look, you seem nice too, and I just want to make sure you understand that some people in Oak Creek are not going to like the fact that you have me working here. So it would probably be best for both of us if I spent most of my time in the back kitchen, out of sight of the fine citizens of Oak Creek."

That was where she would be needed most anyway. "We'll work something out. When can you start?"

"How about right now?"

CHAPTER 17

JORDAN WAS A GODSEND. The woman didn't talk very much, came in and out the back door because she didn't want anyone to see her, and tended to find something to do in the kitchen whenever anyone else happened into the shop. But she was still the best employee anyone could ask for. She worked hard—just as hard as Violet—and was always willing to stay just as many hours as Violet did. Since they were four days from opening, that was a lot.

Jordan was smart too. She may not be college educated, but she was ruthlessly efficient and had quite the head for computers, which Violet found out she had taught herself. When the point-of-sale software Violet had purchased needed some tweaking, Violet had expected to have to spend an entire day learning the system so she could do it or call in a rep from the company. But Jordan had been able to figure it out in under an hour.

So now the front register was linked to Fancy Pants' inventory list as well as keeping track of profits and losses based on pastry types, flavors, and sizes. That would be useful info as they grew. Both Violet and Jordan loved useful info.

They were in the middle of Jordan's third full day, with Violet teaching her some of the basics of the pastry baking she would need to do, when the inevitable happened.

Gabriel showed up.

Violet's relationship with her brother was complicated, especially now. He'd been the adult figure in her life for the past decade. He'd been her legal guardian until she had turned eighteen. He was an amazing, brilliant, and brutally strong individual, both physically and mentally. He'd always been a source of strength for her, a firm foundation.

He'd make a formidable opponent—something she'd never had to worry about. Until now.

Gabe strolled in with Edward Appleton, CT's vice president of operations and one of her parents' best friends before they had died.

Violet rushed up to give the older, formal man a hug, which he returned stiffly. That was nothing new. He'd been returning hugs stiffly her whole life. But he always returned them.

Violet turned and hugged Gabe too. She hadn't seen her brother in nearly two weeks—the longest she'd gone without seeing him since her parents had died. He hugged her back.

"We thought we'd swing by here and see how everything was going," Gabe said in a carefully neutral tone.

"I'm glad. I've been wanting to show you the place." She held out her arms and spun around. "It's great, isn't it?"

Both Edward and Gabe walked around, taking in everything.

"It's definitely got a certain small-town appeal," Gabe eventually said. "And it doesn't look like there are any other shops of this type nearby, so that should work in your favor."

"I finally have it set up the way I want it. We're going to sell almost all sweet foods and high-end coffees. I'm not trying to compete with The Frontier Diner. They have great pies there, so we definitely won't venture in that direction. We'll keep everything more individualized. A lot of petit fours. Do you want me to grab a few of our samples? I'm still trying to finalize what we'll be selling on opening day. I wanted it to be the very best I have."

Violet knew she was rambling, but she didn't want Gabe to start listing all the reasons why opening Fancy Pants was a bad idea.

"Sure," was all her brother said.

She gestured for them to take a seat at one of the tables, then grabbed what pastries she had left over from yesterday from their plastic containers, arranging them artfully on a plate. These were fine, but she wished she had time to go into the back and make some fresh.

"Would you guys like a coffee? I can make an espresso or a cappuccino?"

Both men asked for an espresso, so she made them and brought it all over on a tray, then sat down with them.

She had cooked for Gabe over the years, but not often because their housekeeper had also left meals for them four times a week. They'd both been busy with the company, and her with school, and Gabe was more than progressive enough not to expect her to cook just because she was a woman. Plus, cooking was so much different than baking. Violet didn't mind cooking, but it wasn't her passion.

Surprise lit both their faces as they ate their treats, taking small bites of each.

"You made this?" Edward asked.

She nodded. "Yes. And these are my own recipes. You

wouldn't be able to buy them quite like this anywhere else in the world."

Edward took another small bite of the *canelé*. "Where did you learn how to do this?"

"Eighteen months ago, when I went to that symposium in Paris. I did a food tour just for fun and liked it so much I took a baking class. That was it for me." She shrugged. "I loved it. I've used every spare moment since then learning what I could."

"These are truly delicious," Edward said, reaching out and patting her hand when it became obvious Gabe wasn't going to say anything. "You very definitely have a talent. I should've expected it. You've always been able to do anything you set your mind to."

She smiled at the older man. "Baking and engineering are not as dissimilar as you might think. Both rely on precision and attention to detail."

The men finished the pastries on the plate, looking around as they did. What did they see when they looked at it through their more neutral, businessperson's eyes?

She had no doubt Gabe would tell her. Especially if he didn't like it.

Gabe finally spoke. "So the reason you were in downtown Idaho Falls by yourself in a parking garage at ten o'clock at night when you were kidnapped was because of a baking class?"

She straightened her shoulders, caught off guard by her brother's abrupt statement. "Yes, I had been taking a class for a few months."

"And you didn't think to mention that to me? That it might be a security issue?" He arched a brow.

"That's not fair and you know it, Gabe. I had no idea

there was a security issue, and you never asked me in the past where I was going when I went out."

She could almost see her brother regroup, trying to find the best angle to come at her and make his point without causing harm to their relationship. "I guess what I'm saying is that if this was so important to you, if you were this close to opening a bakery, why haven't you ever mentioned it before now?"

His tone was the very epitome of friendly rationality. Violet knew what her brother was doing: appealing to her sense of reason. He was suggesting that she was latching on to baking because of the kidnapping. That it didn't have a permanent place in her life.

But it did.

"I wasn't hiding it. It just never came up."

He raised a dark eyebrow. "Well, it has certainly come up now. It just all seems like a very sudden change. Nobody knew you baked at all, and then the next thing we know you're opening your own bakery."

"I'm not saying opening this place has nothing to do with the kidnapping." She held her hands out, looking between both men. "How could it not? It affected everything about me, affected how I see the world. The evil that I know is much closer than I used to think."

Gabe put his hand on top of hers on the table. "I know that," he whispered. "And I hate it. I hate that your safe existence had to change at all, much less so brutally. That you had to have firsthand knowledge of that sort of ugliness."

"I know."

Gabe agonized over what had happened to her. He didn't mind facing the ugliness and depravity of an evil world himself—he'd become a Navy SEAL in order to stand in that gap and fight darkness so that people like her wouldn't have to face it. And she loved him for it.

But it still didn't change the fact that her kidnapping had happened. For better or worse, it changed how she viewed *everything*.

"I can't go back to what I was before." She set her jaw. This was nonnegotiable.

He shook his head, eyes softening. "I know. I don't expect you to."

Violet smiled and touched his hand. Good. Maybe Gabriel was finally understanding.

"I'm just saying," he continued, "if you need to take time off, to travel or regroup or whatever, you could do that. But starting a new business, even more, an entirely new *career*? That's a little overkill, don't you think?"

Or maybe he wasn't understanding anything at all. She sighed. "No, I don't think that."

Gabe ran a hand over his face. "You're only doing all this because of your kidnapping."

At Gabe's words she looked over at Edward, hoping for support, but the older man was studying the tabletop as if it held all the mysteries of the universe. He obviously didn't want to get in the middle.

She turned back to her brother. "Baking has been an important part of me for a while. It wasn't something I dove into because of what happened to me."

"Fine." He crossed his arms over his chest. "Not the act of cooking itself, but this whole *bakery as a business* has come up because of your kidnapping."

She slammed her hand down on the table, causing the plate to rattle. Both men startled, then stared at her like she was some unknown creature. She couldn't blame them. They'd never seen her act this way before.

She fought for patience. "No, Gabe. What my kidnapping, assault, and constant fear that I was going to die"—he flinched at her words, but she wasn't going to sugarcoat this for him—"highlighted for me is that even though I'm only twenty-two, I am not guaranteed a tomorrow. Life is too short to spend my time in a career I'm not passionate about."

No more passivity.

"This is what I'm passionate about. Baking. Creating. Providing it for other people and having them be happy for just a moment as the flavors hit their mouths. Supplying a place where they can sit and be part of a community and just eat some fantastic treats. That's what I'm passionate about. Not Collingwood Technology. Not engineering."

Now Gabriel slammed his hand down on the table. "Being passionate doesn't mean you just get to ignore reason and responsibility. You're opening a business, Violet. What if it doesn't make enough to support you? There has to be a lot of overhead in a place like this."

"Fancy Pants doesn't have to make a lot. I used my personal inheritance to pay for the building and make the necessary changes. So fortunately, I'm not under some of the same financial pressures that many new business owners face."

She was pretty sure her brother's eyes were going to bug out of his head. "You used the money Mom and Dad left you to start this business?"

When their parents had died, both she and Gabe had been left individual inheritances that were not tied in with the company. It wasn't so much that they would never need to work again, but it had been more than enough for Violet to buy the building and make the necessary changes.

"Before you start yelling at me about how using my

personal finances wasn't good business sense, I already know that, and I made the choice deliberately. I didn't want to have to worry about cash flow."

Her brother looked like he was about to blow a gasket. Jordan walked out from the back kitchen, halting whatever tirade Gabriel was about to deliver.

"Oh, sorry. I didn't realize anyone was out here with you, Violet." Jordan turned to walk back into the kitchen.

"Stop. Who are you?" Gabriel snapped.

Jordan stayed by the door but turned back toward them. "I just work in the back. No biggie."

Violet walked over and linked her arm with Jordan's, towing her back out toward the table. Both Gabriel and Edward stood at their approach before sitting back down again. Jordan seemed a little surprised at the common courtesy.

"This is Jordan Reiss. She's been an absolute godsend."

Gabriel was not even trying to hide that he was staring at Jordan.

"I just had a question about the tart, but it can wait. I better get back to the kitchen." Jordan turned to leave.

"Reiss?" Gabriel asked. "That's your last name? I've heard that name."

Jordan stopped walking, her back now ramrod straight, and nodded without turning back.

Gabriel's focus moved off Jordan and onto Violet. "Great. Not only are you making questionable business choices, you're also hiring criminals."

Now Jordan turned around, tension evident in the slender woman's frame. "I'm not a criminal. I did my time."

"Come on, Gabe," Violet said. "She fell asleep behind the wheel when she was eighteen years old. But for the grace of God, that could've been any of us."

Gabe leaned back in his chair and crossed his arms over his chest. "I'm not even talking about her jail time. I'm talking about the fact that her father, Michael Reiss, was a con man who cheated a lot of the people in this town out of their hard-earned money."

Violet looked over at Jordan, but she was staring down at her feet, her arms hanging low at her sides. Violet knew it was true without even asking her.

"See, Violet?" Gabe said softly. "You're not processing clearly, not making wise choices. Your abduction affected you more than you think. You need to let the people you trust help you make decisions right now."

For just a second, Violet was tempted to give in. It was in her nature. A twenty-two-year pattern of going along with what other people told her was best for her was hard to break.

"No."

Gabriel hit the table again. "Goddammit, enough already. Think about what you're doing."

"She's an adult." Jordan wasn't looking down at her feet any longer, she was glaring at Gabe. "She can do what she wants. Plus she's absolutely amazing at this. And she loves it."

"Oh really?" Gabe scoffed. "You've been out of prison for what, an hour and a half? That makes you some big authority on human nature? Is that just for honest people like my sister, or do you stick to what you're familiar with?"

"Gabe!" Violet had never heard her brother talk to anyone like this.

"All right now, everyone, let's calm down." Edward was holding out his hands in an attempt to soothe.

"You think you know anything about me, rich boy?" Jordan's voice dripped venom.

Now Violet spun to look at Jordan. She'd never heard the woman speak in that tone either. The other woman had taken a step toward Gabriel like she was going to fight him or something.

Gabriel stood again. Jordan may be tall, but Gabriel's huge arms and shoulders made him look nearly twice the size of the slender woman. "I think I know enough about you to know you don't belong here, tainting someone innocent like Violet."

These two were going to kill each other.

"*Enough.*" Violet said it with enough force that everybody turned their attention to her. "Jordan stays. She already told me about the vehicular manslaughter charge, and what her father did is not her responsibility. So if you don't mind, Jordan, if you could head back to the kitchen, I'll be there in a few minutes, and we can figure out the problem with the tart."

Jordan nodded and turned back toward the kitchen. Gabriel muttered something about Jordan's expertise as a tart, and Violet glared at him. It was obvious from how the other woman's shoulders stiffened even more that she'd heard him.

"You," Violet poked her finger at Gabe's chest, "on the other hand, are welcome to leave. Take your juvenile comments with you. And don't come back until you're ready to support me."

Gabe looked like he was about to light into her again when Edward touched her arm.

"Your brother does support you, Violet. You know that. He loves you, and that's why he is having a difficult time expressing himself." The older man's voice was reasonable. Calm. Edward's voice had always been the one of reason. It had just never been needed between Gabe and Violet.

"Let's just talk for a few more minutes. Both of you will be unhappy if you leave here in anger."

Gabe folded himself into the chair again, mouth tight. Violet did the same.

"Anyone can see this bakery is important to you," Edward said. "I know Gabe and I are both unhappy that you've had this passion inside you and you didn't feel like we would understand it. We hate to think we were stifling you in this way."

She looked over at Gabe, and he gave her a brief nod.

"But the work you were doing at CT, many of your individual projects, like the hydrocarbon fuel cell, are also important," Edward continued.

The micro hydrocarbon fuel cell? Admittedly, she missed that, and she was perhaps at the forefront of the field when it came to that technology. But it was a dead-end project since it could so easily be utilized as part of a weapon. She wouldn't be working on it even if she went back to Idaho Falls with them today.

Which she wasn't.

But she touched her brother's hand where it rested on the table. "Am I truly leaving you in a lurch? That wasn't my intent. Is CT going to suffer without me?"

Gabe rolled his eyes but squeezed her hand. "Yes, we're going to suffer without you. *I'm* going to suffer without you. But no, it's not going to affect the bottom line of the company. Edward just wants you around for his pet projects as always." His finger stroked up and down her hand. "You're a brilliant engineer, and you're my baby sister. So of course I want you around."

He stood up and began walking around the room. "But this place is amazing, Vi. It's so homey, not like your apartment or the office." He studied the bookshelf she'd filled with knickknacks and odds and ends she'd found at various shops and flea markets around the area.

Gabe picked up a small porcelain elephant—so feminine with its pink and purple polka dots. "I made a lot of mistakes with you when you were growing up. I didn't let you be much of a normal teenage girl, rushing you into the engineering stuff."

She stood and walked over to him, putting her arms around his waist and leaning her cheek against his back. "You did your best, and it was more than enough. I was never going to be a typical teenage girl anyway.

"I need to do this," she continued after a moment. "I *want* to do this. I need you to keep CT as successful as it has been, so that if I decide this isn't for me and want to come back, I can."

She knew that wasn't going to happen. But she also understood that giving up Fancy Pants and returning to Idaho Falls was an option if she wanted.

"Okay," he said.

"This might fail, and if it does, then at least I tried. I followed my passion."

He turned so he could hug her back. "You're a Collingwood. You're amazing. Fancy Pants won't fail, fancy pants."

CHAPTER 18

"SO, how does it feel to have two weeks under your belt as the owner of the best bakery in town?" Aiden called out from his bathroom to Violet lying on his bed.

"Not quite as good as what you just did under my belt, but yeah, pretty fantastic."

Aiden grinned. She sounded happy. Sated. Just the way he wanted her.

The past few weeks had been hectic for her. Opening a business was no small feat, but she had excelled. There could be no doubt that everyone loved Violet's edible creations. She had Jordan helping her full-time and Charlie and a couple of other young women helping part-time and on weekends. Fancy Pants had more than enough business to employ them all.

Finding time to spend with Violet had been tough. When Aiden had explained his plan to take it slow, this wasn't exactly what he'd had in mind. But he couldn't begrudge Violet her absolute joy at what she was doing.

"Dates" for the past three weeks had turned into grabbing takeout and eating it at her place or his, or sometimes even him helping her at the shop. Some nights he had to literally drag her upstairs away from her recipes and the new ideas she wanted to try. Even the exuberant and energetic candle of a twenty-two-year-old would only burn at both ends for so long, although there was no telling her that. She needed rest, a chance to be away from the business she loved so much in order to be able to continue working at the pace she wanted.

Aiden happily took on the duty of carrying her upstairs each night and making love to her until she was no longer trying to sneak back downstairs to her kitchen. He had no problem with that job.

Half of Saturday and all day Sunday were theirs. The bakery closed just after noon on Saturday, and each week Aiden had been there ready to pick her up. That first Saturday—in what she had called the worst first date ever— he'd taken her to Linear Tactical and shown her around. He'd wanted to show her where he worked and the place that held such an important part of his life. That, she hadn't minded. She'd enjoyed it, asking question after question about the facility and business.

Go figure, his little baker-engineer had a particular interest in wilderness survival training and wanted to know when she could get in on a class.

After the tour and answering all her many questions, he'd proceeded to drag her into the middle of a self-defense workshop Gavin had been teaching. That was why Aiden had brought her there in the first place.

No, it wasn't a great date, not in the traditional sense of the word. Maybe not in any sense of the word. But when they had left the workshop two hours later, Violet had learned a half dozen methods to protect herself that she hadn't known before. No matter what happened between the two of them, Aiden wanted her to have that knowledge.

She'd been uncomfortable in the class at first. She'd made jokes about it—about his inability to come up with a better date—but he'd known that was a defense mechanism. Some of what was being taught in the class hit very close to home for her. Taking it out on him with sarcasm was an attempt to cope.

That was the other reason why he'd wanted to do this class. So they could do it together. He knew she could have done it with her girlfriends, hell, even with her brother. But he also knew she wouldn't want to tell them all what had happened when she'd been abducted, her worst fears. Aiden had already been witness to a lot of those, so hiding it from him was a moot point.

Still, there had been some he hadn't known about.

She'd been all winks and suggestive comments when they'd gone over the methods for escaping someone who was lying on top of her. Aiden had been more than happy to place kisses on her lips in between bouts. She'd made him wish they didn't have a half dozen people around so they could try the maneuvers naked.

But when he'd flipped her over onto her stomach and allowed some of his weight to rest on her hips and legs, she'd immediately frozen.

The sound of her ragged breathing had been so loud, it had drawn the attention of some of the other people in the class. Gavin had met Aiden's eyes, realizing Violet was having a panic attack. He'd called for a break and had gotten everyone else out of the training room.

Aiden had stayed where he was on top of Violet, crooning her name, even when her tiny sob broke his heart. He wanted to jump off, whirl her away from the situation that was bringing back such hard memories. But if they could work through this now, it would help her so much more in the future.

He kept himself completely still, holding most of his weight off of her on his elbows, murmuring to her softly. Eventually she came back to him.

"Hey there, Firefly."

"Aiden?"

"Just me. We're in the self-defense class, remember?"

She nodded. "I freaked out."

His breath flew out in a rush. He was just glad to get her back. "You were fine when I was lying on top of you and we were face-to-face. What changed?"

"Randy," she finally got the word out. "The night I met you. He told me he was taking me out of the dark room, and I tried to run. He lay on top of me and . . . rubbed himself against me."

Aiden wished Randy were still alive so he could kill the son of a bitch with something much slower and more painful than a bullet to the head.

"It's stupid, right?" she asked with a bitter laugh. "I mean he still had his clothes on, and there was so much worse that could've happened, that *did* happen. Why would the memory of some jerk dry humping me throw me into a panic?"

"There's no right or wrong in recovery," he was quick to tell her. "Your mind latches on to whatever it latches on to. You just fight one bad guy at a time."

Charlie had said that to him once, when he was distraught about not being able to get Violet out. It was fitting that he'd be able to share the same wisdom now.

He kissed the side of her head. "So how about we make

sure you know how to get out of a situation like this so no one can ever trap you this way again?"

"Yes." Her voice was small, but clear.

"I'm going to drop my weight on you, okay?" Slowly he lowered his weight until he covered her legs and hips.

She stiffened, fighting panic, and Aiden held himself still. "It's me. Just me."

Eventually she relaxed enough that he knew she'd been able to take in his instructions. He went over the moves slowly, concisely, and consistently, keeping his tone brisk and instructional.

The first escape option she understood and embraced: twisting with her torso and cracking her attacker in the temple with her elbow. The second option was much less intuitive and went against what her mind wanted her to do.

It required her to actually move her hips up toward her attacker, leaving her momentarily more vulnerable, then flipping around and throwing his weight off of her.

They practiced both ways over and over. Aiden didn't go easy on her, because a would-be rapist wouldn't go easy on her either. She had to be able to defend herself from a full-fledged attack.

By the time they'd finished forty-five minutes later, they were both exhausted. Aiden had the start of a black eye from where she'd gotten in a great hit, and they were both wrung out emotionally.

Gavin had kept his class outside since it was a gorgeous day. Violet was too exhausted—physically and emotionally —to participate in the rest of the class, so Aiden sat against a tree with her in his lap, and they just watched.

For a first date, it had been a little rough, but it had also connected them in ways neither had really been anticipating.

The rest of their dates had been much more traditional, and much less emotionally depleting. Like he'd promised, picnics and dinners. He'd even borrowed Zac's Harley and taken her out for a nice, long ride.

On the motorcycle too.

Aiden rolled his eyes at himself. Now who was thinking like a twenty-two-year-old?

Tonight he was going all out, taking Violet into Reddington City to see the symphony orchestra play the music of John Williams. He'd rented a limo and everything for the thirty-mile ride into the city.

Orchestras hadn't really ever been Aiden's thing until Gavin had dragged the entire team to L'Escolania Choir in Montserrat, when they'd been stationed in Spain. Aiden hadn't been aware music could be that beautiful. From then on, he'd found himself attending as many symphonies and professional choral performances as he could.

He wasn't surprised that Violet was eager to attend the symphony with him, especially when she started talking about the tie between music and math and how it was all combined. She may be a baker by passion, but her brain was always going to be analytically inclined.

Smart was fucking sexy. And she was definitely the smartest person he knew.

CHAPTER 19

DINNER HAD BEEN DELICIOUS. The symphony had been magnificent. Riding in the limo was just damn fun.

But the fact that Aiden had planned it all and made the night—just a normal Saturday night—so special was what awed her most of all.

"What?" He laughed and patted his cheeks self-consciously as she stared at him after the standing ovation for the orchestra. "Why are you looking at me like that? Do I have something on my face?"

"This whole night has been amazing. You're amazing." And she needed to stop saying that word, but it was all she could seem to get out of herself.

She was falling in love with him.

She wasn't going to tell him that, of course, because he wasn't going to accept it as fact. He was just going to think it was another residual part of her kidnapping. White knight syndrome or whatever. Plus, she had no idea how he felt about their whole relationship, or whatever it was.

As he wrapped an arm around her, pulling her tight against his side, her concerns calmed. She didn't need to have all the answers right now. She would just take each day as it came.

"I'm glad you liked it," he said against her temple.

They walked out, and Aiden told her he would call for the car while she excused herself to use the restroom. When she came back out she didn't see him immediately, so she walked toward the giant windows that overlooked a tiny park complete with paths and a lovely fountain in the middle.

The streetlights gave her just enough visibility to watch the people leaving the auditorium, huddled in their wraps and jackets against the brisk, early November night. They scattered in all directions, some toward the parking deck, others across the wide paths, none stopping to enjoy the beautiful fountain in the center.

And that's when she saw him. Dillon. One of the men who had kept her imprisoned in that house. He was standing against one of the decorative street lamps, arms crossed, looking directly up at her.

Terror closed her throat, making it impossible to breathe. He was just leaning there, casually looking at her.

Why was he here? Both Gabe and Aiden had assured her that Stellman wasn't getting out of prison anytime soon. Was Dillon still working for him? Was this just some sort of sick coincidence?

"There you are." She startled at Aiden's voice in her ear. "The car is pulling up at the side now. Are you ready?"

She turned to point out Dillon, but when she looked to where he'd been standing, he was gone.

"I . . ." She rubbed her forehead and looked all around. People were still walking, but it wasn't so crowded that it was difficult to spot someone.

Had that really been Dillon? Why would he be showing up now weeks after her kidnapping?

She had worked with the FBI and Omega Sector to try to identify Dillon, but, despite her descriptions, they hadn't been able to ID him. He didn't match anyone in their bad-guy database or any descriptions of criminals or terrorists on their wanted list.

And since he was just a henchman, they hadn't concentrated too much on him.

"You okay, Firefly? You're looking a little stressed."

She gave Aiden a smile. She wasn't going to let a ghost ruin this wonderful evening. "Just let my imagination get the best of me for a minute. I'm fine."

Those hazel eyes immediately turned serious. "Who? What scared you?"

She could almost see his warrior side take over. Not that it was ever far, but now his awareness and instincts were especially heightened. He turned and looked out the window.

She touched his arm. "Dillon. One of the guys who kept me in the house. But it wasn't him—there's nobody out there. I just got a little spooked."

He was still looking out the window, searching, just in case. She reached up and cupped his cheek, pulling Aiden's face to hers.

"Hey, it's okay. I'm okay. There's no way Dillon would've known I was going to be here." She refused to let it ruin this wonderful night. "It was just someone who looked like him, and my mind ran away with me."

He glanced once more out the window before nodding. "Okay. You're probably right." He led her toward the door but stopped to type a text before going outside.

"Please tell me you're not calling in the cavalry. I promise it was just my imagination."

He kissed her forehead. "I'm not, but I want to make sure there's nothing we need to know."

Evidently a few seconds later, he got whatever information he wanted, because his hand returned to her back and he ushered her out the door. "No change in Stellman's status. Still in prison, no visitors, nothing suspicious."

She relaxed into Aiden. No danger, just her subconscious playing tricks on her. Annoying, but at least it was nothing to be worried about.

As he escorted her back into the fancy limo, his phone chirped wildly. He rolled his eyes, responded, and then flipped it to silent.

"Sounds like some sort of emergency."

"Nope. Just your brother sharing his perfect opinion about us being out on a date. I probably shouldn't have texted him to ask about Stellman, but I knew he would have the most up-to-date info." He rolled his eyes.

"Oh boy. What did you say to him before turning off your phone?"

"In essence, to mind his own business."

"In essence?"

He turned his phone around so she could see his text to Gabe.

Remember when I asked for your opinion? Yeah, me neither.

"I'll bet Gabe loved that." She laughed out loud and reached over to turn her phone to silent too. As soon as Aiden didn't respond, her brother would start in on her.

Aiden leaned back in the seat, obviously not concerned with Gabe's opinion of their dating life, and stretched his legs out in front of him. Violet looked from him up at the glass separating them from the driver, currently rolled halfway down.

"Can that be darkened for privacy?" she asked. "There's something I need to tell you."

He hit a button and the glass darkened and slid up. Aiden's eyes bored into hers, full of concern. "The driver can probably still hear us if we talk much above a whisper, so if it's something really private or important to say, we ought to wait until we get home."

"This can't wait until we get home."

He moved in closer. "What? Tell me."

So serious. Soldier mode. It was her own fault with the seeing-Dillon scare. But it was sexy.

She pressed her lips close to his ear. "I'm ready for the hard and dirty now."

The tension shifting in him was almost tangible. He was no longer preparing to ward off some sort of threat, but her words definitely hadn't caused him to relax at all.

His hand slid into her hair and pulled her head back until they were face-to-face. "Right now, in the limo?"

She flipped herself around so she was straddling him on the seat then reached into her purse and pulled out a condom, fanning it back and forth between them. "I brought this in hopes that there really would be privacy glass."

His breath left his lips in a hiss. "You're being quite the naughty girl, Ms. Collingwood.

She grinned. "But a very prepared one."

She pulled the long skirt of her silk dress up until it gathered around her hips and spread out around their legs, covering them. She ran her fingers through his thick brown hair and brought her mouth close to his ear again.

"I'm even more prepared than you think. I haven't been wearing any panties under this dress all night."

She loved the sound of his groan. She loved it even more when both his hands slid up her thighs to check for the missing article of clothing himself. Then she was the one groaning.

She couldn't stop her hips from jerking against him as his fingers slid along her slit, the shallow caress agonizing in its gentleness.

"So wet," he whispered, streaks of heat spiraling though her as his thumb began to strum across her clit. "But I think we're going to save that condom for when we get back home, and I bend you over my kitchen table as soon as we get in the door."

His words just made her want him even more, and he chuckled as she began to work herself against his hand.

"You're so goddamned sexy on my lap like this in your beautiful dress." His thumb flicked over the bundle of nerve endings she so desperately wanted him to grind against. He worked one finger deeper inside her, then two.

"*Aiden*." She couldn't help the low plea as he took her higher without getting her anywhere near the edge. She was clawing at his shoulders now, riding his fingers.

"That's right, Firefly." He twisted his fingers, and she gasped, eyes rolling back in her head. Every movement of her hips now brushed his fingertips against that place inside her that cranked hot straight into inferno.

She felt his lips hard against her neck as she threw her head back and ground down against his hand, trying to keep quiet. She could feel the fluttering start of an orgasm.

And then he stopped. He slid his fingers away from that spot, took his thumb off her aching clit, and held her hip with his other arm so she couldn't thrust against him.

"Hey!" Her breath was coming in pants.

His smile was wicked. "We've got a while until we get home. Didn't want things to be over too quickly."

She glared at him until his hand on her hip slid up to her hair. He fisted a handful and forced her mouth down to take possession of it. Her eyes slid closed as his tongue stroked long and deep against hers, mimicking the same strokes his fingers had just made.

Damn, the man knew how to kiss. And other things.

It wasn't long before his fingers worked their way inside her again, matching the pace and rhythm of his tongue in her mouth. Instinct took over, her legs sprawling open farther, hips moving of their own volition against him. She gasped his name as need spiraled inside her, threatening to take over.

And then he stopped *again*. Stopped kissing her. Stopped the movement of his fingers inside her. Held her— even as she squirmed, trying to get the last little bit of friction that would throw her over the edge—until the orgasm dancing so happily in front of her slid away.

Her eyes flew open. Even breathing was painful she was so turned on. She gripped his hair in her hands and yanked his head back, no gentleness left in her, so her forehead—just as overheated as the rest of her body—rested against his.

"Enough." She didn't even try to keep her voice in a whisper now. "I'll take Charlie up on her offer to help me hide your body where it will never be found if you don't—"

A dirty grin lit those hazel eyes, but there was sweat on his forehead. He wasn't unaffected by this. "Don't forget to keep quiet, sweetheart," he said against her mouth.

And then there was no more teasing. His fingers thrust against that spot inside her once more, rubbing that patch over and over again. His thumb on her clit sent her the rest of the way over as she jerked almost violently against him.

Her control shattered, and she tucked her head against his neck, gasping, as colors flashed behind her eyes, sensations exploding throughout her body. He continued to work her with his clever fingers, dragging out the orgasm until she was chanting his name into his neck over and over. Finally, she melted against his chest as he slowed his movements.

He held her against him in his lap for the rest of the ride home. She couldn't find the brainpower or willpower to do anything but just rest in his arms.

"You're so damn smart," he whispered against her hair as his hand trailed up and down her spine. "I always love to talk to you because that brain of yours is flying a million miles a minute, and you process everything twice as fast as everyone else around you."

He tucked a strand of her hair behind her ear and snuggled her closer. "That's what makes having you like this, when you can't even figure out how to make a full coherent sentence, even more amazing."

"Hmmm." She wanted to argue, to tell him that she could make a coherent sentence. But finding the words was just too much effort. And she loved having her brain turned off for a while so all she could do was feel.

There was no place she'd rather be.

CHAPTER 20

A FEW DAYS LATER, Aiden had his arm tucked around Violet, walking over from the bakery to New Brother's Pizza to meet some of the gang for dinner. It was Thursday afternoon, the day each week that Violet had decided to close early.

Aiden had tried to talk her into skipping dinner and coming straight to his house—even bringing up the memory of last weekend. As promised, he'd had her bent over his kitchen table about five seconds after the front door had closed behind them, her condom and lack of undergarments making sliding inside of her tight heat much quicker.

The thought of it had made Aiden ache all week for a repeat. But he was flexible; it didn't have to be on the table. He'd be more than happy to bend her over the arm of his overstuffed sofa or the stairs or anywhere she'd let him.

Only after he'd kissed her thoroughly—and forced out her breathless promise to allow him to take her against his choice of surface tonight—did he let her out of her apartment to walk toward the restaurant.

Violet didn't want to stand up her friends, particularly

Peyton Ward. The young, single mom worked part-time at Linear cleaning their office and equipment, part-time cleaning houses around town, and evidently now part-time at Fancy Pants too.

The woman always looked exhausted, even before she'd added this new job. But if Peyton and her vivacious four-year-old daughter, Jessie, would stop in for a minute for pizza, he'd be more than happy to buy one for her. Peyton and Jessie rarely went out.

"Hey." Violet nudged him in the side with her elbow as they walked up to the door of the restaurant. "There's Jordan. I asked her if she wanted to come with us, but she said she had other things she needed to do. But she's here now so why don't we see if she wants to eat?"

Aiden wasn't sure if Violet was aware of how the people in Oak Creek tended to treat Jordan, or if she just refused to accept it. But before he could even begin to explain why it might be a bad idea, she was calling Jordan over. The dark-haired woman stilled when she saw them then jogged across the street to them. Her features became more pinched the closer she got.

"Hey, guys."

Violet immediately linked arms with her. "You look so cute in your skirt! We're just about to grab some pizza. Come eat with us."

Jordan shot both of them a panicked look that Violet didn't seem to notice. She pulled back as Violet stepped closer to the door. "You know, I don't even really like this place."

Violet laughed. "What are you talking about? You order food twice a week from here and have it delivered at the bakery. Adam DiMuzio and I are on a first name basis since

I always seem to be the one out front to pay him when he delivers."

Aiden figured out the scenario quickly. Jordan had the food delivered to the bakery so the pizza place would think it was for Violet. If they'd known it was for Jordan, they'd probably refuse to deliver.

Jordan shot him a look that begged for help.

There were a lot of things he loved about Oak Creek, but how the people here treated this woman was not one of them. The bitterness and hatred for the Reiss family ran deep.

But maybe it was time to face it head-on.

"Come eat with us," he said. "You can sit surrounded by all of us. Finn and Charlie are in there. Peyton. The kids."

Violet turned and looked at him like he was crazy. "Of course she would sit with us. Where else would she sit?"

But Jordan understood what he was saying, what he was offering. There was safety in numbers.

She was about to say yes. It was a little bit heartbreaking to see how much the woman obviously wanted to say yes to a simple dinner, something everybody else took for granted. But as Aiden opened the door to escort them inside, Jordan froze.

Standing just inside the door was Mr. DiMuzio, a big, beefy Italian man wearing a grease- and flour-smeared apron.

Obviously, someone had run to get the owner of the restaurant from the back kitchen when they saw Jordan might be coming in. The older man didn't say anything, but it was obvious Jordan wouldn't be entering his restaurant without a scene. Aiden wouldn't be surprised if Jordan's father had conned tens of thousands of dollars from Mr. DiMuzio.

Jordan immediately caved. She unlinked her arm from Violet's and began backing away from the door. "You know what? I just remembered I have something that I've got to do right now." Her smile at Violet was obviously forced. "But rain check, okay?"

She shot one more pleading look at Aiden to keep quiet before backing across the street without another word before he could talk her out of it.

"What was that all about?" Violet asked as he led her inside New Brother's.

He raised an eyebrow at Mr. DiMuzio, but the older man said nothing, just uncrossed his arms and went back into the kitchen. Aiden decided to just let it drop. Violet knew about Jordan's past, and even about her father, but obviously Jordan hadn't made it evident how the town treated her. He may not like it, but if Jordan didn't want to fight it, there wasn't much Aiden could do to help her.

Hell, even if she *did* want to fight it, he wasn't sure there was much he could do to help her. Some battle lines weren't easily seen.

Finn and Charlie were already sitting inside with Peyton. They didn't seem to have noticed what was happening at the door, mostly because they were too busy laughing at Finn's son Ethan trying to help Jessie win a toy from the crane machine.

They walked over and joined their friends at the big booth.

"Ethan has done extra chores all week to save up five dollars so he can try to win a stuffed animal for Jess," Finn explained. "Even after I explained that he could buy her one for that amount."

"They're strategizing as to which method is their best bet to win a prize with the crane," Peyton said with a roll of her eyes. "I had to make it very clear to my daughter that climbing into the machine, like when she tried last year and got stuck, was not an option."

Everybody laughed, until they realized Peyton wasn't kidding.

"Oh my gosh, she climbed up into the game?" Violet asked, brows going up.

"Yep." Peyton heaved a sigh. "I turned my back for thirty seconds, and she saw some pink teddy bear she wanted and figured she could fit through the hole in the bottom where the prize drops out. Next thing I see is Jessie's head peeking up and looking around for the prize she wanted."

Aiden knew he shouldn't laugh, but he couldn't control it. "At least she wasn't trying to take all of them out."

Peyton shook her head. "Only because it hadn't occurred to her. Squeezing her back out of that thing was a mess."

They ordered their pizza, and the waitress brought them their glasses so they could get their drinks at the soda bar. Before Aiden could stop her, Violet grabbed the tray of empty glasses and stood up.

"Everybody want Coke? I'll get it."

He touched her wrist. "You sit down. I'll get the drinks."

She just smiled as she leaned close and whispered in his ear, "You save your strength. You're going to need it for later. All I have to do is bend over and hold on."

She walked away with a sassy little shake of her hips that had him adjusting himself as discreetly as possible under the table.

Not discreetly enough for Finn to miss it. Charlie was talking with Peyton as the women kept an eye on the kids, and Finn leaned closer so only Aiden could hear him.

"How old are you again, man?" Finn asked, smirking.

"Thirty-three, asshole." Finn knew damn well how old Aiden was.

Finn started doing some sort of complicated math on his fingers.

Aiden rolled his eyes. "Ha ha. Eleven years. That's what you're counting, right? The difference in age between Violet and me?" Because eleven years was a lot, and the knowledge was rarely out of Aiden's mind, especially as things between them were getting more serious.

"Nope. I was actually trying to figure out if she was closer in age to you or to Ethan."

He knew his friend was kidding but couldn't control the wince. "Yeah, yeah. Very funny."

Vaguely, he heard Ethan and Jessie start to complain as their machine stopped working and started buzzing on and off.

"We didn't do it, Dad! I promise," Ethan yelled as the game continued to make the obnoxious buzzing sound.

He heard the loud crash of glass shattering as Violet crumpled to the ground. He was out of the booth in an instant, rushing toward her, his friends just a couple steps behind.

Violet had dropped the tray. Shards of glass surrounded her on the ground. She was curled up in a ball, her arms wrapped protectively around her head.

The animalistic sound of pain and fear coming from her throat broke his heart. Nobody else in the restaurant was talking, just staring, trying to figure out what was going on.

Aiden squatted down next to her and touched her gently on the shoulder, but that just made her thrash around. He stepped back, afraid he was going to cause her to cut herself in the glass.

"It's almost like she's having a seizure," Peyton whispered, concerned.

Finn crouched down next to him. "She seemed fine a minute ago. She doesn't have any history of seizures, does she?"

"This isn't a seizure. This is like some sort of PTSD flashback," Aiden said. "Something triggered her."

And it was getting worse, not better, the sounds coming out of her more ragged than they'd been a few seconds ago.

Charlie squatted down on the other side of Violet and began talking to her softly, soothing words about friends and being safe.

Aiden wasn't even sure Violet could hear her friend.

"I called Dr. Griffin over at the hospital," Peyton said. "I figured she'd get here sooner than an ambulance anyways."

"Did Violet see someone that triggered her?" Finn asked. "You said she thought she saw one of her kidnappers last weekend. Could that have happened again?"

"He didn't affect her like this. Not at all."

His hands clenched into fists at his helplessness. Aiden didn't know what to do. He didn't want to frighten her more by restraining her, but he didn't want her to cut herself on the glass.

And then he heard it.

The crane machine was still giving off that god-awful buzz, turning on and off. Each time it did, it sounded like something was getting zapped electronically.

Not at all unlike what a Taser sounded like.

"Fuck. Get that damned machine turned off, Finn. That's what's triggering her." He bit out the words rapidly.

Finn ran and a few moments later the sound was gone.

The effect on Violet was almost immediate. She didn't

open her eyes, but at least she stopped making that heart-breaking sound of terror.

Aiden tried touching her again, relieved when it didn't agitate her more.

His eyes met Charlie's, and she nodded. She was noticing the improvement in Violet too.

"You're safe, Firefly. I'm here. Charlie is here. Nobody's going to hurt you. Breathe with me, okay?"

He kept saying the words over and over, touching her more and more once it seemed like it helped calm her rather than upset her.

Behind him he could hear little Jessie crying and her mom explaining that it wasn't her fault. Mr. DiMuzio had brought out a broom, and Finn and Charlie were sliding the biggest pieces of glass away from Violet.

She was still lying in that defensive ball, arms wrapped around her head, but she was coming back.

Anne Griffin rushed in, still wearing her scrubs from the emergency room. She dropped beside Charlie.

"What happened? Is she hurt? Did she fall?" She touched Violet's arm to take her pulse at her wrist. "Rapid, but steady. Was she jerking uncontrollably? Did she lose consciousness? That could mean a seizure."

"No. I think it was a flashback," Aiden murmured. "The prize machine was making a sound just like a Taser. I think it triggered her."

Anne's lips pursed. "That could happen. The brain doesn't always process input the way we expect it to. Recovery is never a straight line."

Aiden just kept touching Violet and whispering in her ear.

A few minutes later, he heard her soft voice. "Aiden?"

Oh thank God. "Hey, Firefly." He stroked a strand of hair away from her head.

She blinked up at him. "Why am I on the floor?"

He looked to Anne as Violet began to sit up, wanting to make sure it was okay for her to move. Anne nodded, so he helped her. "Just take it slow. You dropped the tray of glasses."

Violet looked around her. "Yeah, I . . ."

He could tell the exact second that she understood what had happened. The color that had been coming back into her face leached out again. "I . . . I . . . was there a Taser?"

Her voice was so small and frightened, it was all he could do not to snatch her up into his arms.

"No," he touched her shoulder with a gentle hand, "but the prize machine made a sound just like one. It frightened you."

She was becoming more aware of everyone around her. Not just Anne and Charlie, who were next to her in quiet support, but the much wider circle, the patrons of the pizza place all staring at her.

"I just want to go home," she whispered.

Aiden looked at Anne again.

"Violet," Anne said, "can you follow my finger with your eyes?" She held up her index finger and moved it slowly in front of Violet's face. "Good. Does anything hurt? Do you feel dizzy at all?"

"I feel fine. Just stupid." She flushed.

All her friends around her muttered a protest.

"There's definitely no reason to feel stupid," Anne continued. "I don't think it's needed, but we can take you to the hospital if you want me to check you out more thoroughly."

Violet shook her head. "No. I just freaked out. There's nothing wrong with me. I just want to go."

Everyone was starting to go back to their own business as it became obvious nothing else exciting was going to happen with Violet. Anne and Aiden helped her stand, and soon one of the employees was sweeping up the rest of the glass.

"We'll take care of everything here," Finn said. "You just get her home."

CHAPTER 21

AIDEN DIDN'T EXPECT Violet to be chatty after what had happened, but her overwhelming quiet over the next couple of hours worried him.

She would answer if he asked a direct question, which was how they ended up back at his house rather than her apartment. It was how he got her to eat some soup and a sandwich and was how he knew she was okay with him staying with her rather than calling one of her girlfriends or her brother.

He didn't press her to talk about what had happened or what she'd been feeling at New Brother's. When she was ready to talk, she would.

Instead, he wrapped her in the softest blanket he could find in his closet and deposited her on the couch near the fire he'd started in the fireplace.

He wanted to hold her in his lap but wasn't sure that was what she wanted. So, after doing the dishes and trying to give her as much time as she needed to say anything she wanted, he just sat down beside her on the couch, keeping ample distance between them. But he didn't even try to deny the relief he felt when she crawled into his lap a few seconds later. He just wrapped his arms around her and pulled her close.

Even then, she was quiet for so long he thought she'd fallen asleep. It was probably the best thing for her.

He should've known that giant brain of hers was processing everything that had happened, not sleeping.

"You must think I'm so weak." Her voice was thick, her shoulders sagging.

It was the first unprompted thing she had said since they'd left the pizza parlor.

"Not at all." He kept his voice even and calm. "I've seen men twice your size dive for cover because they heard a car backfire, and their brain processed it as danger."

"Hearing that noise . . . It was like my mind was cut in half. On the one hand, I could totally understand where I was and that I was safe. But the part of me that took over . . . I couldn't stop it. I couldn't force the reasonable side of my brain to overcome the emotional side. It was like being thrown back there again."

He just let her talk. There were no words he could say that would fix this.

"I don't consciously think about my kidnapping very often. I mean, I'm much more aware of my limitations and vulnerabilities. Security and stuff like that. But I don't sit around and let it consume all my thoughts."

"You keep busy." He ran a hand up and down her back.

She turned so she could look him in the eye. "But not because I'm avoiding it. I'm not trying to hold it all inside or something like that. I just don't want it to define me. I don't want people to look at me and think, oh that's the poor girl who was kidnapped and held hostage."

"People don't think about you like that at all. Most of

them have no idea anything happened to you, and the ones who do know about the situation are your friends. And you know they don't pity you." He gave her a smile. "Most of the residents of Oak Creek just think of you as the person helping to fatten them up."

"Good. That's how I want to be thought of." She gave him a weak smile.

They sat in silence for a long time again before she eventually spoke.

"It was hard for me to be in the dark at all when I first came home. I still sleep with the light on. I know you know that, even though you've never mentioned it."

She always left the bathroom light on with the door cracked. It hadn't taken a genius to figure out why.

He shrugged. "After being locked in a dark room, it's not unexpected. Trying to force yourself to power through something like that probably isn't a good idea."

She sighed softly. "That's what my therapist said. She said that forcing myself to do things I wasn't ready for, like sleep in the dark when I was scared, would ultimately hinder my progress more than it would expedite it."

"Then you leave the light on as long as you need to. Even if you always need to. That's nobody's business but yours. And I promise I don't think less of you for it. Nobody would." He pressed a kiss to the top of her head.

She nodded, then fell back into silence. Three times she started to say something but wasn't able to get the words out. She was growing stiffer and stiffer in his arms.

"I talked to the therapist about nearly everything having to do with my kidnapping," she finally said. "I talked to her about that dark room, about the masked people at the auction, about how I felt when Randy was shot."

She straightened even further. "But I never talked to her

about that Taser. She never asked, and maybe she never even knew about it."

"Did you not mention it to her for a reason?"

"I didn't want to think about it. I couldn't bear to think about it. I got home and there were all sorts of questions about my emotional and sexual trauma. Had I been raped? Did I need to talk through my assault? Because I *was* sexually assaulted."

He nodded grimly. "You don't have to be raped to be assaulted."

"As humiliated and helpless as I felt naked in front of those people, unable to stop them from touching me or doing whatever they wanted to me, that wasn't the part that I couldn't bring myself to not even think about."

He closed his eyes, trying to swallow the rage inside him. "Being hurt with the Taser was."

She gave him a tiny nod of her head. "I never understood that a person could go through so much pain. Even now, sitting here weeks later completely safe, I . . . I . . ."

He wrapped her tighter in the blanket as she started to shake so badly her teeth were chattering.

That motherfucker Randy should be very glad he was rotting in hell right now, because that was nothing compared to what Aiden would do to him if he could get his hands on him.

"Firefly, you were tortured. There's no other word for it. Just because it didn't involve broken bones or knives doesn't mean it was any less than torture."

A tear slowly slid down her cheek. "H-He shocked me over and over. And there was nothing I could do. *Nothing.* I was completely helpless. I would've given anything to stop him. Promised anything, done whatever he wanted. Do you know what that is, Aiden? To be willing to do *anything* to make the pain stop?"

For the first time in his life, Aiden cursed the fact that he was *Shamrock*—the one lucky member of the team who had never sustained any true injury. He wished he knew exactly what she'd gone through, had some experience he could share that would help make this right for her.

"Violet . . ." He could barely choke the word out.

She was still trembling. "I thought he was going to kill me. God, Aiden, after an embarrassingly short amount of time, I *hoped* he would kill me."

Aiden tucked her up against him as she began to cry, gut-wrenching sobs that broke his heart. He would do anything to carry this for her, make it better, take away the pain of the memory. But he couldn't. Nobody could. It was something she would have to carry her whole life.

Violet Collingwood would always have scars from her kidnapping; they just wouldn't be visible from the outside.

Sometimes those were the worst kind.

He expected her to be exhausted when she finally stopped crying, but instead she was angry. She pushed back from him and onto her feet, keeping the blanket wrapped around her as she began to pace.

He'd take angry, pacing Violet over brokenhearted, sobbing Violet any day.

"I thought I was past this sort of breakdown. But I'm not. They still have power over me, even when I want to pretend it isn't true. I thought I was past this." Her fists clenched.

"I don't know that this is something you ever get *past*. Some things are just with you forever. They become a part of your new normal."

She processed that for a minute, then stopped pacing and looked at him. "Looking back on it all, do you know what makes me the most frustrated? The most angry? *I didn't fight.*"

"The hell you didn't."

She held a hand out to stop him. "I'm not talking about during the T-T-Taser." Her voice still tripped over it a little. "I couldn't fight then. I'm talking about every other moment I didn't fight."

She sighed, pacing once again. "I was held for five days. I was dragged out of my cell, forced to be naked in front of leering strangers. I was molested, groped, and treated like I wasn't human. And I *never* fought back. That's what makes me angry. That except for one damn kick, I just did what I was told. I was so weak."

She needed to get this out just as much as she'd needed to get out the tears a few minutes ago. But there was one thing he had to say. "You survived. That was the most important thing. You survived."

"But I should've *fought*! Every time Randy came into that windowless room, he should've known that I was going to kick, and claw, and bite even if he hurt me because of it. I should've spit on those people at the auction. Punched them, kicked them. Made it so they regretted ever taking me in the first place."

He shook his head. "There were too many of them. They held all the power. You know that. Looking back on it now, it's easy to say you should've fought, should've done more of this or that. But they would've hurt you in ways that nobody could've survived whole." So he was damned glad she hadn't fought.

Her voice broke. "Do you know the story of how Charlie was taken and tortured? She fought back. She was strong. I wasn't."

Yeah, he knew what Charlie had been through. He'd been there when it happened. "Not all strength is in-your-face like Charlie's. But if you don't think she has regrets about what happened to her, how she handled it, if she could've saved herself some of that pain if she'd done things differently, then you're wrong. Charlie sometimes has emotional breakdowns too, just like what happened to you tonight, but in different ways. Just because your strength is quieter than hers doesn't mean it's not just as fierce."

She shook her head, obviously not wanting to accept what he was saying. "I was weak and passive and acquiesced like I always do."

"You were quiet, and adaptive, and focused, which allowed you to get out of there relatively undamaged." Aiden was off the couch and gripping her arms so he could stop her pacing and get right up in her face. "You survived. Maybe that huge brain of yours wouldn't allow you to fight with your body because it knew it was fruitless or could mean your death. But there is no way you can say you didn't fight. You fought with your *mind*, your intellect, and that was even better. There's more than one way to fight."

Those green eyes tore at him, and he just wanted to hold her, but he continued, his voice as firm as his fingers gripping her arms.

"You *survived*. That's what we teach at Linear. It is the number one rule that has no exceptions. Survive no matter what you have to do, no matter if it's counterintuitive to what you *want* to do. *Survive*."

She was too logical to not accept what he was saying, but she didn't like it. So many of the choices she made about the bakery and moving here to Oak Creek made much more sense now. This new need for independence stemmed from what she saw as her failure while kidnapped.

But she had to understand that she'd done the right thing by not fighting.

"I'll be thankful every day for the rest of my life that you didn't try to fight with your body. That you survived and got out of that situation as best you could."

"It's not enough. I should've done more." Her voice cracked on the words.

He pulled her to his chest. He knew what it was like to live with regrets. But just because you couldn't change what was past didn't mean you couldn't make sure it didn't happen again the same way.

"The past is gone, you can't change it. All you can do is move forward. But I can help you with that. Teach you how to defend yourself in earnest. Your mind is always going to be your best weapon, Firefly. You're too smart for it not to be. But I can help you so you're just as confident with using your body as a weapon also."

"Really?"

"You want to know how to stand up for yourself? To know how, when, and where to attack and to defend? Well, it just so happens that I'm in the business of teaching that very thing."

CHAPTER 22

"THE FIRST TIME I saw you with her, you were studying her almost exactly like you are right now."

Aiden glanced over at Gavin from his place at the bar at The Eagle's Nest before turning his attention back to Violet.

He'd been working with her for two months now on the skills she wanted to improve, to use her body to become a weapon and not just her mind.

Watching her come to understand the power she held had been an amazing event to be a part of. Her emergence from her chrysalis—even though she was a firefly rather than a butterfly—had been beautiful. Each day, she woke a little more, understood more of her own power.

Violet hadn't made a big announcement to anyone about what she was going to do. She'd just done it. She worked with him early, late, on weekends. He'd set up a grueling training schedule, and she'd met it without complaint.

They'd worked when she was tired, stressed, or sore. They'd worked on building muscles, endurance, defensive moves, and offensive moves. They'd worked in the cold, in the rain, and even when he was sure she would've shot him in the head if he had given her a gun at that moment.

She may have cursed him out quite a few times, but she had never once come close to quitting. He'd seen soldiers with twice her natural physique give up before she had.

The more he pushed, the more she responded. She was focused and determined. It was a sight to behold.

And probably the sexiest thing he'd ever seen. Even sexier than all the mind-blowing things they'd done in bed over the past two months. Because as Violet's confidence had grown in one area, it had also grown in others. If he had thought she wasn't shy before, her newfound strength and budding confidence had brought him to his knees in the bedroom.

Literally. Multiple times.

Until the day he died, Aiden would feel blessed to be the recipient of that growing confidence.

All of their workouts meant she'd traded her lush curves for sexy, firm strength.

And while he might miss that softness, he could definitely appreciate these new curves just as much. There was still plenty about Violet to drive him crazy.

She could probably drive him crazy for the next fifty years. And that was his problem right now as he stared out at her.

She was currently on the floor, dancing to some god-awful hip-hop song that she and Wavy and Riley had begged the DJ to play. Aiden wouldn't have known how to dance to that if someone had been holding a gun to his head. The way the gals were twisting, grinding, and bouncing was almost comical, although still pretty sexy. Something only the young could get away with.

"Is that music bothering you?" Gavin asked, laughter tingeing his tone. "Definitely not the usual fare here. The DJ probably only played it 'cause your girlfriend is so cute."

Aiden had no doubt that was true. The more people got to know Violet, the more they were willing to do whatever she asked, even if that involved playing Drake.

"I'm head over ass in love with that woman, Gavin."

Gavin chuckled. "Well, then I can see why the music is even more upsetting to you."

He shook his head. "She sings that crap all the time, man. I can't even understand the words, and she's belting it out. And our workouts? We spar in earnest to see who gets control of the playlist, and sometimes I don't win."

Gavin laughed again. "That is grim."

He couldn't tear his eyes away from Violet bouncing and grinding with her friends out on the floor. "She's absolutely amazing."

The other man cocked his head to the side. "Then why the pensive?"

Because it was time for him to stop pretending that he didn't know the truth. That as much as Violet had grown, in order for her to take the next step—the final step—into that warrior she was becoming, Aiden needed to back away. "She wants to grow into the woman she was always destined to be. Strong, smart, beautiful. Fierce."

"And that's a problem?" Gavin asked, eyebrow raised. "You've never been one to be threatened by a woman's strength. You've always encouraged it."

"Hell no, I'm not threatened by Violet's strength. It's the sexiest thing I've ever seen. But I've got to step back for her to make those last steps. I'm too closely tied to what happened to her when she was kidnapped."

Gavin shot him a sideways look. "Don't you think she

ought to make that choice? Are you sure there's nothing else going on here?"

He should have known Gavin wasn't going to let him get away with a half-truth. "She puts her feet up on my dashboard all the time."

Gavin spewed his beer. "Well then you've definitely got to cut that bitch loose."

Now Aiden chuckled. "She likes to chew bubble gum when we're lifting weights. Blows huge bubbles."

"That's not the craziest thing I've ever heard someone doing while lifting."

He took a sip of his drink. "I know. None of this stuff is bad or even annoys me. It's just she's so damn young. Do you even remember what it was like to be twenty-two years old?"

"That does seem like a lifetime ago." Gavin chuckled.

"She and I are in different places in our lives. I just don't want her ever looking back and thinking that I was her crutch, that she wouldn't have found the strength to do all this on her own, because she damn well would have. It's time for me to step back, let her find the rest of herself without me involved."

Gavin wisely didn't say anything. What could be said?

Aiden watched her gyrate to the music some more, laughing hysterically with her friends. His fingertips actually itched to touch her. "If I let it go for now, maybe in a few years this could come back around," he whispered.

A few years without her. The thought punched him in the gut.

"She might not like that thought," Gavin said, taking a sip of his own beer.

"I'm going to talk to Zac about taking some overseas ops. I know there was a company trying to get us to come do some work in Istanbul. Or that firm in Morocco that's been begging us to train their security team."

Because Aiden would have to be out of the country if he was going to keep away from Violet. There was no way he could be here, be around her all the time, and not want her.

Not that being in a different country was going to take the want away. But at least then he wouldn't be able to do anything about it.

He finished his beer and slid the glass away from him on the bar. He didn't want to do this. Every instinct he had told him walking away from Violet was a mistake. And for him, it probably was. It *definitely* was.

But for her . . .

For her, it was the chance to take that last step into what she'd fought so hard to become.

He'd be damned if he let anything stand in the way of that.

Even him.

He stayed at The Eagle's Nest with Violet for as long as he could, way past when both of them should've gone home given the training and work schedule they'd been keeping.

He'd convinced her to stay to put off having this conversation for as long as possible. To give him one more chance to hold her in his arms as they danced. To hear her laugh and talk.

Jesus, he didn't want to have this talk. But if he didn't do it now, it was just going to get harder.

"You're walking me to my house." She'd been humming that same damn Drake song under her breath since they left the bar. "Your bed is bigger than mine. Let's go there."

"I don't think that's a good idea." He winced at the sound of his own words. They sounded stiff, formal.

"I know we've been working ourselves nearly to death the last few weeks, but I'm not that tired." She trailed her fingers up his arm with a smile. "I'll never be *that* tired."

He didn't say anything, but she was too perceptive. It didn't take long for her to realize something was wrong.

"Hey, you're awfully quiet over there. I know you don't particularly care for music that was created in the past decade, but at least I didn't make you dance to it." She ran her fingers up his arm again.

"Yeah, me dancing to hip-hop will never happen, considering you would be the first person to record it and post it online."

She snickered. "*Moi?* Never. But it would go viral."

God, the temptation to just throw her back against the nearest wall and ravish her until they were both in danger of being arrested was almost too much to resist. He looked down at her smiling face and the hand that was trailing up his chest. He took her hand in his and studied it. She'd written some sort of note to herself. On the back of her palm.

"Oh yeah," she smiled. "A new recipe idea came to me tonight while I was at the bar. I decided to jot it down but there were no napkins available. Don't let me forget to transcribe it when we get home."

It was so typical, writing her great idea down on her hand. At least for someone her age.

Jesus, he had to do this now or he was never going to do it at all. And then he would never forgive himself.

Or even worse, she might someday begin to wonder—begin to *question*—if her strength was her own, since they'd been so entwined.

He had to give her time away from him.

Violet stopped walking and cupped his cheek with her scribbled hand. Concern was pouring out of those green eyes. "Aiden, what is it?"

"Sometimes Linear does work out of the country," he said.

"That sounds exciting. Anywhere interesting?"

"Lots of places, actually. We get calls from companies all over the world who want to hire us either for protection or to train their own security services. We don't take a lot of them because most of us got our fill of traveling when we were in the service. We like to have a home base now."

She smiled. "And what a home base Oak Creek is."

He wasn't making this any quicker. He needed to just say what he had to say and make it easier for both of them.

"I think I'm going to be taking a lot more jobs overseas. It's good money and good contacts for the company." He slid back so they were no longer touching, hating himself when she stiffened.

"Oh. I didn't know you were itching to travel again. I can't go anywhere. Not with the bakery."

"I know." His voice sounded stiff even to his own ears.

He watched hurt accumulating in her eyes. At some point she might have stopped at the hurt, worrying, and wondering if she'd done something that had led him to his choices.

He couldn't help but be proud—even as he knew this was going to make the whole situation harder—as she found the confidence to work past that and not blame herself.

Her eyes narrowed. "You love teaching and training. And not just with me, with everyone. So what's this all about? Does Linear really need you to work in a different country?"

He didn't want to lie to her. She picked up on his hesitation immediately.

"If this is what the company really needs," she continued, "then we'll work it out. However long you have to be gone—weeks, months—it will suck, but we'll do it."

This woman. How the hell was he supposed to live without her? "Violet . . ."

Now it was her who took a step back. "But that isn't what this is, is it? Linear doesn't need you to go overseas. You're volunteering."

"I think it would be a good idea for us to take some time away from each other."

One eyebrow rose. "Is that so? It didn't seem like you were feeling that way when we had sex in the shower yesterday after our workout. Or when we were dancing tonight. Is this something that came up on the walk home?"

He drew in a breath. "I'm not trying to be petty. I'm saying this because I care about you."

"You're saying you don't want to be with me anymore because you care about me? Excuse me if I don't quite see the connection. I never took you for a coward, Teague. If you're done with our relationship, just say so."

She turned and began walking away, but he grabbed her arm. "This isn't about me being done. This is about you and what you want to become."

"And what is that?" She put her hands on her hips.

His hands moved up to her shoulders. "Fierce. Independent. Completely your own."

He could almost see the fight drain out of her. "I do want to be those things. I thought we were working toward those goals together. That you wanted it for me too."

He couldn't stop himself. He yanked her against his chest. "I do. Seeing how far you've come over the past couple of months? Your transformation has been one of the most amazing things I've ever participated in."

"Then why stop?" Her words were muffled against his chest.

"You're not stopping. I'm just stepping back so that you can make the rest of the journey on your own."

"What if I don't want to make it on my own?"

He set her back from him so he could look her in the eye. "If I stick around and we continue the way we have been, at some point you may look back and wonder if I was your crutch. You'll worry that it was me who got you through this, not you. I can't stand the thought of that happening."

He could tell that although she may not like what he was saying, it was at least making sense to her.

"I'll take a few jobs away from here, give us both a chance to get some perspective. Give you a chance to try this on your own."

"There's more that you're not telling me, isn't there?"

More, as in he was in love with her and wanted to ask her to marry him? More, as in he was about to turn thirty-four, and she was barely twenty-two, and they were in hugely different places in their lives? More, as in this conversation was eating away at his heart like acid, and he wasn't sure he was going to survive it, much less survive being away from her? He gave her the best smile he was capable of and then turned, wrapping an arm around her shoulder, and moving them forward again.

"You know how it is, Firefly, there's always more. But that's not what's important."

Violet was what was important. And he would give her what she needed, even if it killed him.

CHAPTER 23

THREE DAYS after the talk with Aiden, Violet was pissed.

And sad. Heart-crushingly sad.

She'd thought long and hard about what Aiden had said, and she understood why he'd said it, but that still didn't make it any easier.

She hadn't actually been mad until she'd showed up at Linear this afternoon, ready for her Krav Maga lesson, and was met by Gavin rather than Aiden. She liked the other man just fine, just hadn't expected Aiden to totally bail.

And then an unbearable thought hit her. "Did he leave already?" she asked Gavin, unable to keep the panic out of her voice. "Take a job out of the country?"

"No," Gavin told her. "He just thought you working with someone else would be better starting right away."

Violet had felt like her heart was shattering, but she'd nodded and followed Gavin into the training area.

At least one consolation was how surprised he'd been when she'd knocked him straight onto his ass within the first two minutes of them sparring. Then he'd begun taking her seriously.

An hour of trading blows and the challenge of a new opponent had exhausted her. The hardest part of the lesson was that Aiden had been right. She'd learned more from Gavin in an hour, just because he was new to her, then she would've learned from fighting with Aiden for twice that amount of time. She and Aiden knew each other too well, at least in this particular area, for her not to be able to figure out what he had planned next.

Later that night, she lay in her bed, thinking it all through. Again. God, she missed him. Even understanding why they were doing this, and maybe partially agreeing, she missed him.

How was she going to bear it when he left the country for weeks at a time? The thought had her rubbing her chest against the phantom ache there.

But right on the heels of the sadness was the anger. Why was he the one who got to make all the decisions? Another person who was doing what was best for her, but without asking her what *she* wanted.

And if that was the case, didn't sticking up for herself, being fully independent and fierce as Aiden had put it, mean telling him to go fuck himself?

Or more directly, to fuck *her*?

She honestly didn't know. But just the thought that this was her choice too, that there was more than one option here, helped her relax a little bit.

Aiden was right; she had to know that she wasn't using him for a crutch. But there was one thing she did know, and that was her own mind. It didn't take her weeks or months to come up with the decision. She just needed to let her mind process it and figure out the right way to go.

Yes, not having Aiden around made that a little bit

easier. But hell if she was going to not have him in her life based on sheer principle.

She could be a strong, independent, fierce woman standing on her own.

She could also be a strong, independent, fierce woman with Aiden standing by her side.

Nobody got to make that choice for her except her. Not even him.

Too bad she was having this epiphany at three o'clock in the morning. Since she was wide awake, she decided to go downstairs to try out the new recipe she'd written on her hand at The Eagle's Nest.

Baking always helped center her, almost as much as her newfound skill at kicking ass did.

She slipped into her yoga pants and a shirt and headed downstairs. When she walked into the kitchen and found the light on, she was confused.

She spun around, taking a fighting stance, instincts and training kicking in as the door to the storage room opened. She relaxed when she saw it was Jordan.

The other woman snatched her headphones out of her ears and let out a shriek. "What are you doing here?"

Violet rolled her eyes. "I happen to own this business and live on the premises. What are *you* doing here?"

Jordan had a key and the security code, and honestly, Violet had no problem with her hanging out, but it was the middle of the night.

"I'm not stealing anything," Jordan was quick to say.

"Jordan." She actually snorted. "It never crossed my mind that you would be *stealing* something."

"I just couldn't sleep and my house . . ." The woman shrugged. "I just couldn't be there alone right now."

"Ugh. I don't want to be alone either."

"Why don't you call Aiden? He's got to be up for a booty call from you, even if it's the middle of the night."

Violet leaned against the counter near the sink. "Unfortunately, my boyfriend thinks he knows what's best for me, and that is for us to be apart for a while." A very short while, if Violet had anything to say about it.

Jordan came and leaned on the counter next to her. "I don't have very good luck with guys, so I'm probably not the one to give you advice."

Violet nodded and slipped an arm around Jordan. "I had an idea for a *gougère* the other night. Want to try to make it now? We'll both be exhausted tomorrow together."

Her eyes brightened. "Anything is better than facing my house alone. Let's do it."

Nobody had time to worry about empty beds or sleepless nights when there was a wonderful dessert to be figured out. An hour flew by without them even realizing it while they were busy tasting and reworking problematic parts.

Two times they thought they had the recipe just as they wanted it, but both times on final tasting it wasn't quite correct. Violet decided to just save the trial for another day and they moved on to what they needed to make for this morning's rush. They were both walking into the large walk-in cooler when heat and a terrible noise exploded in the kitchen behind them.

"What the hell?" Violet screamed as they both ran back out of the cooler.

The entire kitchen was on fire.

"What happened?" Jordan asked over the roar. "Did the oven catch fire?"

Violet wasn't exactly sure where the fire had originated, but it didn't look like it was from the oven. It was more like it was from . . . A breeze caught her from the doorway, causing the flames to pick up.

"I think something burning flew through the window." Violet had no idea how that could happen, but the fire seemed to be spreading from the back door.

But it didn't really matter how it started; they had to get it under control or they would lose the whole bakery.

"Where's the fire extinguisher?" Jordan yelled.

"It's by the back door." Both she and Jordan pulled the bottom of their shirts over their face as the smoke became thicker and harder to breathe through. They couldn't get to that extinguisher without going through the flames.

"There's one out front, too, right?" Jordan ran for the door leading to the front of the house, but when she pushed on it, she was knocked back almost onto her ass.

"What the hell?" Violet said, running over to help her friend. That door shouldn't be locked. There wasn't a lock on it. Something was blocking the door.

They both pushed on it together, but it wouldn't budge. They met each other's eyes.

Someone had trapped them here in the kitchen and set it on fire.

Fire was engulfing the whole back wall now. Whereas a few minutes ago Violet was hoping to save the bakery, now she just wanted them to escape with their lives.

"Call 911 and let's get in the cooler," she yelled. "We should be able to keep the smoke out until the fire department arrives." She hoped.

"If we do that, the bakery will burn," Jordan yelled back. The flames were getting higher. "I can still get to the fire extinguisher by the door."

She grabbed the other woman's arm. "No. Those flames are too high. It's not worth your life."

"Yeah, well my phone was hanging by the door. Where's yours?"

Shit. Hers was upstairs in the apartment. There was no calling 911.

Violet began gathering any material she could use to douse flames. Baking soda, salt—she knew better than to use water or flour. A few seconds later, when she had them all gathered, she turned to Jordan. "You throw it, I'll run through the flames."

Jordan shook her head. "Sorry, boss, but even with your workouts, I'm taller and can jump higher. It will be easier for me to get over the flames and grab the fire extinguisher."

She was right, and they didn't have time to argue. Violet nodded once. She would make sure to smother the flames as much as possible with her dry goods.

"On three. Jump high." She got her supplies ready. Timing would be everything. The smoke was getting higher, the heat more oppressive.

"One... two... three..."

Violet dumped as much of the dry materials as she could to make a path for Jordan. The other woman used her height to her advantage and leapt across the flames. Violet kept throwing all the powder she could in Jordan's direction, even when it meant the flames were getting dangerously close to her.

"I got it!" Jordan yelled.

Violet was finding it harder to breathe, now that the baking materials she'd thrown had smoldered some of the flames. Not as much fire, but more smoke.

There was a yelp of pain from Jordan's direction, and then the blessed sound of the fire extinguisher turning on. Jordan sprayed everything she could while Violet continued to pour the last of the flour over the flames.

When they got it under enough control that they could get out the door, they ran outside, both of them gasping for air. Violet took the fire extinguisher from Jordan, wincing at how hot it was, and continued using it on the fire. "Go get help."

Jordan hadn't been gone long when the fire extinguisher ran out, but at least the worst of the blaze was under control. Not long after, Jordan was running back, holding another fire extinguisher awkwardly in her arms. She thrust it at Violet.

"That's from The Mayor's Inn. They're calling the fire department now."

Within just a few moments, the bakery was surrounded. Someone pulled the fire extinguisher from Violet's hands and used it to finish putting out the flames, along with another one that had shown up. Sirens were ringing through the air just a few minutes later. More and more people started milling around as the sun began to rise.

Violet sat down on the curb next to Jordan to watch it all. They had made it out alive. Survival. That was the most important thing.

CHAPTER 24

SHE'D BEEN at the hospital for less than an hour when Gabriel came storming in, Edward on his heels.

"Are you okay? What in God's name happened?" Gabriel walked straight up to her and clutched her against his chest.

She finally worked her way free and hopped up onto the exam table. "There was a fire, obviously."

Violet wasn't hurt, except for a little smoke inhalation. She and Jordan had been ushered into separate rooms upon arrival at the hospital. Violet had already been checked out by one of the doctors—not Anne—who had informed her she would probably have an annoying cough for a while, but that it shouldn't have any effects long-term. It wouldn't be long until she was released. Then she would have to get back and figure out what the hell she was going to do about the bakery.

She needed to talk to the sheriff and figure out if what she thought was true, that someone had deliberately set fire to Fancy Pants.

It just seemed so impossible. Why would someone do that?

And Gabriel was going to freak out when she told him.

"Where the hell are all the doctors in this one-horse town?" Gabe was already pacing.

"I've already been seen by the doctor. I'm okay, just some smoke inhalation, and I smell like the inside of a chimney. Nothing that shouldn't be completely gone in a few days. They should be back to officially release me soon."

Her brother studied her as if trying to figure out if she were being truthful. From her seat on the exam table, she held out her arms and legs in front of her so he could see she wasn't burned. That at least got him to stop pacing.

"What happened, Violet?" Edward asked, moving in closer from the door. "The fire was in the kitchen?"

"Yes."

Gabe rammed his fingers into his hair. "And you just, what, figured out the kitchen was on fire and decided to run downstairs and fight it yourself rather than call the fire department? That's just stupid, Vi. I know you love this bakery, but it's not worth your life."

"Actually," Violet crossed her arms, "I was already in the kitchen when the fire started."

"What?" Edward seemed more upset by that than the thought that she had run down to fight it herself. She couldn't win with these two.

"Why were you in the kitchen in the middle of the night?" Edward asked.

She shrugged. "I had an idea for a new recipe, so we were trying it out."

"We? As in you and Teague?" Gabe bit out.

God, she wanted to see Aiden. She'd wanted to call him

the moment all this had happened. But there hadn't been a chance. And she still didn't have her phone.

"No, actually, it was me and Jordan."

Gabe rolled his eyes. "Of course it was. I should've known if there was trouble, that woman would be in the center of it."

"Cut her some slack. If it wasn't for her, I'd probably be dead right now." She glared at him.

He rolled his eyes. "Because you're both too stupid to leave a fire rather than stay and fight it?"

"Have you always been this much of an asshole, or has this fine personality trait just sprouted recently?"

Gabe shook his head with a wry smile and jumped up onto the examination table next to her. "Both, probably. I've always been a jerk, but you were too much of a sweet little sister to notice. But Jordan Reiss . . . Damn it, I don't trust that woman."

Violet leaned her head against her brother's massive shoulder. "She saved me, Gabe. She jumped through flames to get us both out."

His eyes narrowed. "Then I guess I'll try to keep my assholery in check when I'm around her."

She had to tell him the truth about what had happened. He wasn't going to like it, but he would find out either way. "Somebody set fire to the place on purpose."

He went completely still. "Why do you think that?"

"The fire didn't come from the stove. It wasn't some sort of electrical malfunction. Somebody threw something through the back window."

"Are you sure?" Edward asked, looking alarmed.

"Yes. I know it sounds crazy, but it's not me just being overdramatic."

Gabe slid his arm around her and pulled her close. "I

believe you. Even when I haven't liked the decisions you were making, it wasn't because I didn't trust your judgment. You're not prone to histrionics."

No matter how independent she became, her brother's opinion was always going to matter to her. "Thank you. But what I can't figure out is why. The bakery has been doing so well. I've had to hire more people to help with the business."

There was a knock on the open door. Sheriff Nelson stood in the doorway. "I couldn't help but overhear. And I might be able to assist you with that question."

"Sheriff, come in. Do you know my brother, Gabriel? And this is Edward Appleton. He also works at Collingwood Technology, although he's more of a family member than he's ever been an employee."

The sheriff made his greetings, and everyone shook hands. "I just come from Fancy Pants. The firefighters are finished and out. The fire didn't do as much damage as you might have feared. Bryan Lindsey is the fire marshal for Teton County. He thinks you'll be up and running again in two or three weeks."

That was fantastic news and definitely better than what she'd been expecting.

"So soon?" Edward asked. "Is that even safe?"

"Do you agree with Violet's theory that this might be foul play?" Gabe asked.

The sheriff stepped inside the room and closed the door behind him, taking off his hat. "Should be safe, yes. And, yes, I have no doubt there was foul play involved. Someone threw a Molotov cocktail through the bakery's back window."

"A bottle bomb?" When Violet looked over at him in confusion, Gabe continued, "When I was in Afghanistan, they were used all the time. Basically, it's just a bottle full of kerosene or something flammable with some sort of lighted cloth. The cloth burns, then ignites the accelerant. The bottle explodes and sprays accelerant and flames everywhere. Cheap and easy boom."

Sheriff Nelson nodded. "And the door leading from the kitchen to the front of the shop was blocked with one of the large cabinets you use for decoration."

She just stared at this news. No wonder she and Jordan hadn't been able to get out the door.

"But why would anybody do this to my bakery?" A sudden thought sent fear chasing down her spine. "Do you think this has something to do with Stellman? That he's trying to get to me from prison?"

She saw a look pass between Gabe and Edward.

"What? What do you know?" She hopped down from the examination table.

"Stellman was killed in prison two days ago," Gabe said. "I should've told you right away. I'm sorry."

Violet tried to process it all. "He's really dead?" He hadn't even gone to trial yet. At first she'd been dreading facing him in court. But recently she'd almost been looking forward to it, the chance to look Stellman in the eye, the man who'd tried to destroy her, and make sure he knew he hadn't succeeded.

"You never have to worry about Stellman again," Edward said, tone gentle.

She must be more exhausted than she thought because Stellman being dead was not reassuring her the way it ought to. "Then who threw the Molotov cocktail into the bakery?"

"How well do you know your employee Jordan Reiss?" Sheriff Nelson asked.

Violet rolled her eyes. "I know her well enough to know

she didn't do this. Especially since she was standing right next to me when it happened." She glared at Gabe before returning her gaze to the sheriff. "And before you ask, yes, I know that she used to be in prison."

The sheriff held his hands out in front of him, palms up. "Whoa. I've got no problem with Jordan. And actually, I'm glad to see you defending her so adamantly."

"Why are you even asking me about her at all?"

"Because I think that fire was meant as a message for her to get out or for you to get rid of her as an employee."

That didn't make any sense. "Why would you think that?"

"As much as I don't like it, and I've spent considerable time trying to stop it from happening, Jordan has problems with some townsfolk from time to time because of what happened with her father. He made off with a lot of people's money, and her coming back to Oak Creek is a constant reminder of that." He let out a sigh. "Her place has been vandalized more than once since she got out of jail, and I think this is someone taking it to the next level."

Gabe muttered something foul under his breath. Violet wasn't sure if it was because of what the townspeople were doing to Jordan or because those actions were now linked to Violet.

"Anyway," the sheriff continued, "it might be in your best interest not to keep her as an employee. I've tried to talk Jordan into just moving along. But she doesn't want to leave the house her mother left her."

Silence fell over the room.

"I think we're hoping Violet might decide to close down Fancy Pants for a few months and come back to Collingwood Technology," Edward said. "At least until things settle down a little bit."

It was Gabe she turned and glared at after Edward's words. "Seriously?"

Her brother shook his head and smiled. "I told you it wasn't going to happen, Edward. This is where she wants to be. She's not coming back to CT."

The sheriff put his hat back on. "I'll let you guys discuss this. If you'll excuse me, I need to go question Jordan."

"Can I come too, Sheriff? Jordan doesn't have any family, and I just want to make sure she's okay."

"I think that might be a good idea."

His response didn't reassure Violet, given what she'd just found out about how the citizens of Oak Creek had been treating her friend.

Because that was what she was, Violet's friend. Jordan tended to keep to herself—now Violet understood much better why—but she was more than just an employee.

"I'm coming too," Gabe said. "If there's trouble, I want to know about it. And that woman is the epitome of trouble."

Edward agreed to return to the office when Violet told him she would make sure her brother got a ride back to Idaho Falls.

And she would, if he was nice.

If not, a fifty-mile hike would give her brother a chance to think about his choices.

As soon as they entered the room where Jordan was receiving care for her injuries, Violet knew something was very wrong. First of all, this could hardly be called a room. It wasn't even a curtained-off section of the emergency room, which would also be understandable.

The place they'd stowed Jordan was barely one step up from a goddamn supply closet.

Jordan was sitting on a hard chair near the corner, quietly crying.

"Jordan?" Violet rushed over to her side. "Are you okay, sweetie?"

The other woman immediately tried to pull herself together. She was making a weird gesture with her face against her shoulder, but Violet didn't understand what she was trying to do.

Gabe did. He pulled a tissue from the box sitting on the counter, then walked over and wiped Jordan's face gently. He crouched down next to her.

"Blow," he said as he held the tissue over her nose. She did. Gabe turned to Violet. "Her hands are burnt. She can't do it herself."

"You burned yourself when you picked up the fire extinguisher, didn't you?"

Jordan nodded, her head resting against Gabe's hand as he wiped her face again.

"I-I'm sorry." She was obviously still fighting tears. "It just hurts more than I thought it would, and I can't drive, and I'm not sure what to do."

"I'm sure the pain medicine the doctors gave you will kick in soon," Violet said, rubbing her friend's shoulder.

Gabe was still crouched in front of Jordan, now gently turning her wrists over so they could see the burns.

Violet didn't know a lot about medical stuff, but it seemed like those angry-looking blisters ought to have some sort of ointments or covering on them. "Or maybe they need to give you something stronger if it's still hurting you this badly."

"No, I just want to go home."

"They haven't given you anything at all, have they?" Gabe asked in a low voice.

"I—I . . ." Her big gray eyes blinked at them.

Gabe stood and tucked a strand of Jordan's hair behind her ear. "You hang in there a few more minutes. I'm going to handle this for you."

Her brother was every bit the Navy SEAL as he walked out of the room.

"They haven't given you any pain medicine? Why didn't you tell them how much it hurt?" Violet asked. She hated to see her friend in pain.

"I haven't seen anyone."

Violet didn't understand. "You haven't seen anyone since your hands started hurting so badly?"

"No, I haven't seen anyone since they brought us in. They took you to your room and brought me here."

"They did *what*?" Violet turned to stare at the sheriff.

He shook his head. "This is the sort of thing I was talking about. The staff will come in here and eventually treat her, but there will be all sorts of excuses about limited space and emergencies if anyone even bothers to ask why she wasn't treated right away."

"Oh hell no." Violet was about to go use some of her favorite tae kwon do moves on the nearest medical professionals.

"No, you stay here," the sheriff said. "I have no doubt your brother is taking care of this and that heads are rolling quite efficiently right now."

Just a few minutes later, Anne came rushing down the hallway and into the room.

"Jordan, my God, I just got here for my shift and found out what happened. I'm so sorry. We're going to get you to a room right now and get you started on some pain medication."

Anne dropped down in front of the other woman and began looking at her wounds and taking her vitals. A few minutes later, a sullen-looking nurse showed up with a wheelchair and gestured for Jordan to get in.

Anne spun toward her and poked a finger right in the nurse's face. "I don't care what your problem is, but if you expect to continue working at this hospital, you will treat this patient just like we treat all patients: with care and respect."

"Her father stole all my parents' money." She sneered over at Jordan before returning her gaze to Anne. "My dad still hasn't been able to retire because of what happened, and he's nearly seventy."

"I don't care if this woman pulled a gun on you this morning, much less something she didn't do and has no responsibility for. As long as she is in this hospital needing care, she will receive it. You and everyone else who worked the shift today, whether they had a part of sticking her in this closet or not, can consider themselves on disciplinary probation."

The nurse's eyes got big and she began blustering. "You can't do that."

"Oh, I damn well can. No one comes into my hospital needing medical attention and doesn't get it because of a ten-year-old grudge. Now do your job or consider yourself fired."

Violet and Jordan both just stared at Anne. Violet had never seen her quiet friend speak to anyone like that.

The nurse assisted Jordan, with great care, into the wheelchair. Anne was already calling out orders for preparation as they wheeled Jordan into an actual room. Within minutes Jordan was in a bed and hooked up to an IV. She still looked like she was in pain, but at least she wasn't distraught.

Gabriel was back, standing guard at the door, arms crossed over his chest. Violet was at Jordan's side, leaving room for all the hospital staff hovering around the woman. Anne kept watch from the foot of the bed.

Gabriel looked like he couldn't decide whether to come in closer or not. Indecision wasn't something she was used to seeing on her brother's face. Neither was the helpless anger that crossed over his features every time there was a hiss of pain from Jordan as they tended to her wounded hands.

He looked like he wanted to fight everyone in the room to protect Jordan. Which was interesting, considering last time Violet had seen them together, they had looked like they were going to fight each other.

Once Jordan was more comfortable, and her wounds had been wrapped, Anne turned to Violet, searching her face. "Are *you* okay?"

"I've already been checked out and will be leaving as soon as someone signs the paperwork."

Anne nodded. "I'll do that and leave it at the nurse's station. Sorry I can't stick around with you. I've got some asses to kick." She walked up the side of the bed so she could touch Jordan on the shoulder. "Again, I'm so sorry, Jordan. How you were treated was completely unprofessional. If you'd like to write up a formal complaint with the state, I would understand."

"No," Jordan said softly. "I'll be fine. I just want to go . . . I just want to get out of here."

"There's no reason for you to stay overnight. I'll give you a prescription for pain medication and an antibiotic ointment. But you're going to need someone to drive you. You won't be able to drive with your hands like they are."

"I'll have someone bring me a car, and I'll get her home safely," Gabriel said from the doorway. "I've set up triage care for burns before. I'll make sure she has everything she needs and is able to access it before I leave."

Jordan looked like she might argue for a moment, but then frowned down at her bandaged hands. "Okay, um, thank you."

Anne nodded and left. Violet almost felt like she should leave also, give them privacy even though there was very little privacy in the emergency ward. Gabe and Jordan were opposites in every way, but she'd never seen her brother look at anyone outside of family with such protective fury. Like he would tear apart anyone who tried to hurt Jordan.

Violet didn't need anyone to look at her like that, but she wanted someone to. Wanted Aiden to. Wanted him to burst through the door and sweep her off her feet.

Not because she needed him to, but because she *wanted* him to.

"I'm going to go check myself out at the nurse's station. I'll call you later, Gabe, after I get my stuff and—"

As if her thoughts had conjured him, Aiden walked through the door—hazel eyes laser focused on her.

"Aiden," she whispered.

He was here.

CHAPTER 25

WORD TRAVELLED fast in a small town.

When Aiden got a text that there had been a fire at Fancy Pants, but no one had been hurt, he bolted out of bed, ready to fly over there and take care of it all but stopped himself at his front door.

This was exactly the sort of thing Violet wanted to be able to handle on her own. She didn't need someone rushing in to fight her battles for her.

He forced himself to walk back into the kitchen and make coffee and breakfast with fists that kept clenching and feet that kept turning toward the door of their own volition.

When he found out an hour later that the fire had been deliberate, and that Violet had been trapped in the kitchen as it was burning, he didn't give a flying fuck about independence or strength or her ability to fight.

He wouldn't fight her battles for her, but he would damn well be by her side as she was facing them.

He was scheduled to travel to Greece next week for Linear. That would not be happening. He texted Zac as much as he ran out the door toward the hospital, thankful he was close enough not to need to take a car.

He slowed himself to a walk by the time he got to the entrance of the emergency room, forced himself to calm down as he asked at the nurse's desk about where he could find Violet. The temptation to just blow right through was strong, but he resisted. That would just get him kicked out anyway.

He wasn't getting far with the person at the desk, since he wasn't really anything to Violet. Not a family member, not even her boyfriend.

That, he planned to rectify immediately. Even if he had to beg her.

It was only because Anne walked up, looking more pissed than he'd ever seen her, and told the nurse to let him back that he made any headway at all. Anne gave him a brief wave, then turned, calling for a meeting in the back for anyone who wasn't actively working with a patient.

She looked like she was about to unleash hell. Aiden didn't know what had happened, but he was glad he wasn't being called into that meeting. The nurse grimaced, then gave him Violet's room number before muttering something to another nurse about Jordan Reiss.

He wanted to ask what was going on but honestly didn't care. At least not nearly as much as he cared about getting to Violet. He was rushing down the hall toward her room when he heard her in another room.

He immediately turned inside. He'd already known she wasn't seriously hurt. But she *could've* been. Trapped in a fire? No amount of training prepared somebody for that.

He stopped and just stared at her.

No injuries. She was filthy, that gorgeous red hair

tangled and matted, clothes ruined, and soot and dirt streaking every inch of available skin, but no injuries.

She was the most beautiful thing he'd ever seen.

"Aiden."

His name slipped out of her lips, like he was the answer to a prayer, the exact same way he felt about her. He crossed over to her and didn't stop until he had her pulled up against his heart, where she belonged.

Gabriel cleared his throat from the far side of the room, but Aiden didn't care.

"Are you all right?" he whispered.

Before she could even answer he caught her lips in a kiss, mouth plundering hers, one hand rooting itself in her hair, the other gripping her hip. When her arms wrapped around his neck and pulled him even closer, he took advantage of every bit of her hot, wet, open mouth.

When Gabriel cleared his throat even louder, Aiden finally eased back, leaning his forehead against hers.

"Are you even going to let her answer the question, asshole?" Gabe muttered.

Aiden could only vaguely remember what the question was.

"I'm fine." Violet smiled up at him. "Jordan was hurt, but I'm fine."

"I'm okay too," Jordan said from the bed. "No need to kiss me."

Gabriel muttered something about how he better not kiss Jordan, but Aiden ignored him once again.

"Take me home," Violet whispered. "I know things are weird with us right now, but I just need to be with you."

"Yes."

Yes, he would take her home with him. Yes, he would do his damnedest to convince her to never leave there again.

Yes, this woman was it for him, and there was no way he'd ever find the strength to walk away from her again, even temporarily.

He helped her finish the paperwork and escorted her out. He expected more of an argument from Gabe, until Violet explained he was going to give Jordan a ride home. Evidently Oak Creek's ugly side had made an appearance in terms of Jordan's care.

"Did you know they treat her like this?" she asked after explaining what had happened.

"I know a lot of people around here still hold a grudge. I wasn't trying to keep it from you, I just figured it was Jordan's choice about how much to say. Her trauma to talk about or not."

She sighed. "I guess I can understand that. I just wish I had known so I could have helped her."

He wrapped an arm around her as they walked out onto the sidewalk from the hospital. "Everybody has to choose how to fight their wars. So far, Jordan's MO has been evasion. If she decides to make an out-and-out stand, she'll know she can count on you beside her."

She nodded, her arm wrapping around his waist. "I probably shouldn't get this close to you. You're going to smell like a kitchen fire."

"I've got a shower and a lot of shower gel. The smell will eventually come off."

She peered up at him. "I might need some help scrubbing off in the shower. But you'll have to promise to be very, very thorough."

This woman. She was everything. "Firefly . . ."

She heaved a sigh. "I know. I know. We're on a break. We need distance. I need to make completely sure my big-girl panties work. You're going to work in Timbuktu so we can stay away from each other."

He stopped walking and turned to face her. This wasn't a conversation he'd planned to have in the middle of the sidewalk, even if it was relatively empty. But it couldn't wait.

She hadn't stopped talking. "Showering together is a bad idea because of all the mind-blowing sex it leads to. Yada yada yada. But you know wha—"

He put a finger over her mouth because if she said one more word, he would throw her down on the sidewalk and take her right here.

"*You* know what?" he said. "Screw all that stuff I said before. My intentions may have been good, but I don't care anymore. You're the most amazing woman I've ever met. You're strong in every way a person can be strong—physically, emotionally, mentally. You're strong with me, without me, it doesn't matter."

"Aiden . . ."

He cupped both her dirty cheeks in his hands. "I'm never going to be your crutch. You're never going to *need* a crutch. Every gain you've made has been your own. And if you start to doubt that at some point, we'll just take it to the mat, and you can beat on me until you prove yourself wrong."

He kissed her tenderly. "Take me back, Firefly. Come home with me, not just for a shower, not just while they repair your bakery. Come home with me and stay. Let's figure out where this—*us*—leads."

She let out a soft sigh that had him worried.

Shit. "What? Too much, too fast?" She was twenty-two fucking years old, for Christ's sake. What was he doing, besides scaring the shit out of her? He scrubbed a hand over his face as an even worse thought hit him. "Too late?" he croaked.

What if the time apart had made her realize that she wanted things to be casual between them, if she even wanted anything at all?

She folded her arms over her chest. "What I've said from the very beginning in your kitchen is still true. I refuse to take a passive role in my own life ever again. I refuse to blindly conform to what other people want for me any longer or let them make decisions for me and just go along with them. That includes you too."

He could barely breathe through the pressure squeezing his heart. How had screwed up the most important thing in his life so badly?

"Violet, I . . ." He trailed off, not even sure what direction to take. Should he try to explain? To reason? To beg?

She reached out and poked him in the chest with one small finger. "Lucky for you, I'd already decided what I wanted before your little speech. Hell, before the fire even broke out. I was coming for you, Teague. You weren't getting away from me that easily."

There was finally enough oxygen in the world again. "I wasn't?"

"You were right about some of what you said the other night. I probably do need to continue my training with someone else if I want to take it to the next level."

He nodded.

"But I get to choose who's by my side. Just like you get to choose who's by *your* side. Nobody makes that choice for us. Don't try to make it for me again."

He held up his hands in a gesture of surrender. "You're right. I'm sorry."

She reached up and grabbed the back of his neck and

pulled him down so their foreheads were touching. It was more like the opening stance of a wrestling match than an embrace.

And somehow all the more perfect because of that.

"We stand by each other's sides. And we're stronger because of it."

"Yes."

She kissed him gently, softly. "I'm learning how to follow my instincts. And all my instincts point directly to you. We'll figure the rest out on our way."

He let out a sigh of relief and threaded his fingers in her hair. "You're young. Every time I hear a damn Drake song, I realize how young you are. I'm not trying to rush you. We'll take all the time we need."

"I know my own mind. That's the good thing about having been so mature all these years. I may not have done a lot of the stupid things that are traditional for people my age, but I've never been flighty. I know what I want. I want you." She grinned. "Even if you are like *Off my lawn!* old."

He threw his head back and laughed. He really was in love with her.

And he had to have her right damn now.

He put an arm around her again and started walking so fast she almost had to jog to keep up with him. "Just wait until I get you into the shower. I'll show you the difference between being old and having enough experience to make you scream my name multiple times."

She smiled. "So we get clean first, then we'll get very, very dirty."

CHAPTER 26

VIOLET ROLLED her eyes at Aiden five days later as she spoke into the phone at breakfast. Aiden couldn't blame her; Edward had called at least half a dozen times since the fire.

He was pretty desperate to get her to come back. Aiden stood up to get them both another cup of coffee. If this conversation was anything like the last few, Violet would be on the phone for a while. She'd just been making vague agreement sounds—obviously in an attempt to listen and pacify Edward—for the last few minutes.

She set her cell phone down on the table and put it on speaker so she could eat while continuing the conversation. She held her fingers up to her lips to tell Aiden to keep quiet.

As if he wanted to get caught in the middle of this argument.

"We just need you for a few days, Violet," Edward said. *Again.* "Your work is so important."

"I'm not the only person who can work on these projects," she responded, taking a sip of coffee. "And there's no way I'm coming back for a whole week. You're going to have to find someone else."

"Fine. Not a week. Just three or four days. Gabriel needs you. You know how he is, doesn't want to talk about it or admit that he needs help. But he does."

Aiden smirked under his breath. Edward knew just what strings to pull with Violet. She may be all independent, but she wasn't going to leave a loved one in a lurch.

"Fine. One day. That's all you get. And then that's it, Edward, I'm done. CT is not my life anymore." Those emerald eyes looked up from her food to meet his with a smile. "My life is here in Oak Creek now."

Aiden flashed her a smile back. It sure as hell was. They didn't have to know what the future looked like, they just both knew it started here.

"Fine." Edward sighed. "Thank you. I know Gabriel will be happy to have your help. He's looking forward to working together with you."

"I'll head over to Idaho Falls as soon as I'm done with breakfast."

They said their goodbyes, with Edward all but gushing his thanks.

"I guess we don't get to play hooky anymore," Aiden said.

"I'll go do this one thing, and then I'm done. Gabe wouldn't have asked if he didn't really need my help, and I'll get to work with him, which will be fun. Besides, if I don't do it now, Edward will just keep asking, especially while the bakery is out of commission. I don't think he or Gabe really want to accept that I'm gone." She got up and came around and sat on his lap, tucking her feet under one of his legs. It was a habit she'd developed once it had gotten colder.

His arms wrapped around her automatically. "Change is hard, but they'll come around. I need to get into Linear anyway and figure out the new winter schedule. Everything is in a little bit of disarray since I decided not to go overseas."

"And I'm very happy about that." She relaxed against him.

They'd spent the last three days in an odd mixture of training, sex, and baking. Since Fancy Pants wouldn't reopen for at least another two weeks, and that was with Violet paying out of pocket for the repairs until she was reimbursed by insurance in order to speed things up, she'd turned his kitchen into her own pastry test facility. It had never smelled so good in his house. Neighbors, including Mrs. Mazille, were constantly stopping by.

Aiden needed all the training and the sex to burn off the calories from the new creations she'd made him try.

There hadn't been much progress on who had thrown the bottle bomb into the bakery. Sheriff Nelson had brought in three or four guys who'd been known to give Jordan a hard time in the past. But they'd all had alibis.

Aiden wouldn't be giving up and wouldn't be letting Violet stay there alone. Gabe felt the same, and Kendrick and his team would be back on security detail once Fancy Pants reopened.

They finished their breakfast, and Violet got ready to leave.

"If this is the last day I'm giving them, I'm sure it's going to run pretty late. They'll try to milk me for every hour they can."

He grabbed her by the collar of her shirt and pulled her close. "I'll be waiting up, no matter how late it is."

She smiled. "That's just what I was hoping you'd say."

Violet was barely out of Oak Creek before she got another call from Edward. She sighed and hit speaker again.

"I'm still coming, Edward. I said I would."

The older man chuckled. "Actually, I'm calling to ask if you can meet us at the research and development warehouse in Irwin on Highway 26."

"CT still owns that? I thought we got rid of it a couple years ago."

"No, we still have it, we just don't use it much anymore. But at least it means less of a drive for you."

That was true; it would cut her drive nearly in half.

"Okay, I'll see you there." She disconnected the call before Edward could start thanking her again for agreeing to work.

She put the directions into her GPS and headed toward the lab, wishing even now that she were headed back toward Aiden. She might be pissed as hell about the fire, more because of the hatred aimed at Jordan than the damage to Fancy Pants, but she would always be a little glad it had happened, since it had forced her and Aiden to confront their real feelings about each other.

Finding the old R&D lab was a little trickier than she remembered. This place really was out in the middle of nowhere. Edward's sedan was parked out front, but there was no sign of any of the three cars Gabe drove depending on what mood he was in.

She walked inside, shaking her head. If CT was paying for this place, they needed to keep it up better. And most of the inside looked just as neglected as the outside. Only one small section of the lab, where Edward and a lab tech were already waiting for her, held any of the equipment they would need to do significant work.

"It would've been worth it for me to drive all the way to Idaho Falls," she said in lieu of a greeting. "There's only so much we're going to be able to do here."

"It has what we need," Edward replied. The stranger standing next to him didn't say anything. He had on a white employee lab coat like many of the CT techs wore. The coat barely covered the muscles on the guy.

"Where's Gabe? And what the heck was he thinking, sending us here? I can't believe he let a lab we own get so run-down."

Edward shrugged. "You know your brother. He always has his reasons, but he doesn't tend to share them with anyone. This is Matthew Learson. He's a new employee and isn't very familiar with many of the CT projects, so I'm not sure how useful he'll be."

Learson still hadn't said anything, so Violet just shrugged. She wasn't here to make friends. She slipped on the lab jacket Edward handed her, and she had to admit, it felt a little nice. Not what she wanted to be doing all the time, but good for today.

"Well, let's get started. I'm on your dime, and it's a very limited one. I don't want to waste time waiting for Gabe."

"I was hoping you'd feel that way." Edward sounded about as excited as he ever got.

Violet literally rolled up her sleeves and got to work. Gabe had sent her a dozen files, each with a problem that needed to be sorted out. None of them were easy, but none of them should've been anything that Gabe or any of CT's higher-level chemical or mechanical engineers couldn't have figured out on their own.

By midmorning, when Gabe hadn't shown up—despite

asking her to come help him—Violet felt no guilt at all about her decision to make this the last time she worked for CT. Especially when what they were giving her to work on didn't actually need her expertise.

She was beyond angry at her brother when they stopped for a short lunch. Edward assured her he was on his way, and man, was she going to let Gabe have it when he got there. Not only for being late, but for giving her this crap work.

After lunch they moved on to the next task Edward shoved into her hands. Her microhydrocarbon fuel cell project. Now *this* was something that truly needed her expertise. The project had been her baby, and she'd made advances on it before they had sent development in a new direction.

Until she and Gabe had realized its strong potential for weaponization.

"Gabe wants me working on this?" she asked.

Edward nodded. "He wouldn't have sent it if he didn't."

She had to admit, she had everything she needed here to take those final steps on the project she'd stopped working on a couple months before the kidnapping.

"Hand me the DMFC," she said to hulking tech guy. He'd been hovering over her shoulder most of the day, but she had yet to see him do anything of any real use. He just looked at her blankly now.

She shook her head. "The direct methanol fuel cell?"

The guy had no idea what she was referring to. She mentally added "screening lab techs" to the list of things she was going to chew her brother out for. If he ever actually got here.

Edward pushed Learson out of the way and handed her

the cell she needed, which she began to dismantle so she could basically strip it for parts.

Edward rubbed his hands together. "Yes, now we're getting somewhere."

She didn't pay him any attention, her focus now on the work at hand. She'd enjoyed this project but hadn't minded moving away from it when it had become necessary. Partially because of the danger, but partially because she'd known this one was going to be more long-term. Developing it as a weapon was going to be easy—she was almost there now. But continued development so the fuel cell couldn't be used as a weapon was going to take years of research and testing.

She smiled as she continued to work, the hours now flying by. Even back when she'd been itching for a change, she'd known to back away from the projects that were longer term because she wasn't going to be here to finish them.

But she could finish this one component now. It would be the most important aspect of the micro fuel cell. It would be fully functional after today, and she would have to trust Gabe to make sure the prototype and research were protected and kept secret until he and the R&D staff could develop the rest of the technology to keep it from being used as weapons.

But Gabe wasn't here to assure her of that, was he?

She looked at Edward, who had been hovering over her shoulder. "Are you absolutely positive Gabe wanted me focused on this?"

"One hundred percent. He left very explicit instructions that this was what you were supposed to work on."

Her stomach dropped. "I thought he was going to be here. Why would he leave instructions for what I was going to work on if he was going to be here to tell me himself?" she asked softly.

For the first time she could ever remember, Edward looked shaken. Not like the rock he'd always been. "I just meant until he gets here."

There was something wrong. "Why don't we just take a break until Gabe arrives? Or even better, I'll call him and cuss him out for forcing us to work when he didn't even show up."

"I'm sure he'll be here any moment. Why don't we just keep going until he does get here? You're so close."

Edward wasn't an engineer. He worked on contracts and finances for CT. He knew enough to understand the basics of what she was doing, but maybe he didn't understand the potential danger of what was in front of them.

"I think there's been a mistake, Edward. I started my testing on the hydrocarbon fuel cell last year and made a lot of progress. But then Gabe and I agreed that it needed to be shelved indefinitely. A normal-sized hydrocarbon fuel cell has a number of legitimate uses. But a micro-sized one, engineered the way it would be here, is nothing but a deadly bomb that would be very difficult to detect. It would make it easy and cheap for terrorists to do as much damage as they wanted."

Edward shook his head. "That's so unfortunate."

Violet let out a sigh of relief that Edward seemed to understand. She'd really been getting worried for a moment. "Good. So let's just shelve this until Gabe gets here and we can talk about it more. I'm not comfortable moving forward without him. To be honest, I'm not sure I'm willing to move forward even if he wants me to. But I don't think he will once we talk about the potential dangers again."

Edward was still shaking his head, his shoulders

drooping now. "No, I mean it's unfortunate that you're not willing to continue without talking to Gabe. I had truly hoped you would. It would've made things a lot less painful for all of us."

"I don't understand. Do you mean arguing with Gabe? I can handle him. Besides, he agrees with me. This is not something CT wants to be a part of. We don't want to set this loose in the world. In the wrong hands, it would be devastating."

She felt something hard and metal press up against the back of her head.

"No, it's unfortunate that we have to do this the harder way," Edward said. "The way that definitely doesn't end happily for either of us."

She spun around and found Learson pointing a gun at her.

She flipped back to Edward. "What the hell is going on?"

"As you no doubt suspected long before Learson pulled out his weapon, he's not actually a lab tech. He's here to ensure you continue to work even if I'm unable to convince you."

She looked at the man she'd known nearly her entire life. "What have you done, Edward?"

"What do you want me to do with her, Mr. Stellman?" Learson asked.

Stellman?

Her blood turned to ice in her veins. She stared at Edward, shaking her head. "That's not possible. Stellman was arrested after my kidnapping and was killed in prison last week."

Edward shook his head kindly. "Stellman was never just one person, my dear. That's how he remained undetected for so long. There were three of us who embodied the name. Jonathan Stellman, the man who was arrested and who law enforcement knows as Stellman, was the face. He was paid very well over the past decade to do nothing but enjoy being rich and powerful. But he always knew if he were ever caught, he would have to stay in prison."

Violet just shook her head, hearing Edward's words but unable to truly process them.

"When Jonathan decided to renege on his agreement and threatened to provide law enforcement with the information he had on the other two of us, he had to be eliminated altogether."

Violet wrapped her arms around herself, voice shaking. "*You* had me kidnapped? *You* had them do all those terrible things to me?"

Edward shook his head. "Those other things were never my intent, I promise. You were meant to be kidnapped and held for a few days. You'd been getting off track, refusing to work on the micro fuel cell. The abduction was supposed to help refocus you on your research."

"Kidnapping was supposed to *refocus* me?"

"Ever since Paris, you haven't been concentrating the way you once were. I thought you were having an identity crisis of some kind. Turns out you were, just not the one I thought. *Baking*." He spat the word. "Who would've figured that this would all come down to you wanting to cook?"

"Not focusing on the fuel cell project had nothing to do with that." She shook her head. "It's too dangerous. You have to see that, Edward. This could be used as a weapon to kill thousands of people without being detected."

He held up a hand. "Anything can be used as a weapon. You know that. Don't concentrate on the ethics of it. Focus on the science of it. That's all you can control. It's all you need to control. Now I need you to finish, Violet. I've gone to great lengths to get you back here, even setting fire to your precious bakery."

"That was you? You almost killed us!" she shouted.

He sighed, weary. "Again, that wasn't my intent. You should've been upstairs in your apartment, not down in the kitchen. The fire was meant to damage the empty kitchen area, not hurt you. The intent, once again, was to get you back to CT and focused on your research."

He'd gone to such extreme lengths to get her back in the lab and on this project. But now he had exposed himself. She knew he was Stellman. Was this man, who she'd considered family her whole life, going to kill her?

She wasn't going to ask, and she wasn't going to wait and see.

"Finishing this project is of the highest priority," Edward continued, voice tight. "Life-threatening priority, Violet. Both mine and yours. It was promised months ago and still hasn't been delivered. The buyers have grown impatient, and they're not the type who handle that well."

Violet still couldn't wrap her head around what was happening. But she could tell Learson was relaxing his stance just slightly as she and Edward continued to talk. He was big, but she could take him. At least enough to get his weapon away from him and get out.

"Fine, Edward. None of this is worth dying for." She pretended to turn back toward the work table, distributing her balance equally on both feet the way Aiden had drilled into her for the past two months, then whirled back around to make her move against the hulking giant behind her.

CHAPTER 27

AIDEN SPENT the entire morning after Violet had left working at Linear: first talking Gavin into taking the assignment for him in Greece, which admittedly hadn't been terribly difficult, then teaching Gavin's concealed carry permit class.

He'd be teaching all of Gavin's classes for the foreseeable future, and probably doing the man's laundry, but it would be worth it if it meant he didn't have to leave Oak Creek. The class went by without a hitch, and later that afternoon Aiden was heading back into town. He wanted to be home in case Violet got there earlier than planned.

He stopped by the drug store to grab some more condoms—he wasn't going to take a chance on running out since Violet was going to be living at his house for the foreseeable future—and froze as he walked down the aisle and saw Gabe standing there.

Buying condoms in front of Violet's brother was so *not* what he wanted to do. He tried to back away without being seen, but no such luck. Shit. Aiden continued walking down the aisle. No way around it now.

"Gabe."

"Teague."

The look in Gabe's eyes was wary, almost a little panicked. Then Aiden saw what section Gabe had been looking at.

Feminine products.

Now condoms didn't seem so bad. Aiden wasn't going to ask why Gabe was studying feminine products. He *was not* going to do it. Was. Not.

"Looking for something specific?" He did it.

Gabe actually shifted from foot to foot and combed his fingers through his hair. Aiden couldn't help but chuckle at the man's obvious discomfort. He'd seen this warrior face down death on the battlefield without faltering, and now it looked like some boxes of tampons were about to send him crying.

"It's not fucking funny," Gabe muttered.

Aiden both didn't and really, *really* did want to know what Gabe was looking for. Hell, they had a box at tampons at the Linear gym for bloody noses, but no one actually ever volunteered to buy it.

He would just leave the man to his misery. He crossed behind Gabe to the condoms.

"Are *you* looking for something specific?" Gabe asked. Aiden glanced back at him. Now he no longer looked uncomfortable, he just looked pissed.

"I generally like ribbed for a woman's pleasure." He grabbed a pack, not the normal brand he would buy, just to egg Gabe on.

Gabe just raised an eyebrow, his tone dry. "If you need ribs on your condom for a woman's pleasure, you're doing it wrong."

Aiden just laughed. "Touché." He grabbed his normal brand. "I'll leave you to your . . . feminine items."

"Fuck off."

Aiden laughed again. "Why are you even here? I thought you were working with Violet today in Idaho Falls."

"What?" Surprise was clear in his tone.

"Edward called this morning—*again*—begging her to come in. Said you two would be working together. This was the last time she was planning to work for Collingwood Technology, much to Edward's dismay."

Gabe's eyes narrowed. "Plans must have changed because I didn't know anything about it. I'll check in with Edward. But I don't want my sister working for CT anymore. She's happier here." He grimaced. "With you and her bakery. And despite what you may think, I want Violet to be happy. But also safe."

"I'm going to keep her safe. Linear is working with the sheriff to find out who threw that bottle bomb into Fancy Pants. It might not have been intended to hurt Violet, but I'm not going to let her be collateral damage in someone else's asinine war."

Gabe's eyes narrowed. "I'm looking into that situations for reasons of my own. It's time for this to stop."

Aiden didn't think that decree had anything to do with Violet, but it would help nonetheless. "So it looks like we're on the same side."

Gabe studied him. "How about I don't kick your ass about those condoms and save that beating for if you hurt my little sister."

Aiden rolled his eyes. "Why don't you finish picking out whatever tampons you need and save your speech. Your sister can kick my ass herself if I hurt her. She's become more than capable. And fucking call her. I think she was looking forward to working with you today."

Gabe's eyes narrowed once more. "I'll get that worked out immediately."

Aiden paid at the front before walking the few blocks back to his house. When the front door was unlocked, something inside his heart eased.

Violet was home.

"Hey," he called out as he walked in and closed the door behind him. "I just ran into your brother at the drug store, and you'd never believe what he was buying."

No answer.

"Vi?"

He walked into his living room and found a man pointing a Beretta 92 at him. A second man at his three o'clock caught his attention. That guy didn't have a gun out, but that didn't mean he didn't have a weapon on him.

"Violet isn't here, but we'd like to take you to her," Beretta said.

Aiden kept his hands in plain view—condom bag hanging off one finger—as he stepped into the room. They had the advantage in weaponry and numbers, but they obviously didn't want him dead or they would've taken him out as soon as he walked through the door. "Violet's working at her brother's company. I don't need you to take me to her."

Beretta grinned in a way that made the bottom of Aiden's stomach drop out. "Actually, there was a change of plans. Violet was directed somewhere else."

Shit. Now the fact that Gabe hadn't known anything about her working with him was starting to make more sense.

"Oh yeah, where is she?" Aiden took another slight step

toward the man with the gun. Another couple of feet and he'd be able to make his move.

"Like I said, we'll take you there."

Another step. "Well, you'll have to excuse me if I don't really want to take your word for it. My mother always said something about not getting into cars with strangers." He kept his voice calm and easy. "So why don't you get Violet on the phone, and then I'll go with you."

The guy finished Aiden's job for him by getting mad and a taking a step forward. "How about I have the gun and—"

Aiden didn't wait for him to finish the sentence, just tossed the bag of condoms at the man. When he automatically went to catch it, Aiden jumped forward, popping the gun out of his hand with a hard swipe of his fist, then brought the palm of his hand upward, breaking the guy's nose. Without stopping, he swung his leg around, hitting the second man in the jaw with a roundhouse kick that knocked him backward into the wall as he was reaching for his gun. Both men howled in pain.

Aiden immediately turned his focus back to Beretta to finish the job. He only got a step toward him before he heard a soft sound behind him. Before he could even turn, a burn in his shoulder sent him stumbling.

There'd been a third man in the house. As he turned, he recognized the guy. Dillon, one of Violet's kidnappers.

And he'd just shot Aiden in the shoulder.

"I'm going to have to ask you to stop picking on my men, Teague." Dillon lowered the gun with the silencer attached. "We need you alive, but not necessarily in one piece."

Aiden brought his hand up to his shoulder, finding his fingers covered in blood almost immediately. Shit.

Before he could move, the guy whose nose Aiden had

broken grabbed Aiden by the hair, putting a knife up to his jaw, voice hard. "This fucker broke my nose, Dillon."

"He threw a box of condoms at you, Luke, and you dropped your guard. You deserve more than a punch in the nose. So put the damn knife down."

Luke did but not before slicing it along Aiden's cheek. "That's to remember me by. For what little time you've got left." He followed it up with multiple shots to Aiden's gut with his fist, his other friend joining him.

Aiden did his best to protect himself from the blows that rained all over his body, but with his right arm basically useless, it was nearly impossible.

"Enough," Dillon finally said when they'd beaten Aiden to the ground. "That should be enough to scare Violet into doing what we want."

Aiden could barely hold himself upright. "What the hell are you talking about?" Blood splattered the ground as he spoke.

"As entertaining as it was to watch that idiot Randy drag Violet around and parade her to make a few extra dollars, that was never the real goal. She was needed for something else. And now, you're going to help us get it from her."

"Like hell I will."

Dillon just smiled and shook his head. "When she sees you like this, I think she'll be willing to do just about anything."

Aiden dove for Dillon. He wouldn't be used as a tool to hurt Violet. But he was slow, his reactions mushy. Dillon just stepped to the side. He nodded at one of the men behind Aiden.

Something crashed on the back of his skull, then darkness fell over everything.

CHAPTER 28

VIOLET SPUN AROUND, knocking the gun out of Learson's hand with a sudden knock to his arm, then she drove the heel of her other palm up into his nose, just like Aiden had taught her.

She was a little sickened but strangely satisfied at the crunch Learson's breaking nose made under the pressure of her blow. And thankful that Aiden had explained what would happen when she did this to someone so she wouldn't be thrown off guard.

Someone coming at you with the intent to hurt you is your enemy. To show them any mercy is more than they are going to show you.

So as Learson was crying out in pain, she spun her body around and finished him with a spinning roundhouse kick to the head.

Learson fell to the floor, unconscious.

Staying where she could see him out of the corner of her eye, she turned to Edward. She was completely satisfied and not at all sickened by the stunned look on his face.

"I suppose I have you to thank for my new strength and

power of will," she said, forcing a smile. "If you hadn't had me kidnapped, I never would've become this person. What's that saying? You never know how strong you are until strong is the only choice you have?"

He shook his head sadly. "Believe it or not, I never wanted it to be this way. I never wanted you to get hurt, never approved the death of Jean and Carson. They were my friends."

She swallowed hard. "*You* killed Mom and Dad? But they died in a car accident."

"Not me, but my partner. I always hated that you blamed yourself for their deaths, my dear. It had nothing to do with getting you those concert tickets you wanted. The next time they entered the car for any reason, the brakes were going to fail."

Oh God. Her parents' death hadn't been an accident. Edward had been some sort of criminal mastermind for *years*. "You killed them."

He shook his head. "No, I argued against it. But we needed control of Collingwood Technology. My partners and I didn't dream Gabe would come back and raise you and become CEO of the company. So our plans here had to change, become more long-term, focus on other things until the time was right to get what we needed. That time is now. The micro fuel cell can't wait. You're going to finish it today."

"Like hell I am." She'd taken down his goon. If she could take him, she would have no problem getting away from Edward. He was older, untrained.

Edward just shook his head. "I'm afraid you're not going to have any choice in the matter. Like I said, Stellman has always been made up of three people. The face, who is now dead. The brains—that would be me. And the brute force.

He's the one who killed your parents, and the one who allowed those horrible things to happen to you when you were kidnapped. I never would've had the stomach for that, Violet."

She heard a voice from behind her near the doorway. "I think he's referring to me."

Dillon.

She spun around, gripping the table behind her. "Wh-what are you doing here?"

"C'mon, Violet, you're quicker than that. I'm also part of Stellman—the brute force, as Edward calls me. He assured me he could get you to do what he wanted the easy way. But since he can't, we'll try it my way. The hard way."

It was like facing down the devil from her nightmares. He just watched her from across the room, just like he'd done when she was kidnapped.

"You killed my parents?" The words were barely audible.

Dillon didn't flinch. "I did. And I allowed Randy to do whatever he wanted when you were kidnapped. Then, of course, I had to make sure he didn't talk to anyone, so he had to be eliminated when Edward let me know your brother and his band of soldiers were coming to your rescue."

She pushed all this information to the side. It didn't matter right now. All that mattered was getting out of here alive. Taking out Dillon would be harder than Learson, but she could do it.

"I'm still not going to build the fuel cell."

Dillon tilted his head to the side. "You sure about that?"

She stepped closer. "Are you going to pull a gun on me too? If you shoot me, you won't get what you want. And putting together the cell requires a steady hand, so hurting me means I won't be able to do it either." She shrugged and took a step closer to Dillon. She had to get closer to take him out.

Learson groaned on the floor. Before she could even figure out how she was going to divide her time between Learson and Dillon, Dillon pulled out a gun and shot Learson where he lay on the floor. The man's body jerked before stilling.

Violet bit her lip, trying to suck in enough air in a room that suddenly felt stifling. This was Dillon trying to intimidate her. She couldn't let that happen. He'd actually just done her a favor—one fewer bad guy she had to fight.

She had the upper hand. He couldn't hurt her as long as he needed her to finish the fuel cell. The work was too delicate.

She feigned like she was getting farther away from Learson's body, but the move brought her half the distance to Dillon. She tried to keep Edward in her peripheral vision.

"Killing him doesn't scare me," she lied. "You can't do that to me if you want to get what you want."

Dillon surprised her by smiling. "Look at you, taking a step closer as you talk so I won't notice. What do you need, another ten feet before you're close enough to make your move?"

Shit.

"You've obviously been well trained. By, let me guess . . . Teague? I only ask because I just saw him do the same thing to my men and almost completely get the drop on them. I had to step in."

Dillon moved farther into the room, and her stomach dropped out when two more men entered, dragging a barely conscious Aiden between them. Dillon pulled a chair to the middle of the room, and they dumped Aiden into it.

"Aiden!" She ran over to him, dropping down on her knees in front of him, trying to figure out where he was most hurt. Blood was oozing from a bullet wound in his shoulder, and his face had been cut badly along the cheek. One eye was swollen shut.

"Firefly." The word was slurred, and his head hung low.

"Aiden." Panic welled up inside her. She ripped off her lab coat and held it against his bleeding shoulder. "Okay, hang in there. I'm going to get us out of this."

"It's time to get to work, Violet," Dillon said. "Because I'm not going to hurt you if you don't finish the fuel cell. I'm going to hurt *him*."

Aiden rallied. "Violet, no. Don't do it."

Dillon calmly took something out of his pocket.

A Taser.

Violet couldn't help herself, she scampered back from the weapon. Dillon shook his head, smiling almost gently.

"You obviously remember this." Dillon shook his head. "Randy, what an overzealous bastard he was. But don't worry, it's not for you."

He walked up behind Aiden and put the electroshock weapon against the back of his neck. Aiden's body jerked violently as the electrical current blasted through his body.

"Stop!" Violet screamed. She couldn't let Aiden go through this. She could remember with crystal clarity the Taser against her own skin. The brutal agony.

Dillon stopped for just a moment, then placed it back against Aiden again, turning it on.

"Stop! I'll do it. Just stop. Please!" She was begging. Crying. She didn't care.

Dillon switched it off. Aiden was moaning in the chair, barely conscious. He couldn't take much more. Violet wouldn't let him take more.

"I'll do it." She stood and walked over to Aiden, touching him softly on the head. The two men behind him had their weapons drawn, pointed at Aiden, ready if she made some sort of defensive move. She couldn't take them both and Dillon before one of them shot Aiden.

She put his hand over the lab coat against his shoulder. "Try to hold this against your wound," she whispered to him.

She turned back toward the table and got to work, not wanting to give Dillon any excuse to hurt Aiden further.

But he did it anyway, stunning Aiden every ten or fifteen minutes just to get her to work harder, faster. Aiden didn't cry out, but she could tell he was getting weaker. He'd stopped trying to hold the lab coat to his gunshot wound, and the white material had fallen to the floor, stained red with his blood.

Aiden was running out of time.

As she continued to work, she tried to figure a way out of this. If she finished the micro fuel cell and handed it over, they would just kill both her and Aiden. There was no way they'd let them live knowing what they did.

She glanced over at the men. Four of them, including Edward. Maybe he wasn't a problem, but taking out three armed men by herself? She couldn't do it.

Panic and anger warred inside her. Why hadn't she trained more? Learned how to handle multiple attackers? Her inability would end up costing her and Aiden their lives.

Dillon shocked Aiden again, and he moaned then slumped to the side.

"Enough!" She turned and glared at Dillon. "You want this done right, then you leave him alone. Every time you do that, it sets me back."

Dillon just shrugged.

God, she wished she had a weapon. Any weapon would help level the playing field. But unless she was going to throw the fuel cell equipment at them, there was nothing.

Your mind will always be your best weapon.

She heard Aiden's voice, almost like he was standing beside her. She looked down at the delicate equipment in her hands, which were shaking. She couldn't fight her way out of this, but maybe she could buy herself and Aiden a little time to do . . . something.

She went to work, completely focused now on the equipment in front of her. Evidently, Dillon was convinced she was legitimately trying now because he stopped hurting Aiden.

Or maybe Aiden wasn't conscious and couldn't be hurt any more.

They wanted a micro fuel cell? Violet was going to give them one. But it was also going to be more than they'd bargained for. Edward had set her up with more than enough equipment and supplies to do so.

Would it be enough for her to get Aiden out of here alive? Doubtful. But it wouldn't be because she didn't try. And it wouldn't give Edward and Dillon—freaking *Stellman*—what they wanted.

She continued to work, focused on what was in front of her. Everyone was watching her, but nobody knew enough to know what she was going to do. When they turned the fuel cell on for a trial run, which they undoubtedly would do, it would blow up in their faces. Literally. Plus provide a nice little electromagnetic pulse to take out all the electronics around them—including the lights in the lab.

She couldn't stand the thought of Aiden's poor face, the abuse his body had been through. She had to push it completely out of her mind in order to function, yet allow part of her brain to consider how she was going to try to get him out when hell broke loose.

Within thirty minutes she had it finished. She turned, sparing a look at Aiden, who definitely wasn't conscious.

"Here." She picked up the fuel cell in her hand—it wasn't any bigger than her fist—and walked it over to Edward, who was standing with Dillon. "It's finished."

She gave it to them and rushed over to Aiden, leaning over him to try to support his slouched body.

"How do we know it works?" Dillon asked.

She didn't even look up from Aiden, her voice flat. "Try it for yourself."

"If you're lying, I will wake him up, then torture him until he dies right in front of you."

Now she looked up, glaring at them. "I'm not lying." And she wasn't. It worked. It just did more than they expected.

Dillon turned to Edward. "What do you think? Would she lie?"

Edward shook his head. "No. Not about this. Not when his life is at stake. She did what we wanted."

Dillon nodded. "Well then, I guess you've served your purpose, Edward. It's time for Stellman to die. No one will ever know I was even part of this."

Edward's eyes grew big. "What are you talk—"

Violet couldn't hold back her surprised scream as Dillon pulled out his gun and shot Edward in the head.

Oh God.

Violet was struggling to hold it together. Dillon's men were stirring, undoubtedly wondering if they were going to be the next ones he shot.

It was a reasonable fear, given that he'd already shot two of his own men today.

"He's going to kill you too, you know," she said to them, anything to help spread confusion and panic. "It's just a matter of time."

"Nonsense, Violet," Dillon responded calmly. "These are my trusted men. I'm not going to kill them. I'm going to give you to them as a reward. As soon as I make sure your fuel cell really works."

This was it.

"Oh God, Aiden, wake up," she whispered. They were going to have to run, and she couldn't carry him.

Then, amazingly, his fingers gripped hers. He was awake.

"Bomb," she said while Dillon was distracted with the fuel cell, loud enough so only he could hear her. "Get ready to run."

Two squeezes of her fingers. "You run."

She didn't know if his words were so soft because of his injuries or because of stealth, but it didn't matter.

"No. Soldier's creed. You don't leave a fallen comrade behind."

He squeezed her hand again. She knew he would argue if he could, but it didn't matter.

He hadn't left her. She wasn't leaving him.

Dillon was about to test the device. He looked over at her. "You better hope this works."

"It will." Approximately five seconds after he turned it on.

She could feel the muscles in Aiden's legs tense. She knew him well enough to know he was going to do his damnedest not to slow her down. Even if it killed him, which at this point, she had to consider was a distinct possibility. But staying and doing nothing was a surety.

A few seconds later, Dillon let out an angry, pain-filled screech as the fuel cell exploded in his hand. The tiny EMP blast was enough to blow out all the lights in the lab, leaving everything in darkness.

Aiden's arm wrapped around her as he bounded from the chair, moving faster than she would've dreamed was possible with his injuries. Shots rang out in the direction where they'd just been standing.

If they had moved two seconds later, they'd be dead.

She wrapped an arm around his waist and sprinted with him toward the back door. They zigged and zagged, trying to avoid giving Dillon and his men a stationary target as they shot into the dark.

They made it to the door, and Violet threw it open. Aiden pushed her through as bullets began to fly their way now that it was clear where they were. She heard Aiden grunt as his body fell forward.

Oh God, he'd been shot again.

"You have to run," he said as he hit the ground. "Please, Firefly. You can make it."

His breathing was already labored. She couldn't tell where he'd been shot, but he obviously wasn't going to be able to go any farther.

"Violet!" Her head whipped up as her brother's frantic yell came from the other side of the lab. He must have come in the front door.

More gunfire erupted inside the lab, but it was no longer just coming toward her and Aiden. She grabbed Aiden's torso in her arms and pulled him against her, sheltering his body the way he'd once sheltered hers at that house.

Kendrick came running at them from outside. He gently touched the top of Violet's head before rushing inside through the back door.

Three shots later and everything fell silent.

"Clear," Kendrick called out.

"I'm good too," Gabe responded. "Where's Violet?"

"By the back door," she yelled, panic lacing her words. "Call an ambulance, Gabe. Hurry!"

Aiden's breathing was becoming more and more erratic. She looked down at him.

"You're not leaving me, Teague. You got that?" she whispered, stroking her fingers along his forehead. "Breathe with me, soldier. In. Out. I'm not going to live without you, Aiden. I love you. Breathe with me. In. Out."

The one eye that he could open, cloudy with pain, he kept pinned on her. Within a few seconds his breathing was evening out. Following hers.

"That's right. In. Out. You and me together. Every breath. Always."

CHAPTER 29

THREE DAYS LATER, Aiden was finally awake and sitting up in a hospital bed, surrounded by most of his Linear friends. Violet was perched on his bed by his side.

He'd never been on this side of a hospital visit before. Always the visitor, not the visitee.

"You know we called you Shamrock because you'd never been shot, stabbed, or blown up," Finn said. "If you didn't want that name anymore, you could've just told us. You didn't have to go and have all three done to you in one day."

Aiden chuckled, wincing a little, because, damn it, everything still hurt. The second bullet had hit him in the fleshy part of his waist. The doctor said if it had been half an inch over, he would've bled out before anyone could have stopped it, but as it was, it wasn't going to give him many problems. The shoulder wound was going to take a lot of physical therapy to regain a full range of motion.

But all things considered, he would take it.

Dillon Bassler and his two cronies had been arrested after being shot and subdued by Gabe and Kendrick. If it hadn't been for Gabe's quick thinking and suspicious nature, Aiden and Violet would've been dead. Gabe had immediately called CT to find out what was going on after their meeting in the tampon aisle, and when no one could get ahold of Violet or Edward, he'd tracked Violet through an app he'd placed on her phone.

Both of them were taking Edward's betrayal and death hard. The man had been in their lives for as long as they could remember.

Stellman was gone for good now, but the price for taking him—*them*—down was much higher than Aiden had thought it would be when he'd first gone undercover months ago.

One by one his friends began to leave, cracking jokes as they went. He assured them he had no plans to be in the hospital regularly for them to visit.

"Actually, if you wouldn't mind getting shot a couple more times, there's a nurse I have my eye on, and that would give me a legit reason to stop by," Gavin told him on his way out the door.

Aiden flipped him off and Gavin blew him a kiss as he walked out.

Violet shifted on his bed, looking at him with concern, like she had since he'd woken up and found her at his side.

"You can go, too, if you want. I know staying here has to be boring."

She shook her head. "I'm staying. I'll go home when you do. It was bad enough when you were in intensive care, and they wouldn't let me in at all. So I'm staying."

"Firefly—"

She raised an eyebrow. "Want to spar for it?"

He laughed. "Seeing as how you can kick my ass half

the time when I'm one hundred percent, I think I'll concede."

"Good. Because I'm not leaving you." She scrubbed her hand over her eyes, her voice cracking. "I thought we were going to die, Aiden. I didn't know how to fight that many people, and you were so hurt. And I had no weapon."

He reached up with his good arm and wrapped both her hands in his. "But you did have a weapon. One you'll always have with you."

She brought his fingers up to her lips. "I kept hearing you say my mind was my greatest strength."

"It's always going to be, fight or not. And besides your kindness, sense of humor, zest for life, lips, boobs, and ass, it's what I love most about you."

She smiled, then reached out and cupped his injured cheek gently over the gauze. "The doctor said this was going to scar because of how long it went untreated. But I've been looking into possible reconstructive treatments if you want."

He shook his head. "I don't mind the scar if you don't."

"No, it doesn't bother me. But what about being Sham-rock? All luck, no scars."

He crooked his finger at her, so she came in closer. "I'll look at this scar in the mirror every day and be damned happy to see it. Because the people who gave it to me were the same people who brought me to *you*."

Those green eyes filled with tears, and he wiped them away as they fell.

"The luck I had not ever being wounded is nothing compared to the luck I have from loving you. And I do love you, Firefly. From the first second I saw you, I knew I was yours. Watching the warrior you've become has just made me love you more."

As more tears fell from her cheeks to his, she kissed him, her touch gentle, soft, full of every promise in the world.

He would take that too.

She lay down next to him, cuddling up to his uninjured side. "Since you were so brave and somehow found the superhuman strength to get yourself out of that chair despite what you'd been through, I'll even let you choose the music while we're doing all your recuperation training together."

He kissed the top of her head. "See? Shamrock's luck lives on."

∽

ACKNOWLEDGMENTS

As always, writing is never a lone endeavor.

I am ever thankful to my family for putting up with my crazy when deadlines come along. I'd like to particularly thank my mother, who saw I was drowning under the weight of what I'd taken on, and basically came and took over all household and kitchen duties for *weeks* so I could finish.

And she did it without making a big deal of it or taking any credit for herself. If that's not the best mom a girl could ask for, I don't know what is. Love you, Mimi.

Again, my undying gratitude to my tribe: Marci, Girl Tyler, Anu, Stephanie, Regan, Nichole, Julie, Beth, Lissanne, Elizabeth. Thank you for the encouragement, the support, the tough love when needed. And Marci, for the best pillow ever—you are so special to me!

Once again, to my editors and alpha readers: Elizabeth Nover, Jennifer at Mistress Editing, Lissanne Jones, Marci Mathers, Elizabeth Neal, Stephanie Scott, and Aly Birkl. I *really* think we've created a winner with this one. Thank you for your diligence.

To everyone who has given the Linear Tactical books a try...thank you! I never dreamed these books would be as popular as they have and I am tremendously blessed to create stories for a living. Without you, there's definitely no Janie Crouch, author.

With love and appreciation,

Janie Crouch